WINTER WARNING

WINTER WARNING

AN ISAAC SIDEL NOVEL

JEROME CHARYN

PEGASUS BOOKS
NEW YORK LONDON

WINTER WARNING

Pegasus Books Ltd.
148 W. 37th Street, 13th Floor
New York, NY 10018

First Pegasus Books edition October 2017

Interior design by Maria Fernandez

Library of Congress Cataloging-in-Publication Data is available.

ISBN: 978-1-68177-348-3

10 9 8 7 6 5 4 3 2 1

Printed in the United States of America
Distributed by W. W. Norton & Company

DON QUIXOTE WITH A GLOCK

1

I began the saga of Isaac Sidel in 1973 . . . only the saga wasn't about Sidel. Isaac was a minor character in his own series. *Blue Eyes* (1975) was devoted to a blond detective, Manfred Coen, who was Isaac's adjutant. He was modeled on my older brother, Harvey Charyn, who didn't have blue eyes, but did have Coen's penchant for silence. Harve was a homicide detective in the NYPD. We both grew up on the mean streets of the South Bronx. Harve was my survival kit. Gang leaders left me alone because they didn't want to tangle with my brother, not because he lifted weights and had biceps as big as ostrich eggs. That wouldn't have mattered much to the Cherokees or the Minford Place Maulers. What mattered to them was that Harve didn't have a pinch of fear in his brown eyes. He would have taken on every member of the Maulers, one by one, each with his zip gun and South Bronx claw—a hammer with a spike attached to its head with a battalion of rubber bands.

And so I led a charmed life, and was never scalped or bruised by a makeshift tomahawk. Harve was the artist in the family and a great reader of books. But he didn't get into Manhattan's celebrated High School of Music and Art; he had to loiter around at some lowly trade school, where he didn't have a whiff of Picasso or Cézanne, and studied industrial design instead. But I had all the cunning of a billy goat. I got into Music and Art, where I was introduced to middle-class culture and buxom girls from Central Park West. And later, while I studied Russian lit at Columbia College, Harve soldiered in Alaska, having to drive heavy-duty trucks on long hauls. I never touched a rifle, a bayonet, or a ten-ton truck. My prize possession was a bookcase that housed my collection of Modern Library classics. I was already hooked, a rabbinical monk who believed in the holiness of the written word.

I lived in a closet in Washington Heights, tacking pages together until I published my first novel in 1964. Meanwhile, Harve got married and became a cop, and I taught contemporary lit at Stanford, published a book of stories and five more novels, each one with less sales than the last—my life as a writer had become one great vanishing act.

So I went to Harve. He was a Mafia expert, stationed in the wild lands of Brooklyn, and I wanted to resurrect myself as a crime novelist. Hammett had the Pinkertons, and I had Harve. I tried to cannibalize him and his little band of detectives, learn their lingo. I traveled with them in their unmarked cars, listening to their hatred of the street—everyone outside their own orbit was either a "mook," a "glom," or a "skel." They weren't much like the warriors I imagined detectives to be: they were civil servants with a gun, obsessed about the day of their retirement. I sat with Harve in his station house, saw the cages where all the bad guys were kept. I visited the back rooms where cops would sleep after a midnight tour. I was Charyn's kid brother, the scribbler, and radio dispatchers flirted with both of us.

My brother drove me to the Brooklyn morgue since I needed to look at dead bodies for my novel. The morgue attendant took me and Harve around. All the dead men looked like Indians. Their skin had turned to bark. I distanced myself from the corpses, pretended I was touring some carnival with refrigerated shelves. It was Harve who sucked Life Savers and seemed pale. I was only a stinking voyeur in the house of the dead.

But I had the beginnings of a crime novel. I chose my hero, Blue Eyes, aka Shotgun Coen, who raced into battle with a shotgun in a shopping bag. I made him a graduate of Music and Art, as if I was grafting my own life onto Harve's. Coen had all the sadness of the South Bronx, that brittle landscape of long silences. Coen was divorced, like me. He worked for Sidel, a volatile chief in the first deputy commissioner's office, known as Isaac the Brave. Isaac had gone undercover, disgraced himself, joined the Guzmanns, a tribe of Peruvian pimps, with their headquarters in a candy store on Boston Road, in the heartland of the Bronx. And Manfred was left out in the cold. Isaac could no longer protect him. Coen had also committed a sin. He fell in love with Isaac's voluptuous daughter, Marilyn the Wild. And Isaac was filled with an ungovernable jealous rage. Blindly, he maneuvered to get Coen killed. Manfred dies in the middle of his own novel, and the rest of the story unravels, as Isaac pounces on the

Peruvian pimps and redeems himself. He's some kind of a villain in our first encounter.

I didn't realize that there would be a second. But I had to continue the tale and get to the *fundament* of Isaac's feud with Coen. Hence, I wrote *Marilyn the Wild* (1976), a prequel to my first crime novel. I figured my job was done. But that very year I got a phone call from movie star Richard Harris.

"Do ya know who I am?" he asked.

"Do I not?" I answered, trying to imitate his Irish brogue.

I loved Richard Harris in *This Sporting Life* (1963), where he's an oddly poetic brute of a rugby star fresh out of the coal mines. Harris himself had played rugby at school in Ireland, and one could feel the pinpoints of tension in his body. He was the closest *anyone* would ever get to Marlon Brando's subversive charm on the screen.

He adored *Blue Eyes*, he said. And he wanted me to create another character like Manfred Coen, a brooding Irish version of him. I sat with a galaxy of lawyers in a glass tower on West 57th Street to iron out the details of my "indenture" to Richard Harris. Who would own the character I created, particularly if I wanted that same character to appear in one of my own novels?

Harris flew in from Hollywood. We were scheduled to meet for breakfast at the Palm Court in the Plaza Hotel. I arrived first. I'd never seen such opulence—palm trees and exotic plants and a vaulted skylight—in the middle of Manhattan. Harris arrived a few minutes later in his bare feet and filthy white pants. Who would have reprimanded him for violating the Palm Court's dress code? Whatever rules the Plaza had didn't pertain to Richard Harris. My mind was on the prowl, and I immediately had the character I wanted to create: Patrick Silver, a barefoot Irish-Jewish janitor at a crumbling synagogue—Congregation Limerick—on Bethune Street, in Greenwich Village.

Manfred Coen was long dead, but I would rekindle Isaac Sidel in this novel and his feud with the Guzmanns.

The first scene of *The Education of Patrick Silver* (1976) takes place in the lobby of the Plaza Hotel, with a barefoot Patrick Silver guarding one of the Guzmanns. The novel has its own surreal flavor, a noir *Alice in Wonderland*, with Patrick as my Mad Hatter. With Richard Harris in mind, I wrote and wrote. Of course, my novel was in want of the usual fabric for a Hollywood film. It would have needed the madcap metaphysics of someone like Quentin Tarantino, and Tarantino was thirteen years old at the time.

Harris would never get to play Patrick Silver. But Sidel was back with a vengeance, still a somewhat shadowy figure, cursed with a tapeworm after the death of Manfred Coen. And then, in 1978, he would have a novel all his own, *Secret Isaac*, where he makes a magical trip to Dublin to commune with James Joyce's ghost and meet with Dermott Bride, an Irish-American gangster exiled at the Shelbourne Hotel. Isaac himself may have unwittingly launched Dermott's career. He's risen in the ranks, with his tapeworm, and is now the first deputy commissioner of the NYPD.

Sidel must have fallen out of mind, since I abandoned the series for twelve years. I didn't publish *The Good Policeman* until after I had moved to Paris in 1989. What was a wild child from the South Bronx doing near all the mythic cafés along the Boulevard Montparnasse? Even as a small boy, I'd loved the *idea* of Paris, with its one recognizable totem, the Eiffel Tower. At junior high, while all my classmates chose Spanish as a foreign language, I studied French with a few other misfits and stragglers. My French teacher, Mrs. Maniello, kept repeating how lucky we were. She herself was an incurable Francophile. She would tell us tales about Fantômas, the king of crime, a hero of French fiction who was the wickedest man alive. Fantômas rode across the rooftops of Paris, leaving a pile of corpses in his wake. He used all the tricks of a detective to capture his prey. Fantômas murdered at will. He had a daughter, Hélène, who was his one mark of vulnerability. And I wondered if part of the inspiration for Isaac Sidel had somehow risen out of Mrs. Maniello's class. Sidel wasn't evil per se. But he did use many of Fantômas' tricks. He wore disguises and got rid of his enemies one by one. And he had his own Hélène—Marilyn the Wild.

No matter. I moved to Paris. But I was in the middle of an identity crisis, like some Candide stunned by a stick, or perhaps a French Pinocchio adrift without his puppeteer. I walked around in a daze, with a kind of residual terror. The apartment I had rented was as schizoid as I was. Its front rooms faced one of Paris' ugliest and busiest boulevards, the Avenue du Maine, while the kitchen and bathroom overlooked the Montparnasse Cemetery. It was strangely soothing to stare at that green graveyard while I was on the pot. But my own writer's engine was impaired. I couldn't traverse the least imaginative landscape. Previously, I'd written novels about Wild Bill Hickok, FDR, and Rags Ragland, a maverick fictional third baseman who was tossed off the Boston Red Sox, banned from baseball, and had to play in the Negro Leagues. My mind had been voyaging for twenty-five years, moving from target to target, and then it all stopped. I couldn't commune with my own creative ghosts and gods. I'd start a novel, and would have to abandon it after several tries to sculpt a décor. I'd lost touch with my own language. I worried that I'd start dreaming in French. Yet there was one subject I could still write about—New York, one landscape I could still traverse, one décor that was mine. And so I returned to my very own Fantômas, Isaac Sidel, and wrote *Maria's Girls* (1992). Isaac was now police commissioner, but the novel swirled around detectives from Sherwood Forest, as I dubbed the precinct in Central Park. I'd never realized there was such a precinct until I returned to Manhattan on a short trip and went on a pilgrimage to that mysterious police station. It made a lot of sense. Sherwood Forest was where the horses had once been stabled when there were horse patrols in the park. The precinct itself existed in its own time warp.

Meanwhile, comic actor Ron Silver had read *The Good Policeman* and wanted to play Isaac Sidel in a television series devoted to Sidel's adventures and mishaps. And now I was involved in the warp of a television series as a writer-producer, which meant I had to remain in Manhattan for six months. Silver had been marvelous in Paul Mazursky's adaptation of Isaac Bashevis Singer's novel, *Enemies: A Love Story* (1989), where he plays Herman Broder, a Jewish refugee from Hitler's Europe who's involved in multiple love affairs. Broder had enormous, sad eyes that seemed to watch the world at a slant and suck up all our sympathy. And Silver was an excellent candidate for Sidel. He grew up on the Lower East Side, like Sidel, and his father was in the clothing business, like Joel Sidel, Issac's errant dad. But Silver had grown a beard since he'd played Herman Broder, and must have seen himself as a seductive Mephistopheles. All that comic empathy was gone, and the beard seemed to camouflage his emotions and obscure those enormous eyes. He did look a little like Fantômas, but Sidel's warmth and wackiness had disappeared.

"Ron," I said, "you gotta shave off that fucking beard."

"Why?" he asked, as if he were talking to a pet snake.

"Because it's like wearing a mask."

I told him how wonderful he'd been in *Enemies: A Love Story*.

"Terrific," he said. "That movie lost millions."

"It doesn't matter. That guy in the film is Sidel."

Ron kept his beard. The series about Sidel was canceled. I returned to France.

I continued my own series, novels devoted to Isaac Sidel and his rise from police commissioner to mayor of New York. He kept murdering bad guys as he built his own makeshift ladder of success.

I began teaching at the American University of Paris. I started a film department and felt comfortable around kids who were vagabonds like myself, commandos between two cultures. And when *another* vagabond, Quentin Tarantino, emerged as a filmmaker with *Reservoir Dogs* (1992) and *Pulp Fiction* (1994), I realized he was sculpting his own novels on the screen, just as I was directing my own films on the page, with jump cuts and words that were able to conjure up multiple décors. I had my cinematic language the way Tarantino had his. He was his own Alice, his own Mad Hatter; he could kill off a character in one scene and bring him back to life in the next. He was Glenn Gould playing with his eyes shut, Bobby Fischer dancing blindly with his back to the board. Perhaps I couldn't reach the perfection of *Pulp Fiction* in my crime novels, but I wanted them to explode with an absolute sense of play.

I quit teaching in 2008 and returned to Manhattan. I felt like Candide venturing into a wilderness of words. A whole new language had been carved in my absence. It hurt the most whenever I watched a Knick game. I knew what "drop a dime" meant when it related to a snitch. But how did you "drop a dime" during a basketball game? And when I heard Knick announcers talk of "3-and-D" and "dead-ball rebound, " I wondered if I was Rip Van Winkle or Methuselah. I had to gather in this new vocabulary, become my own "dead-ball rebound." It didn't hurt as much when I dug deep into the nineteenth century and wrote *The Secret Life of Emily Dickinson* (2010), or *I Am Abraham* (2014), a novel in Lincoln's own voice, or when I slipped back into the 1980s to write *Winter Warning*, the ultimate encounter with Isaac Sidel, where he becomes, almost by accident, President of the United States.

It's the twelfth novel in a crime series that's occupied my psyche, waking and dreaming, for over forty years. The series has a ripple effect that builds from book to book like a curious mosaic, but each of the novels can be read on its own. I didn't provide a reader's bible for *Winter Warning*. Blue Eyes is never mentioned. Isaac's tapeworm has fled, but he *feels* like a character who's in constant mourning. There's a sadness that accompanies his every move. And I realized that the rhythm of the book, as in all the Sidel novels, grows out of the cosmic sadness of my childhood. I'd always been an outlier. I didn't belong to Manhattan's middle-class culture at Music and Art, or any culture at all. And perhaps that's why Fantômas resonated so deeply when I was at junior high. He was a breaker of boundaries in that mask of his. Murder was a form of poetry to Fantômas. And his many disguises were like language itself—words could kill.

Yet Isaac was rabbinical, a profoundly moral man. He didn't have a penny in his pockets. He wasn't fueled by greed. He never uses the presidency for his own personal gain. Perhaps that's why all the politicos in *Winter Warning* are scared to death of him. He can't be bought and sold. He wears his Glock in the White House, like a frontier marshal on Pennsylvania Avenue.

He's haunted by one man, Abraham Lincoln. Isaac doesn't believe in Lincoln's "better angels." He's been wrestling demons all his life. He prefers to have his Glock, even if it falls out of his pants and bumps along the carpets. But Lincoln was his own better angel, who held the fabric of the country together with the force of his beliefs. Lincoln also had a mad wife and a boy who died in the White House. Isaac's wife abandoned him years ago and has become the queen of Florida real estate. And so Isaac shuffles across the White House residence in his shaggy slippers, with Lincoln's ghost to keep him company. He doesn't have Lincoln's aura and never will. His own political party would like to stage a coup and get rid of him. His only allies are a Russian crime boss and a pair of Israeli fugitives. His first trip abroad is to a former death camp in the Czech Republic. But he doesn't feel at home until he rides Marine One to Rikers Island and puts down a revolt among the inmates. He's Don Quixote with a Glock rather than a lance. His own music has been inside my head ever since I can recall. If the world has darkened around him since he first appeared in *Blue Eyes*, he's always been a noir character in a noir world, and always will be.

WINTER WARNING

PART ONE

PART ONE

1

His honeymoon was over before it began. He didn't even have his ninety days of wonder, that period of immortality granted all modern presidents, the good, the bad, and the mediocre. He'd swept his party back into power in what was soon known as the Slaughter of '88, as he captured sixty-two percent of the popular vote on his credentials as a cop. People thought they'd elected a mayor-sheriff with a Glock in his pants, not Spinoza with a bald spot. They couldn't seem to remember that he was a political philosopher as well as a sleuth and had once been called the Pink Commish.

Isaac Sidel wanted to eliminate poverty on his first day in office; he talked of subsidies for the disenfranchised. His top aides had to hem and haw. Finally they cleared their throats and hinted to Isaac that the disenfranchised hadn't catapulted him into office and created a Democratic landslide, hadn't cast a single vote.

"So what?" Sidel said. "It's still a crying shame."

He'd lost his hand-picked chief of staff, Brenda Brown, who was even more of a maverick than Sidel. She wanted the Big Guy to sidestep Congress and govern by presidential decree. Brenda was preparing executive orders that would have overturned rulings of the past three Republican presidents. But Brenda had a breakdown after a month, as she realized that the White House was a hornet's nest of compromises, and she ran off with a summer intern, a voluptuous magna cum laude from Mount Holyoke—it was the first scandal of the Sidel administration.

The Democratic National Committee climbed on Isaac's back and thrust Ramona Dazzle upon him, a Rhodes scholar who wouldn't stray into uncharted waters at the White House. And soon Isaac began to suspect that his own party had planted a spy in the West Wing; where once he'd had a tapeworm he now had a dybbuk, who gobbled his intestines piece by piece. Ramona handled all the details of his daily life; she hired and fired until he couldn't recognize a soul. The White House had become an alien hotel. It was Ramona who presided over the menus—the Big Guy had to feed on crumbs—and had furniture shunted around to suit her fancy. The Oval Office was a hovel compared to Ramona's suite of rooms. Isaac had no sense of décor. But Ramona had plucked Dolley Madison's music box and chiffonier out of a secret storage facility in Maryland that collected the residue of former First Ladies, and her own corner office had become the jewel of the West Wing, half museum and half war room for skull sessions with her brats.

Isaac could have defied the DNC and kicked Ramona out on her ass, but it would have caused another crisis. Yet he could feel himself grow invisible, become the Shrinking Man of Pennsylvania Avenue. He was Ramona's shadow, the proxy president, swimming in his pants. He had a hard time carrying his Glock under his belt. It would crash to the floor and alarm the Secret Service. The Big Guy could barely look at himself in one of the White House's antique mirrors; his cheeks were hollowed out, and the curl that once covered his bald spot had disappeared. So he marched across the hall to Ramona's enclave.

It was a queen's residence, with antechambers for her brats, all furnished from that secret storage facility. Her aides treated Isaac like an intruder, an unwanted desperado. "You fuckers," he growled, "you work for me." They still defied the president, dared him to make a move. He was an orphan in his own palace, an outcast, like King Lear, with a trove of poisonous daughters and sons. He didn't want to look ridiculous in front of these retainers. He clutched the Glock to his belly, so it wouldn't land on Ramona's cream-colored carpet, did a curious entrechat, and found himself in the queen's corner office. It was roomier than Isaac's, with a grand mahogany conference table, a relic from FDR's White House. Isaac was still haunted by that crippled president. He'd seen Roosevelt ride down the Grand Concourse in 1944, when he himself was a young delinquent, a dealer in stolen goods. He'd given all his swag to Roosevelt's reelection monitors. He was born at the very beginning of Roosevelt's reign and it seemed logical to Isaac that FDR would rule forever—at least for a fifth and sixth term. He was like a big baby who couldn't quite recover from FDR's sudden death in 1945.

He didn't covet Ramona's conference table, but it conjured up a past that left him like a permanent mourner in a mourner's ripped coat. His chief of staff ignored him, pretended he wasn't in the room.

She was on her speakerphone, surrounded by interns and aides. She had her own defiant charm, sat with her legs in the air, in black panty-hose. Isaac had to look away from the knitted wrinkles of Ramona's crotch. She had large brown eyes, like a doe's, and very thin nostrils.

"Yes," she said, "POTUS doesn't like to travel. I can't get him to sign anything. We've been feuding from day one."

"Ramona," Isaac whispered, "get off the fucking phone."

She swiveled slightly in her chair. "POTUS doesn't want campaign contributors sleeping in the Lincoln Bedroom. He says it's sacred ground. Lincoln never slept there, for shit's sake."

"But it's where he signed the Emancipation Proclamation," Isaac shouted into the speaker and pressed the mute button on her telephone console.

"Idiot," she said, rolling her big brown eyes. "That was one of our biggest donors. We've been bleeding hard cash ever since you were sworn in. Our first Yid in the White House, and I can't get him to visit the Holy Land. K Street calls you an anti-Semite. I can't battle the whole Jewish lobby, not while we have Hamlet's ghost on the second floor."

He was a ghost, wandering about the White House residence, falling asleep in different bedrooms when he could fall asleep. Half the time he drifted in and out of his dreams. Harry Truman had called this presidential palace "the great white jail." And Harry wasn't wrong. Isaac was homesick for the wilds of Manhattan. He no longer had his pied-à-terre on Rivington Street; the building had burned to the ground while he was on the campaign trail. And he couldn't tour the Lower East Side as some invisible guy with a Glock. He would snarl traffic for an entire day with his Secret Service caravan, even if he landed at some remote heliport on the East River; his very presence caused chaos and confusion. And God forbid if he wanted to dine at some little Italian dump on Ninth Avenue—he had to sit with the Secret Service in his lap, while other diners were scrutinized as potential terrorists and saboteurs. And he ended up playing patty-cake with his own retinue of Secret Service agents, plus a doc from Bethesda, a speechwriter or two, a policy wonk, members of the White House press corps, and Isaac's military aide, who carried the "football," a black briefcase which held the doomsday codes that would allow the president to launch a nuclear counterstrike. This satchel accompanied Isaac everywhere. And he wondered if the President of the United States—POTUS—was a mountebank, who had to live near a doomsday satchel, like a character in one of Gogol's surreal tales.

"You ought to be nicer to me," Isaac said. "I have all the codes to the football."

Ramona dismissed her aides with a swanlike flap of her hand and then she burrowed into Isaac with her brown eyes. "Don't you come in here with your swagger, Mr. President. I'm more concerned about your Glock than the football. You could shoot off one of your toes. You're an accident waiting to happen. And we might not be able to afford you much longer."

Isaac knew Ramona was conspiring with his own vice president, Bull Latham, former director of the FBI, who still pulled all the strings at the Bureau. Ramona and the Bull were preparing some sort of a coup and had to wait for Isaac's numbers to drop. His popularity could vanish in the blink of an eye. He'd forsaken the middle class, talked of food stamps and housing subsidies. But Ramona had to be cautious. Isaac was flamboyant and fearless. He might ride anywhere aboard Marine One, land on the roof of a rural high school, where some madman was holding a class of tenth graders hostage, and talk that gunman down—that was Isaac's enigma. He could connect with people in some primitive way. Ramona had to chop at him by degrees until little was left of the Big Guy. She outmaneuvered him at every turn. Democrats didn't want him in their districts. He was a president with a growing rebellion within his own party.

"Sir, you can't have federal marshals arrest teenagers for smoking cigarettes. You'll involve us in a million lawsuits. You'll bankrupt your own government."

"But I want to bury Big Tobacco," Isaac said.

Ramona didn't have to perform in front of an absent audience. All the innocence had gone out of her doe's eyes. She treated Isaac like a boorish child rather than the president, looked right past him and pictured Bull Latham in the Oval Office.

"You're sitting where you are, sonny boy, because of Big Tobacco. You couldn't have had much of a campaign without those three giants. They abandoned the Republicans and backed us to the hilt."

Isaac wanted to rip Ramona out of her Renaissance Revival chair. "I never said a kind word about the cigarette companies."

Ramona mocked him without mercy. "They're not looking for a sympathetic glance, darling. They'll continue to thrive with or without you."

"What did you promise them?" Isaac had to ask, like a beggar in his own palace.

"Nothing. They like to be on the winning side."

"That's grand," Isaac said. "And I sit here and watch people cough their lungs out?"

"Make your speeches—I'll help you write them. But you'll never get a piece of legislation passed against Big Tobacco. Jesus, we took *every* tobacco state. Do you really think senators from those states will badmouth Lorillard and the others?"

The Big Guy shouldn't have left Gracie Mansion. He knew how to govern the maddening whirlpool of Manhattan. He overrode his police commissioner; he built school after school, and created Merlin, a program where kids from firebombed neighborhoods could mingle with the wizards of Bronx Science and Brooklyn Tech. Real estate barons shivered in his presence. They couldn't get near a city lot without Isaac's approval. He was the master builder, not the barons. He flourished, despite the chaos and the crime. He could march into City Hall and break the will of rebellious council members. But the White House was a mansion in the middle of nowhere. It couldn't connect him to the nation's pulse. He lived in a presidential park surrounded by ripples of poverty. Yet Isaac couldn't have created another Merlin in the District of Columbia. Congress held sway over Washington, ruled its budget, wouldn't relieve its slums.

"Wake up," Ramona said. "You're not Santa Claus. You can't *gift* a whole population of slackers. You have certain responsibilities. If you abandon your warriors, Mr. President, they'll abandon you."

Who were these phantom warriors? Ah, her minions and volunteers on the DNC. Isaac was never a party politician—he was a Roosevelt Democrat at a time when "entitlement" and welfare programs had become taboo. Isaac should have been vice president, but the Dems had to get rid of their own president-elect, J. Michael Storm, a serial philanderer and a thief. It was Isaac who picked Bull Latham, a Republican, as *his* vice president. He liked the idea of a pistol like Bull at his side, a former linebacker on the Dallas Cowboys, who bent the law while he was at the Bureau. Isaac had also bent the law, had used the resources of the Mob to help him solve the thousand riddles of *disorganized* crime. But Bull was a bigger gangster than Isaac had ever been. Bull had plundered to feed his own pocketbook, while POTUS had a ravaged bank account and five dollars in his pants. Isaac rose higher and higher, like a big fat fireball, with every bad guy he killed. He'd glocked his way to the White House.

"You have no idea," she said. "I never volunteered to be your baby-sitter, but that's what I am. POTUS is everyone's personal target. I'm the gal who has to keep you alive."

Isaac wasn't fooled by this grandiose picture of herself. Ramona was there to keep him tucked away in a closet while she ran the country from her corner office. He didn't give a damn that she'd sacrificed her status as a killer attorney at a killer law firm. She would be welcomed back after Isaac's wake. But he was jealous of her other credentials. She'd studied literature and philosophy at Oxford, had written a book on Saul Bellow, while Isaac had one stinking semester at Columbia College. He'd devoured *Augie March*, reveled in the tales of Jewish swindlers and lowlifes from Chicago, but she was the one who had dined with Bellow.

The Big Guy had a sudden brainstorm. "Why don't we ask him to the White House? We'll have a banquet in his honor. I'm sure you can drum up some kind of medal."

Ramona smirked at Isaac, hoping to make him suffer. "If you mean Saul," she said, "you're a little too late. He was given the National Medal of Arts last year. I pinned it on him myself, in front of President Cottonwood."

Isaac groaned. He despised Calder Cottonwood, who'd had his own hit squad at the White House and declared open season on Sidel. But that's not what troubled Isaac. "You had a son of Chicago hobnob with Republicans?"

"Indeed. He sat with the nation's best conservative philosophers. Saul wouldn't have accepted an invitation from you, Mr. President. He calls you a Stalinist. He hardly set foot in Manhattan while you were mayor. The subways were filled with hoboes, and he says you allowed petty criminals to run rampant."

Isaac had a touch of vertigo, having to defend his tactics to the father of *Augie March*. "Yes, I cleared out some of the holding pens at

Rikers every six months. I couldn't let young men and women—half of them children, really—linger at Rikers while they were awaiting trial on trumped-up charges that could have been settled out of court in five minutes. I wasn't that kind of a mayor."

"And what kind of president are you?" Ramona asked with a stingy smile. "You've lost the respect of your own constituents. You're a clown with a Glock. I had to quash a wholesale mutiny within the ranks, and it wasn't fun. I'm not your private hammer . . ."

She paused for a second, and Isaac knew where that hammer would drop next. She'd been dreaming of this moment, nursing it along.

"You can't invite Ariel Moss to Camp David," she said. "That's final. The party won't allow it."

"Didn't he win the Nobel Peace Prize? He was prime minister for six years."

"But he's become an outlaw—and a hermit."

"He was always an outlaw," Isaac said. *Ariel Moss* was the alias of an alias. No one knew Ariel's real name. He was born in some lost territory of the Pale, a Polish enclave ruled by the tsar. His father was a timber merchant who owned an entire forest, while his mother was descended from a royal line of rabbinical scholars—at least that was the tale Ariel told of his lineage. He claimed to have studied law at the University of Lodz, but none of the students remembered an Ariel Moss. The first time that name surfaced was in 1942, when he joined a ragtag of Jewish commandos within the Free Polish Army, a suicide squad that went into Nazi headquarters in some provincial town and killed the local commandant. Ariel was the only one to survive. The Nazis put a price on his head, and the Poles sent him to Palestine, where he was meant to train with a bunch of British saboteurs. Here the myth began that Ariel Moss was a double agent, striving for both the radical Jewish underground of Irgun and the masters of British intelligence.

If so, Ariel must have been the best damn double agent around. He robbed British banks in Jerusalem, kidnapped British officers, bombed the headquarters of the British high command inside the King David Hotel, broke into the impregnable fortress of Acre Prison, and walked out with captured members of Irgun. This anonymous man with one lazy eye would become the boss of Irgun, as he plotted to kick the British colonials out of Palestine.

Isaac grew up with a picture of Ariel on his wall; actually it was a mug shot of the terrorist under yet another assumed name, Sasha Klein, at a Soviet labor camp in Siberia; he looked like a common criminal, an *urka* with a shaved head. He'd been arrested some-time in 1940, as a *zhid* who was trying to smuggle other *zhids* out of Poland. Sasha Klein escaped from the gulag with a band of thieves and morphed into a resistance fighter and member of the Jewish underground.

He visited the U.S. in November 1948, now the leader of his own political party in the new state of Israel. He was trying to raise hard cash, but Ariel Moss was attacked by Albert Einstein and other illustrious Jews as a right-wing fanatic who had brought a reign of terror to the Holy Land. Isaac, who was fifteen at the time and still a purveyor of stolen goods, attended a rally for Ariel Moss in Seward Park. Socialists from Brooklyn and the Bronx had come to the Lower East Side to taunt and spit at the renegade who was locked in a long struggle with Israel's ruling socialist party. Ariel didn't look like much of an outlaw. He had stooped shoulders and a narrow chest, and his eyes were hidden behind thick lenses that gave him the aura of an owl.

"Satan," shouted one of the socialists, "did you murder children?"

Ariel peered at the socialist with his owlish eyes. "Yes, there were children in the debris when we bombed the King David. I held one in my arms. I couldn't revive him. I was a demolition man, not an angel of mercy. But I warned the manager of the King David, told him to clear the hotel of all his guests. He didn't listen, comrade."

"I'm not your comrade," said the socialist. "You're a killer and you come here begging for money."

Isaac put whatever loot he had into Ariel's collection box. And Ariel returned to Israel, still an outcast. It took him thirty years of finagling to discover mainstream politics. He appealed to the downtrodden, Jewish refugees from the Muslim countries of Africa, descendants of Babylonian tribes—grocers from Iraq, bakers from Uzbekistan—rather than the educated Ashkenazi of Eastern Europe, and this ghostly graduate of the law school at Lodz was elected prime minister in 1977. He startled his own nationalist party when he signed the Camp David Accords with Anwar Sadat in 1978, promising to hand back the Sinai Peninsula in return for Egypt's recognition of Israel's right to exist. The Egyptians were no more pleased with the accords than the Israelis were. Sadat was assassinated three years later by a jihadist in the military, and Ariel escaped one assassination plot after the other by fanatics among the religious right and gunmen within the moribund Irgun. He was hospitalized six times. His own children stopped talking to him. His wife died. He grew more and more morose and resigned in 1983. No one could reach him, neither journalists, nor his wife's relatives, nor the few friends he once had. He moved from location to location, from a shack in Haifa to a shed in the Jerusalem forest. There were reports that he had become a beachcomber and a vagabond, perhaps had even gone back to robbing banks, but that the internal security agents of Shin Bet protected Ariel Moss from harming himself and others.

Ramona Dazzle wondered why this hermit would reach out to Isaac Sidel.

"Did he ever visit you while you were mayor?"

"No," Isaac had to insist. Ariel seldom came to Manhattan while he was prime minister. He shunned the UN and every sort of lobbyist. Perhaps he couldn't recover from the ferocity of the socialists on his first trip to America in 1948. But he did come to New York while Isaac was still police commissioner. Ariel had been mugged in the street and landed on the ward at Lincoln Hospital in the South Bronx. Isaac was shy about disturbing his boyhood hero. But he couldn't understand what Ariel Moss was doing in the badlands, and without a bodyguard. So he crept onto the ward out of curiosity. He had no desire to interview Ariel, just to sniff around on his own. He spoke to a nurse and a few of the residents. They had no idea who Ariel Moss was, thought he might be an amnesiac wandering about in the most dangerous square mile in North America. And while Isaac sniffed and sniffed, Ariel opened his lazy eye.

"I know you—you're the Pink Commish. But we met once before, at a rally in Seward Park. The socialists were tearing off my flesh, and you gave me some *gelt*."

Isaac was startled by the hospital patient's prodigious memory. How could Ariel recollect one lone boy? "That gift wasn't kosher," Isaac said. "I gave you money I got from stolen merchandise."

Ariel laughed in his blue hospital shirt. His teeth were all black. He looked like a vampire who relished black blood in his mouth.

"Well, then we're both a couple of desperados. It's no secret. I was once a bank robber."

"But there are no banks along this stretch of Southern Boulevard. Very little happens here. Why did you come to such an unholy place?"

"I was on a pilgrimage," said Ariel Moss.

Isaac was even more perplexed. He wondered if that mugger had rattled Ariel's mind.

"You must have heard of Sholem Aleichem, the Yiddish Mark Twain. When I was in the gulag, it was his stories that kept me going. He spent his last years in the Bronx, on Kelly Street. He couldn't write. He was a legend who'd lost his substance. He had diabetes and tuberculosis, among other ailments. If a few of his devoted readers hadn't left food outside his door, he and his family would have starved. Yet he had a hundred thousand people at his funeral. And I never got to Kelly Street."

That was the last encounter Isaac had with Ariel Moss, in his blue hospital shirt. And then a week ago, out of nowhere, the Soviet acting deputy foreign minister, Pesh Olinov, whispered in Isaac's ear at a reception in the East Room that the Hermit of Haifa had fled his chicken coop and wanted to see the Big Guy. Those were Olinov's exact words—fled the chicken coop. Why should a Soviet diplomat, whose sudden success was tied to the KGB and the crime bosses of Moscow and Kiev, have become the messenger of a derailed ex–Israeli prime minister? It made no sense. Egypt was Soviet Russia's client, not the mad Jews of Tel Aviv. But then Isaac recognized the tattoo on Olinov's knuckles—a dagger piercing the eye hole of a skull. Isaac had seen that tattoo before, among the *cheloveks* of Brighton Beach. It was the mark of a werewolf. And Isaac realized the connection. Ariel and Pesh Olinov must have served in the same gulag, many years ago, must have belonged to the same crime boss, and must have escaped together. But the *cheloveks* wouldn't have gathered among themselves a Jewish intellectual from the law school at Lodz—unless that law student was as much of a werewolf as they were. Intellectuals and *zhids* always died first. That was the rude sign of Siberia. Ariel Moss couldn't have survived the brutish life of a labor camp without the protection of a *pakhan*, or crime lord. And Olinov must have been that lord's lieutenant. Born in Siberia, the son of a whore and a *chelovek* at the camp, he was raised as a werewolf who sat at his *pakhan*'s knee. He had scars on his face from knife fights with rivals of his *pakhan* and other *cheloveks*. He looked like a gourd with ruts down the middle; his eyes, a luminous green, were half hidden among all the marks. Isaac felt an immediate kinship with Pesh Olinov; they were like bounty hunters in a sea of diplomats and politicians. Yet this former KGB colonel and intimate of crime bosses was Mikhail Gorbachev's deputy foreign minister; Olinov had helped shape *glasnost* and *perestroika*, was instrumental in making overtures to the West and bringing about social and political reform in the Kremlin's bewildering bureaucracy.

The Pink Commish wasn't blind. Moscow ranted against alcohol consumption, destroyed distilleries, while it lost billions of rubles to Olinov's pals in the black market. Pesh grew richer with every one of his decrees. He spent months in our capital, like any lobbyist from K Street. He lived across from the White House, at the Hotel Washington, where he dined with six bodyguards surrounding his rooftop table. He still had to step out of explosions, his body covered in bits of glass. Who knows how many Moscow gangsters and graduates of the gulag were gunning for Pesh? Having become one of the masterminds of *perestroika* had made him an easy target among conservative politicians and members of the Politburo. So a day after this mysterious encounter in the East Room, Isaac met with his intelligence chiefs in a dungeon under the Oval Office to discuss Olinov's overtures. Bull Latham had been there with Ramona Dazzle. Isaac felt like a schoolboy having to repeat word for word his conversation with Pesh.

"The deputy kept saying that Ariel wouldn't come to the White House—the walls had too many ears. He would only come to my dacha. I didn't know I had a dacha."

Isaac remembered the chiefs chortling among themselves. His national security advisor, Tim Vail, spoke first. Vail was a boy genius, a graduate of Harvard and Georgetown, who had published the definitive paper on Soviet geopolitics. "Olinov meant Camp David, Mr. President. That's where Ariel signed the peace accords with Sadat. That's where he must have felt most comfortable. But why would Pesh volunteer to be his angel? There's nothing in the chatter we've picked up so far that links them. And we've been diligent, sir. That's why we don't trust this gambit. It's some kind of a stunt to suck you into Ariel's orbit, whatever it is."

But Isaac trusted Ariel's roundabout summons more than he did the advice of his intelligence chiefs. And Ramona must have sensed this. Her boss was a hopeless romantic and a loose cannon. And now she tried to ruffle Isaac, catch him off guard, while he stood in her office with his Glock.

"Ex–prime ministers don't come out of hibernation like that and suddenly decide to visit POTUS at his dacha in Maryland. He must have a motive. And I don't like it, particularly when the SOS is from that thug at the Kremlin. Ariel hasn't revealed himself yet. And when he does . . ."

"You'll have *our* thugs leave him to wander as much as he likes."

Her lower lip trembled. She couldn't find her magic potion with Sidel. "We're not like the Russians," she said. "We don't employ thugs. Some of our best agents have PhDs."

Yes, Isaac muttered to himself, *they can whack you on the ears while they recite one of Hamlet's soliloquies.*

"He shouldn't have been allowed to get on a plane. He has forged documents. We'll find him."

"That's what the Brits said after he bombed the King David. He's landed, Ramona, and he's much too clever to be found. He's been a hunted animal half his life."

An ancient, ravaged prime minister on the lam must have caused havoc among the ranks of Shin Bet. Perhaps Ariel Moss once had his own nuclear football, with all the doomsday codes, and Shin Bet didn't want this Hermit of Haifa to fall into the wrong hands with whatever codes he still had. Isaac could tell that Ramona had been in touch with Israeli counterintelligence, and she'd kept it a secret from him. Shin Bet didn't trust the Pink Commish, even if he was a *zhid* from the Lower East Side. His horizons were too far to the left. His own intelligence chiefs were suspicious of him, fueled by all the neoconservative think tanks. The neocons were convinced that President Sidel was a sleeper who took his instructions from Moscow. The Secret Service had dubbed him the Citizen, and that name stuck. Fanatics on talk radio took to calling him Citizen Sidel of the Soviet Union. He couldn't light out for the territory, like Huck Finn, his favorite character in American lit. There was no territory now, in Isaac's mind, except perhaps Antarctica and Tierra del Fuego, and he had little desire to go there. He was stuck in this "great white jail" with a chief of staff who was plotting to dismantle him. She sat with her pantyhose in the air, as if he was some sidebar she had to tolerate for a little while longer.

He hated her smugness, her certainty that he was a transient who would fall into ruin. He had to resist tugging at her pantyhose and spinning her around until she couldn't recapture her comfort zone. But Isaac would have ended up in handcuffs, charged with assault.

So he smiled that errant smile of his—like a Chinese mask that couldn't be pierced.

"Ramona, I bailed you out," he said. "You would have shoved me into the tar pits if your own candidate had survived his inauguration. But he couldn't, and now you're stuck with me. Either we have a marriage, or it's civil war, and it will ripple right through the DNC. You'll lose all your donors."

Those thin nostrils of hers flared. "Are you threatening me, Mr. President?"

"Yes," he whispered. They were all alone in her labyrinth of rooms. Ramona's brats must have fled to a bar in Georgetown, where they could mock Isaac's torn cuffs and bald pate over whiskey sours and a pot of British ale.

Ramona tugged at her pantyhose, stood up, strode around her antique desk, and walloped Sidel. His jaw tingled. His mouth bled, and he had a roaring in his ears that was like the crash of the Atlantic against Ramona's private seawall. The Big Guy didn't bother to wipe the blood from his teeth. The ground had shifted. He'd riled Ramona Dazzle.

"We'll have that Russian dwarf Olinov recalled to Moscow. He won't play Mercury for a miserable old man from Haifa."

"Pesh isn't a dwarf," Isaac said, with a sudden lilt to his voice. "And you can't have him recalled—it's the age of *glasnost*, the era of cooperation between East and West. We're downsizing our nuclear arsenals, in spite of their generals and ours. If you let your hatchet men go near Olinov, I'll have their peckers cut off and hung on display in the Rose Garden. You can watch their wrinkled remains from your patio."

"You're disgusting," Ramona screamed into the void. "You're uncouth."

She walloped him again. The Big Guy tottered for a moment and grabbed her wrists. It was his first moment of pleasure since he'd arrived in the White House.

"Let go of me," she screamed at Isaac, who had to sidestep her flicking heels like a matador and also protect his groin. A Secret Service man arrived, his .357 Magnum unholstered, like an obscene toy. With him was Isaac's naval aide, carrying the nuclear football. And behind them both was the vice president, Bull Latham, barreling in and shoving everyone out of his way, until Isaac's naval aide and the nuclear football landed in the dark well under Ramona's desk.

"Can this lovers' quarrel, Mr. President. There's been some disturbing chatter."

He sat Isaac and Ramona down at her conference table. "It's not a joke. Oh, we've heard rumors about Colonel Gaddafi sending hit men after your hide—that's been going on for months. But he wouldn't want his ass bombed out of Tripoli. He'd have to retire to the desert in a woman's scarf and join my list of favorite cross-dressers." The Bull was basking in his new glory. He'd set his own rules as Isaac's vice president. He reigned over the FBI and went into the deepest pockets of Isaac's other agencies. His Herculean shoulders held him in good sway wherever he happened to poke around. "The Colombian drug lords hate you because we've been busting up their cartels. But they consider themselves crusaders. And you're popular in the barrios. They call you the *israelita* with a Glock, so the clamor comes from another direction. We don't bother with anti-Semitic dreck—fruitcakes who rant against that 'Heimie in the White House.' "

The Bull paused to lick his lips and capitalize on his own sense of drama.

"Something came in from the Aryan Brotherhood, those jailhouse freaks. It's a fucking tattoo. They're tattoo artists, I know. But this one is a little scary. It's a caricature of you, Mr. President, with an ice pick in one eye, and your neck sewn onto your head, like some Frankenstein, with the stitches as fat as a finger."

"Then we ought to round up those tattoo artists and teach them a lesson," Ramona rasped.

"Whoa," said Bull Latham. "They're only the clerks. That's why we have to shake their little tree."

Isaac was wary of Bull Latham. The Secret Service should have notified him of any danger, not his vice president. And Matthew Malloy, chief of the White House detail, hadn't said a word.

"What sort of tree?" Isaac asked, with that false naïveté of an ex-cop.

"A poison tree, Mr. President, but the tree's not important. We should concentrate on the gardeners who've been watering it. They're the ones who would profit from your demise. They lured the Brotherhood with a secret load of cash."

"And who are these ghostly gardeners?"

"There's the rub," said Bull Latham. "I haven't a clue. I'd squeeze the neo-Nazi bastards, but most of them are lifers who are loyal to one another, and they'd only lie. Could be anybody under the sun with a grievance against you, yet tough enough to tangle with the Brotherhood and relieve them of their art. That's no small accomplishment. The Brotherhood doesn't like to part with their tattoos."

Now Ramona saw her chance. "I'll bet Ariel Moss is involved. He could be one of the gardeners."

The Bull chuckled to himself and chided her. "That hermit? He has to wear diapers—that's in my logs, swear to God. He was always incontinent, even during the Camp David Accords. Shin Bet had to run up and down the paths with a fresh pair of nappies for their prime minister. He had some sort of dysentery when he was in the gulag, and it was never cured—a horrible case of the worms. He's not one of the gardeners. I can guarantee that."

"But he's out there doing mischief," Ramona chanted, like a little helpless girl, while the Bull winked.

"We'll catch him. All we have to do is sniff the wind."

Isaac grew weary of his vice president. He left Ramona's labyrinth without a nod to the Bull, walked under the colonnade that Thomas Jefferson had built, rode upstairs to his private quarters in the president's elevator, two Secret Service men at his tail. He had his own labyrinth of rooms. He couldn't seem to settle in. He inhabited the entire second floor of the White House, with its rosewood tables, astral lamps, satinwood commodes, its cut-glass chandeliers that left irregular shadows on the walls, and a little treasure of Cézannes with clumps of earthlike color that crinkled against the fanlight windowpanes. The residence also had a kitchen, sitting rooms, a balcony, and a beauty salon, with a salmon-colored lounge chair, multiple hair driers, a manicurist's stool, and a porcelain shampoo bowl, meant to accommodate the First Lady. Somehow, Isaac preferred this room, with its coral-colored rug. He wasn't wifeless. But the wife he had, known as the Countess Kathleen, a voluptuous redhead whom he had married when he was nineteen and had never bothered to divorce, preferred an empire of Florida real estate to the White House. She was five years older than the Big Guy and a rabid Republican. He could never have become mayor or police commissioner without Kathleen, who had stroked the Irish mafia of the NYPD for Isaac. She might have slept with a few of the chiefs before her own marriage, bewitched them with her wild Irish ways.

The Countess was an embarrassment to Ramona and the DNC, having donated millions to Republican coffers during Isaac's campaign and not a dime to the Democrats. But Isaac never abused her, never sang an unkind song, even when Ramona's detectives came up with every sort of dirt about Kathleen's land deals in the Florida swamps.

"Sweetheart, leave my wife alone," Isaac had to warn. "Whatever you uncover will only come back to haunt us." Isaac was clever enough to see the Countess's own cleverness. Who would be dumb enough to prosecute a president's wife for some arcane land deal in the Okefenokee? And it gave him pleasure to sit in the White House's Cosmetology Room and dream of the Countess rinsing her red hair.

The Pink Commish was about to shut his eyes when he noticed a slip of paper beneath one of the hair driers, like a primitive greeting card. On the front was written in a very ragged script:

Welcome to the Brotherhood,
Big Balls

That's what his enemies would call him when he was police commissioner and had locked up badasses in every borough. They meant to mock him, but Big Balls soon became a mark of respect. He followed child molesters and bank robbers and sadistic gang leaders across the landscape until he cuffed them. He went into a burning warehouse once to capture a homicidal maniac and had to be hospitalized for six weeks. But that couldn't sideline Sidel. He simply moved his office into his hospital room, and was surrounded by detectives and assistant DAs.

His nom de guerre didn't follow him to Gracie Mansion. He wasn't Big Balls on the mayor's circuit. So why should that name suddenly haunt him at the White House? He unfolded the greeting card and saw an imprint of the tattoo that the Bull had described, a sample of the Aryan Brotherhood's art in bold red ink—Isaac with his bald patch, an ice pick stuck in his left eye and his head sewn onto his body with a thick cord.

The artist had captured Isaac's stern look, as if the Pink Commish had sat for his own portrait somewhere in hell.

Below the drawing were the habitual swastikas and runes of the Aryan Brotherhood. Isaac brooded over this greeting card. How did it get here? Who had sneaked it into his sanctuary? Someone had to be aware of Isaac's habits and haunts. He didn't shout for the Secret Service, didn't alert Bull Latham. He plucked a telephone out of its cradle near the manicurist's stool and had the White House operator dial the Hotel Washington and ask for Pesh Olinov's suite. Some Soviet gorilla answered the phone.

"Who is talking? Please to answer, yes?"

"Big Balls," Isaac shouted. "Tell that to Pesh."

2

He couldn't cross the street without his caravan. He would have stopped traffic cold on Pennsylvania Avenue for an hour, as District detectives and the Secret Service scrambled about and lined the gates of Lafayette Park. Every one of his moves had to be mapped out and diagrammed, his destination logged in. It would have taken him five minutes to travel on foot from the White House to the Hotel Washington, but he'd never have gotten out the North Portico on his own. He was embalmed in his own trappings as president. The White House operator must have snitched to Ramona and Matthew Malloy. Isaac's chief of staff flew at him like one of the Furies.

"Imbecile," she said. "Do you want to create an international crisis? The dwarf's thugs could shoot you in the shoulder—just for fun. You can't amble into the Washington. You have to follow protocol. Tell him, Matt."

The head of the White House detail rocked on his heels. Ramona had managed to henpeck him after she first strutted into the West Wing. He was almost fifty, and intended to retire. He must have looked like a blue-eyed Apollo once, but Calder Cottonwood had involved him in some shady deals, and that blond handsomeness was gone; his face had turned soft, as if he'd begun to rot like an exotic flower.

"I'll put a package together, sir. We'll have everyone in place, and we'll secure Dragon."

Dragon was Isaac's armored Lincoln Town Car with bulletproof glass; he'd have had to exit the White House in a fleet of sedans and ride two blocks, with his own "double" sitting in one of the sedans.

"That'll take an hour, and Pesh will have time to prepare a whole scenario. I want to catch that prick with his pants down. We're going on foot, Matt."

He'd still lose precious time. Matt would have to alert the hotel and secure the perimeter, which meant agents outside Pesh's room and on the floor above and the floor below. It was like the choreography of a mad king, and Isaac had to reside within the pretense of Matthew Malloy's "chaos control." He refused to strap on a fiberglass vest. His Glock was good enough. But he had to wait and wait for his protective team to gather its gear—the magnetometers, the .357 Magnums, the button mikes, the Ray-Bans, the metallic cups—and rise out of its roost in the cellars of the West Wing.

Matt and his men never wore topcoats in the winter chill. It would have slowed them down considerably if they had tried to reach for their .357 Magnums. They'd discovered a thing or two from Shin Bet. The two secret services liked to trade professional tricks. And last year Matt invited Shin Bet for a week of exercises at his own training facility near Laurel, Maryland. "They're tough customers, those Izzies," he said. "I wouldn't want to fart around with them." And now Isaac's protective team scrambled across the leafless landscape of Lafayette Park, with its little world of windswept trees with rotting silver bark, and rushed into the lobby of the Hotel Washington like a human sledgehammer, with the Big Guy wedged in the middle. They looked sinister in their Ray-Bans—and slightly comical.

The entire lobby was in their thrall. POTUS and his protectors had just entered a slow-motion paradise, where all movement stopped and not a sound was heard. They commandeered an elevator for themselves, while two agents fell away from the team and guarded the elevator bank. The others rode up with Isaac. They leapt out on the sixth floor and surrounded Isaac again. Two of the agents were carrying portable magnetometers. It didn't matter who Pesh was—diplomat, crime boss, or king of Siam. They would still have to shake down his suite. There had been no preliminary search, and they couldn't allow POTUS to enter uncharted territory.

Isaac himself knocked on Pesh Olinov's door; for a moment he felt like a young deputy chief inspector out on his first raid. One of Pesh's gorillas opened the door with a growl. He had a shaved skull with a red birthmark on its crown that could have been a map of Siberia.

"What you bother, eh? Pesh asleep."

"Wake him," Isaac said, as the Secret Service barreled through the door in their Ray-Bans and button mikes. Pesh Olinov appeared from the bedroom of his suite in a magnificent velour robe. Another bodyguard stood behind him, waving a document in a leather wallet.

"You cannot interfere. We are Soviet diplomats."

"It's no use, Sasha," said Olinov with a smile that moved like a trembling worm across his mouth. "We are with the barbarians."

"Sir," said Matt, "we'll have to sweep the room and give the Russkies a toss with the magnetometers."

"Not now," Isaac said. "Forget the body searches. I have business with Pesh."

He turned to the acting deputy foreign minister, bowed, and whispered in his ear, "You'll have to forgive my own protectors. They have their protocols. It can't be helped."

He walked into the bedroom with Pesh and shut the door, just as Matt began to scream, "You can't go in there, sir. It isn't safe."

Isaac had expected to meet a couple of call girls under the satin covers of Olinov's king-size bed. He'd heard about his kinky habits from Bull Latham's informants at the FBI. But Isaac was bewildered by Olinov's companion. She wasn't even undressed. She sat in a rosewood chair that could have been a replica of his own prize furniture at the White House. It was Renata Swallow, the doyenne of Georgetown, and one of the principal Cave Dwellers, the elite of Washington's elite. The Cave Dwellers had never had much truck with presidents or their wives. They and their ancestors snubbed Mary Lincoln, Eleanor Roosevelt, and Mamie Eisenhower with the same icy venom. They were listed in their unique social register, the Green Book, had their charity balls and concert subscriptions, and rarely meddled in politics. But Renata wasn't like the other doyennes, or Queen Bees. A recent widow, who hadn't relied on her late husband's fortune, she was thirty-seven years old, defiantly blond, preferred martial arts to charity balls, and was a buoyant member of the Republican National Committee.

She despised Isaac's chief of staff and never missed a chance to hurl a poisoned dart at "Dizzy Ms. Dazzle."

Isaac had met Renata once before, not in the District, but at a gala honoring George Balanchine and the New York City Ballet while Isaac was in his honeymoon as mayor. He was captivated by her voice. She spoke to the *maître* in a lyrical Russian that was like the cry of a desolate bird. He'd never realized how sad a language could be. And it seemed out of place with her almost masculine beauty and clipped blond hair. He was delirious about this matron of the arts from the District until she grabbed him by the shoulder and roared at him in a voice with its own martial music—"What are you doing here, Mr. Mayor? Have you ever seen a ballet in your life?"

Issac's tongue twisted, and he couldn't utter a word in front of Renata, who went right back to Balanchine and warbled in Russian. She had only daggers for Isaac Sidel. To spite her, and displace his own curious attraction to this Cave Dweller, he began to attend the New York City Ballet, and he marveled how the prima ballerinas danced only for Balanchine, who sat in the last row of the orchestra, his nose twitching incessantly, while he watched like a warrior hawk. Balanchine was hospitalized soon after that and never returned to his seat. Without Balanchine's gaze to guide them, the primas fumbled through their dance, like moribund, frenzied dolls, and Isaac stopped going to the ballet. He meant to write Renata, but somehow he couldn't seem to find the vocabulary. And here she was, in the bedroom of a Russian gangster-politician, who was Gorbachev's conduit to the crime lords of Moscow and Kiev.

Renata wasn't even embarrassed. She extended her hand to Sidel. "How lovely," she said, staring at his Glock. "I'm delighted to see that you haven't lost your affection for firearms."

She'd already disarmed Isaac, and he hadn't said a word.

"Balanchine," Isaac managed to whisper. "I saw my first ballet thanks to you."

The doyenne fondled the soft material of the Russian gangster's robe for an instant, then turned to Isaac as if to remind herself that he was still there. "I'm so glad. And what did you learn, Mr. President?"

"That it's a catastrophe if you separate the creator from his creation. The ballerinas were all in a trance after Balanchine died."

"Yet the company still exists, and I'm one of its patrons. I'm sure you have a lot to discuss with Pesh. Goodbye."

And she marched out of the bedroom in her lambs' wool coat, as if she'd spent the afternoon with her fellow bluebloods at the Salamander Club rather than with a political pimp. But Isaac wasn't as courteous with the gangster as he had been with the lady from Georgetown. He grabbed the lapels of Pesh's robe.

"What was she doing here? Are you selling caviar to the Cave Dwellers?"

"No, Madame Renata was worried about the Kirov and the Bolshoi—Russian ballet. She knows how inflation has been tearing up the roots of my country. We've been eating into our foreign reserves, and—"

"Since when are you a cultural commissar?"

"You shouldn't belittle me," Olinov muttered. "I'm one of the last allies you have left. Why did you settle in the White House? You won't survive very long, my friend."

"Congratulations, Pesh. You've become a mind reader."

Isaac took the greeting card from the Aryan Brotherhood out of his pocket. "Those jailbirds smuggled this into my quarters. Are they sending me a kite?"

Pesh savored the word "kite," allowed it to settle between his teeth. "This didn't come from those amateurs at the Aryan

Brotherhood. The work is much too fine. *Their* tattoos are primitive and childish. They never had access to a master artist, and they never endured the endless winters of Kolyma. None of them was born into the craft. They're copycats. You've received an epistle from the Sons of Rossiya. And you should be proud."

Pesh explained who the Sons were: orphans plucked from the streets of Moscow and shipped to Siberia, they had grown up in the gulag, protected by one *pakhan* or another, or else they would have become the sexual toys of the camp guards and the *cheloveks*. They all had a specific talent, either as engravers or tattoo artists, or experts with the pickaxe and the knife. Mostly, they were counterfeiters, and they made millions for their *pakhans* and for themselves. And when the camps began to close down during the political upheavals after Stalin's death, they felt lost, abandoned, homeless. They were werewolves, like the other *cheloveks*, reborn in the camps, but still, they managed to survive. They didn't tear at each other's throats, didn't wage mortal combat between Moscow and Kiev. They remained neutral and half dead. They were the Sons of Rossiya, counterfeiters and killers with an unbroken loyalty oath. Many moved to the West, settled in Milan, London, Madrid, crossing borders with all the agility of a werewolf.

"Then why haven't I heard of them?" Isaac asked.

"Because these were the *besprizornye*—street children. You must have had your own *besprizornye* in Manhattan."

Yes, Isaac recalled; wild boys who stole from the pickle merchants and lived on the brine. They had a perilous existence in the back alleys of Hester Street. They perched on the rooftops like gargoyles with warm blood. Isaac could never tame these orphans no matter how hard he tried, never get them to attend school at Gracie Mansion and become Merlins, like children from the South Bronx he managed to rescue from the oblivion of broken streets.

"But these boys perished," Isaac said. "They couldn't survive the Manhattan winter year after year." Big Balls nearly broke down and cried at the recollection of these winter boys. "I had to bury most of them in Potter's Field, without a name tag, and nothing to eulogize them with but a primitive pine box."

"Not our *besprizornye*," Olinov said. "They survived Siberia. Their greatest feat, once they left the camps, was to exist without an identity, recognizable only to themselves. And as the Russian empire falls into ruin, with rubles that aren't even worth enough to copy, they're the ones who have had to pick up the pieces. That's why they sent you a kite, as you say, only they would call it a winter warning—it was always winter in the taiga, you see."

"And that greeting card is some kind of a threat?"

Olinov appraised the portrait of Isaac with an ice pick piercing his left eye.

"I don't think so. They consider you a werewolf, like themselves. And that's a mark of respect. Perhaps they would like to meet with you—the presidency means nothing to them. It's not your power that interests the *besprizornye*. In their eyes you have none. Perhaps it is a real winter warning, and they are telling you to be more careful with your steps. The Secret Service cannot protect you with their magnetometers, my friend."

Isaac was still baffled. The Sons of Rossiya were as remote to him as Teutonic knights. "How did they smuggle their greeting card past all the lines of security? We have bomb-sniffing dogs in the mail room. We have X-ray machines. Every damn letter is sifted and unsealed. And that card ends up under a hair drier in the White House beauty parlor."

Olinov laughed. "The *besprizornye* have all the money in the world—they bribe and kiss and kill. On top of that, they're wizards. Their souls could probably pass right through an X-ray machine."

Pesh's mystical ballyhoo didn't appeal to Isaac. He wouldn't have been surprised if this gangster invented the *besprizornye*, orphans with a magical twist. "And where does Ariel Moss fit in? He's no wizard."

"But he's become an orphan in his old age."

"Who escaped his keepers at Shin Bet."

Pesh frowned for the first time. "Don't patronize me, Mr. President. It was Ariel who created the model for Shin Bet when he was with the Irgun—silent ghosts with a protective shield. Didn't he float into Acre Prison and float out with half his gang? Shin Bet worshiped him when he was prime minister. The same silent ghosts kept him alive. How many suicide attacks did they thwart? At least a dozen. They were his family, my friend, his shield. Shin Bet would never harm Ariel Moss."

And now Isaac was the policeman again, prickly as ever. "So where did you bump into the Hermit of Haifa? At a Black Sea resort?"

Olinov scratched under the collar of his robe, and Isaac glimpsed at the paws of some imaginary beast tattooed on his chest, like a marvelous totem. "No, my friend—not the Black Sea. The old man knocked on my door. He was starving. But he couldn't swallow American roast beef. We had to scour the markets for Russian rye bread, blackened potatoes, and *balanda*."

"What's that?"

"Prison soup," Olinov said. "Once you've feasted on such watery slop, it destroys your appetite for anything else."

Isaac didn't believe a word. "Where did you find your precious soup ten thousand miles from Siberia?"

"I prepared it for him on a hot plate at the hotel. We're all *zeks* from the same zone. My *balanda* revived the old man."

Pesh revealed how emaciated Ariel Moss was, and how he and his own gorillas—all graduates of the same penal colony—had to feed the recluse with a wooden spoon, how they sang their favorite prison songs about cocks and cunts and Stalin's swollen testicles. But Ariel kept insisting that he had to see the Pink Commish.

"Your enemies, the old man said, will eat you alive. And it was only safe for him to meet at your dacha."

It made no sense to Isaac. Why would that hermit leave his private garden for Isaac Sidel? He could have gone to Shin Bet. He must have been on familiar terms with half its retired generals. Yet he went back to robbing banks, or something close to that, to help finance his own disappearing act. He crosses two continents like a silent ghost, knocks on the gangster's door at the Washington, fills himself with *balanda*, and talks about cannibals in the White House. It made no sense.

Isaac could hardly trust anything the dwarf said—yes, Ramona Dazzle had been right. Pesh was some kind of a dwarf. He didn't even reach Isaac's shoulder blades. Perhaps all that *balanda* had stunted Pesh's growth. And the Cave Dwellers' Queen Bee hadn't come here to talk with Pesh about the Bolshoi. All the scars on his face—the souvenirs of knife wounds gathered in the gulag—hadn't suddenly turned Pesh into a balletomane. Renata was searching for something much more enigmatic, something she couldn't find among all the bluebloods at the Salamander Club—it was the tattoos of a Russian gangster. That's why he stood in his velour robe, while she sat around in her winter coat. Isaac had interrupted a striptease act.

"*Chelovek*," Isaac said like an inmate at Kolyma, "get undressed."

Pesh stared at Isaac with that face of a mottled gourd. "Are you crazy?"

"Strip, little man. I want to see your colors."

Pesh lunged at Isaac with a sailor's paring knife cupped in his hand. The Big Guy smiled. This was a world he understood, not the invisible knife-throwing of all his military and intelligence chiefs, where it was useless to dodge; the knives always landed in some forlorn spot under his ribs, and Isaac had to survive with that perpetual nagging pain. But an ex–wild boy from the gulag was another matter. Isaac cracked Pesh's knuckles with the blade of his hand, and the tiny hooked knife fell to the carpet. Then he grabbed Pesh's velour collar and spun him out of his robe. And there was the bird that rippled across the gangster's chest—a griffin of some kind, with majestic, multiple claws, a lion's haunches, a feathery tail, and a half human head, with whiskers, a wolf's ears, luminous eyes, and a cavernous mouth that seemed to stifle a scream.

It must have been a creature born in the gulag, the personification of a werewolf, with symbols that only other wild boys and their *pakhans* could master—stars with seven points on the griffin's shoulder blades, swastikas on its expanding wings that ruffled in front of Isaac's eyes. The gangster had mesmerized Renata, made her dream. That's why she'd come to this hotel—not to flirt or do business with a Moscow minister without much of a portfolio.

"You cannot look at me," Pesh whispered. "It is sacred. You could be killed. Only the *besprizornye* are permitted to stare and count the stars. Each star tells a tale."

"And yet you stripped for Renata."

"As a special favor. She has powerful friends. And we are beggars with an abundance of nuclear warheads. The Kremlin has become a whorehouse for hire. There's talk every week of a coup. Look," he said, kicking a gigantic suitcase near his bed. "Open it, Mr. President, and you will understand our plight."

Isaac sprang the lock with a click of his thumb; the suitcase was crammed with rolls of toilet paper, like packaged snow.

"My bodyguards went on a shopping spree in Chinatown. It was God's country to them. You know, we have every flavor of ice cream in shops along the Arbat—peach, white chocolate, caramel—but a singular absence of toilet paper. In Moscow you learn to wipe your ass with *Pravda* or with the back of your hand . . ."

They heard the thump of a warring army outside the bedroom. Pesh wrapped himself up in his robe, covering that strange, grounded bird on his chest, and the two of them leapt into the parlor, where the Secret Service was engaged in a battle royal with Pesh's bodyguards, fighting over the magnetometers—like wild boys, Isaac muttered to himself. *Besprizornye.*

"That's enough," Olinov said, slapping at the shaved skulls of his men. "Sasha, let them have their toys."

And Isaac marched out of the room with his detail, their Ray-Bans all awry.

He was overwhelmed by the wanton crush of people in a lobby crammed with spectators and members of the White House press corps, and stragglers who'd wandered in from the street—it seemed as if the whole damn capital knew of POTUS's impulsive peregrination across Lafayette Park. Isaac was no less a recluse than the Hermit of Haifa. Washingtonians seldom had a chance to catch him in the flesh. He must have looked a bit ragged and drawn in his suit and tie from the clothing barrels of Orchard Street. He wouldn't change his habits, no matter what his advisors said. He would have felt ridiculous in an Armani label.

Isaac was trapped in a swirl of bodies, and his detail couldn't help him now. He had to bob and weave with the prevailing rhythm, or he would have been swept back toward the elevator bank. Hands gripped at him like the colossal talons of that mythical bird under Olinov's robe; his face was scratched; he was beginning to suffocate amid that furnace of human flesh. It was Matt Malloy who had the presence of mind to reach for his holster and shoot into the ceiling with his .357 Magnum. His superiors would crucify him for firing his hand cannon in a crowded hotel. But that explosion—like the crack of a whip in an echo chamber—smashed the relentless rhythm of the mob. Isaac lurched forward and tumbled out of the hotel. There was an aura of irreality about the episode. Isaac, Manhattan born, could have been a minor character in *Augie March*.

"Sir, are you hurt?" asked Matt Malloy, with anguish in his eyes.

"Matt, I'm fine. I had the time of my life."

But his team wouldn't let him recross Lafayette Park on foot. Matt hunched over and kept nibbling instructions into his ear until Dragon arrived, Isaac's bulletproof Lincoln deluxe. And now he'd have to ride two blocks in his chariot, with a Lincoln behind him and a Lincoln in front.

Back to the asylum, he muttered, as he stepped into the chariot.

3

olonel Stefan Oliver, code name Rio, was in the rec room at Quantico, immersed in a monumental ping-pong match with the base champion, a sergeant from the Philippines, when he heard a crackle in his earpiece and instantly halted the match. He had to wear a button mike whether he was wielding a ping-pong paddle or sitting on the crapper. The duty officer at the White House was communicating with him on one of the Secret Service's encrypted channels. "Tango One to Rio, clear the decks. The Citizen is riding high."

"Roger that, Tango One, but what the hell is going on?"

"You have to arrange a lift package in about twenty minutes."

"That's absurd," said the commander of the most elite unit in the helicopter corps. "I'm wearing silkies, and I'm playing the match of my life. I can't put together a lift package in twenty minutes."

"Sure you can, Rio. You're the president's fucking pilot. Now clear the decks. The Big Guy is at your facility, sir."

He had to banish the Filipino sergeant and every other player from the rec room—clear the decks. Then he heard that unmistakable clatter of the presidential detail. Son of a bitch. POTUS had come to Quantico.

Sidel walked into the rec room in a blue sweatshirt and silkies—the Marines' traditional nylon running shorts. He had to borrow a paddle.

"Hit with me, Stef. I always think better when I hear the sound of the ball. That's why I came to fetch you. I couldn't wait."

He knew firsthand of the president's fabled softness for ping-pong. Sidel had the Seabees and the gardeners at Camp David rip up the miniature golf course that earlier gardeners and engineers had cut out of the forest exclusively for President Eisenhower—it was modeled after the grounds at Burning Tree, the capital's premier private golf club. Every president after Ike had used it as a putting green. But Sidel couldn't bear the sight of that golf course outside his picture window at Aspen Lodge—it offended his proletarian pride. And he had Ike's little green turned into a bumpy playground with marble-topped ping-pong tables that summoned up his childhood in Manhattan, when every park had its own ping-pong tournament, summer and winter. Isaac hadn't counted on the perpetual wind off Catoctin Mountain that sent the ball sailing after every shot.

And so Stefan Oliver, the thirty-seven-year-old commander of Squadron One, stood in his silkies at Quantico and slapped at the ball with his president. He wasn't trying to score points. For whatever reason, the Big Guy had glommed onto his personal pilot, and the Marine generals at Quantico were uncomfortable about this sudden coziness. The colonel was a widower; his wife, Leona, had died of a blood clot that had gone to the brain, and left him with Max, a moody eleven-year-old boy. And since the colonel had complicated hours, with the added complication of a boy who attended a school for the learning disabled near Rock Creek Park, Isaac insisted that father and son sleep at the White House on those days when his pilot was too involved with lugging him around. Stefan Oliver had a bedroom in the "attic," on the third floor; he and the boy were the White House's semipermanent guests.

But Isaac hadn't come to Quantico before; the visit seemed strange, almost a kind of burlesque. He'd never involved himself in his pilot's lift packages, and he had his own ping-pong table in the White House attic, where he could have scheduled a match with members of the Secret Service and won in a sneeze. Yet he'd come to the rec room at Quantico, where he could be alone with Stef and risk losing point after point.

"Kid," Isaac said, "I'm being set up."

"Then shouldn't we tap Malloy and Bull Latham? I'm an amateur when it comes to intel."

"But you have a keener eye than Matt. And the Bull is compromised. He's loyal to his own career. He'd love to watch me stumble. No, I need your calibrations, Stef. You were at Camp David during the accords."

"Yes, sir, but I wasn't involved with the big show. I didn't have any presidential lifts. I was a babe in the woods, the youngest pilot on the watch."

Isaac studied him for a moment, pursed his lips. "Did you meet the Israeli prime minister?"

"A couple of times. He liked to ramble, but his security was tight as a rat's ass. I did carry him once. He wanted to go up on one of our Night Hawks. Shin Bet had a fit. But they couldn't stop him. He wouldn't stay aft with all the generals. He sat in the cockpit with me, sailed right through the mist."

"And what was your take on him?" Isaac asked. "Was he suicidal, or in complete control?"

Stefan Oliver stared at his boss. "I'd say he was a prisoner of protocol—a lot like you."

Isaac laughed and tossed his paddle into the air. "I knew it! You're a natural, much more clever than Matt and the Bull. Colonel, let's get cracking."

"I wasn't told about this lift package. Where to, sir? What's our destination?"

"My dacha."

Sidel wouldn't change out of his silkies, and Stefan had to give him fatigues and one of his own flight jackets. He'd consult the weather charts, talk to the tower. If the fog was too thick, they couldn't approach the mountaintop. They'd have to land at Thurmont, and drive the rest of the way to the presidential retreat. The military team at the White House had choreographed this damn lift, and the colonel had been left to piss in the wind on his own command. He didn't like it at all. He radioed the duty officer.

"Tango One, can you hear me, Tango One?"

"Loud and clear."

"Weather uncertain. Will Dragon be at the Thurmont rendezvous?"

"Dragon on target, Rio. Not a worry in the world. Roger and out."

Why had they bothered to include him in this mystery tour? The entire crew had assembled without him. His crew chief and copilot were in place. Stefan scowled, and they busied themselves with the control panels like a couple of innocents, while the president climbed the air stair, and the helicopter with the distinct white top assumed the designation of Marine One the moment he was aboard. There were two Hawks on this lift package, Marine One and a decoy.

Stefan had the stick between his legs, but the Hawk seemed to hover on invisible strings. He didn't like it at all. Still, he couldn't soliloquize to himself while he was in the air. He cruised toward Maryland and the mountaintop. The weather had begun to break. He could see clear to Gettysburg and some of the battle sites, like little green bumps. He confirmed his coordinates with the tower and radioed the duty officer.

"Tango One, we'll survive without Dragon. I'm heading toward Camp David."

"Are you sure, Rio? What if the sky falls on your head?"

"Then you'll suffer, son. I didn't authorize this lift. I was never briefed. I'm a ghost rider. Roger and out."

It was always a bitch to land on the mountaintop. It didn't matter how many times he'd been in the captain's seat. You still had to squint like a hawk to spot the landing zone that had been cut out of the forest and that also served as a skeet range. He worried all the time that some son of a bitch of a sharpshooter would be out on the range popping at clay pigeons like Buffalo Bill while Stef was bringing in a White Top. And sure enough, a sharpshooter was right on the range with headphones and a target gun, as if he was lord and master of these bucolic grounds and there had never been or would never be a metal bird known as Marine One.

Stefan had to radio the camp commander. "Shoofly, Shoofly, what the fuck is Buffalo Bill doing on my lawn?"

And the commander shot back at him, "Rio, you have God's word, the lawn is bare-assed."

Stef had to squint again at the skeet range—Buffalo Bill was gone. Neither the copilot nor the chief steward had seen him. And Stef began to doubt his own instincts, that sixth sense he had of the terrain. He allowed his craft to hover a bit as he surveyed the lawn and then landed Marine One on a dime, as he always did. The president didn't stride into the cockpit to chat with Stef and thank him for the lift, which had become his "protocol" on board Marine One, but climbed down the air stair instead with his military aide and Matt Malloy. There were the usual motorized golf carts that would carry the Secret Service men on board the second White Top to their cabin. But Isaac detested these carts and everything that reminded him of golf and all the aristocrats at Burning Tree. And unless he arrived from Thurmont on board Dragon during a foul-weather lift, he preferred to hike from the landing pad to the presidential digs at Aspen Lodge.

The Big Guy could relax a bit. He didn't have to follow the protocol of a full presidential detail, since his dacha on the mountain was a fenced-in fortress. And the airspace above this fortress had been dubbed "the doughnut of death," considering that no unauthorized craft couldn't possibly penetrate it.

Isaac had deposited the colonel's flight jacket on his seat and wore one of the traditional blue windbreakers that were coveted by all those who visited the mountain.

So he was almost invisible at his dacha, since everyone—from the Seabees to the carpenters and the kitchen patrol—was decked out in identical windbreakers with the words CAMP DAVID stitched in gold on the back.

Stef couldn't accompany POTUS on his little pilgrimage to Aspen Lodge. He had to button up the aircraft, put it to bed. He was tired and also pissed off at the president. He'd always been informed, even when there was a sudden shift in POTUS's schedule. If something went wrong on this ride, and Marine One had been knocked about in a blizzard, Stef would still bear the blame, even though he hadn't designed or approved the lift package.

He rode in a caravan of golf carts across the wooded terrain, past the camp commander's quarters, past the dispensary, past the nurses' station, past a row of horseshoe pegs, past the primitive cabins with their green-painted boards and shake roofs, and leapt out at Walnut Lodge, his own digs at Camp David, this hidden resort with roads that were hard to find, where the sun could sink behind Catoctin Mountain and leave a blood-red trace, and where time had a lulling yet ferocious tug that was beyond the clockwork of any president and his keepers. FDR was the first president to visit the mountain and he'd dubbed it Shangri-La, where he could escape the furor of politics in wartime Washington and have his own rustic paradise. His aides had to live without running water and wash themselves in wooden troughs, while Stef had all the perks of a Marriott at Walnut Lodge.

He couldn't even settle in. The duty officer at Camp David was on the horn: POTUS wanted to see him at his dacha.

"How soon?" Stefan asked. "Can I unwind a bit? Have a cup of fruit cocktail out of my fridge?"

"Colonel, the boss expects you to come riding into Dodge as pronto as you can. If you're screwing one of the nurses from Chestnut, tell her to diddle herself." There was a deadness on the line, as the duty officer realized his blunder. Stef was still in mourning. "I didn't mean to be untactical, sir . . ."

He put on his own windbreaker and a Baltimore Orioles cap and went out into the winter chill that had settled on the mountain months ago and would last until spring. It could make a man crumple up on a bad day. He had no official status at Shangri-La once the lift package landed. He was one of the president's invited guests, marking time on the mountain until the president decided to leave and Stef had to prepare another package, like a mummy called back to life. That was the strangeness of the squadron commander's role once he arrived at Shangri-La.

He kept seeing other men in windbreakers and Oriole caps, men he had never seen before. They didn't mask their gaze. They saluted Stef.

"Evening, Colonel."

It still unnerved Stef. They were his duplicates or triplicates, who rode the wind, like he did. He could have had a dozen twins out there—two dozen. Dammit, he knew his own Marines, and he was familiar enough with the Secret Service. These weren't Park Rangers, who had clearance at this site, who gardened a lot and often provided mounts for the president's guests.

He stopped one of these strangers. "Who are you, son?"

"Chief Petty Officer Tatum. I'm with the Seabees, sir. I belong to Captain Cotter's detail."

Tatum's tags were in order, and he knew the abracadabra that the Secret Service had arranged with Naval Intel to spirit out any rogues on the mountain: *Blood on the Moon.*

So Stef passed the swimming pool that President Nixon had the Seabees build for him near the patio of Aspen Lodge; Nixon had kept the pool heated summer and winter during his stay at the dacha—it was called Dickie's Birdbath, since crows seemed to populate the pool more than presidents, riding over the surface with their raucous chatter. Isaac also kept the pool heated, and might go for a midnight dip when there wasn't too much blood on the moon. POTUS was a mystery unto himself, a ping-pong playing police chief who had become president by mere chance because the president-elect, J. Michael Storm, had to resign. Still, it was Isaac who had gathered in the votes, who had campaigned with a Glock in his pants, while J. Michael hid out at the Waldorf. But Isaac was beginning to suck up more and more of Nixon's habitat. He'd become as reclusive as Nixon after Watergate. Isaac wasn't plagued by any scandal. But he withdrew into the mountain mist, and allowed Ramona Dazzle to run the palace.

Aspen Lodge was barely visible in the steam clouds that rose above the water, even with the spotlights that surrounded the president's cabin. The colonel had to climb the patio steps through a shroud of wintry air—it was like holding a moist web in his hands. POTUS was on the patio with his chef, Charles, a huge black man with scars on his face as vivid as tattoos. Charles was a Seabee assigned to Aspen Lodge, and had also been with the Seabees in Nam. He'd had a concession booth at the Polo Grounds when he was still a boy. Isaac loved to talk with his Seabee chef about the late New York Giants. POTUS was still grieving Willie Mays, who was plucked from the Polo Grounds and sentenced to San Francisco. But Charles had another tale to tell.

"Look, Mr. President. I was there. I saw Willie walk down the steps of St. Nicholas Terrace and slide into the Polo Grounds on his own two feet. I watched him play stickball with kids in the Valley. He took to Harlem, and Harlem took to him, but you won't catch Willie walking on St. Nicholas Terrace—gone is gone."

Charles marched back inside the cabin, and Isaac was left in that wintry web, as the colonel climbed onto the patio.

"You know, kid, I can always see the deer at first light—from this porch. They come to the salt lick. The Seabees replenish that lick whenever I come to the mountain. Those whitetails were all bled out by local hunters, but I suspended the hunting season on this mountain, put a moratorium on whitetails. That's the last bit of power Ramona's left me."

"You could always fire her," the colonel said.

Isaac smiled in that curl of steam clouds. "And risk a coup? The military's on her side."

"I doubt that, sir."

"I didn't mean to *dis* you, Stef. But I had to get out of the Hotel"— that was the Secret Service's code name for the White House. "And I didn't want Ramona here. So I improvised and covered my tracks. She won't find this little maneuver in the logbooks."

Stef had to grin at Sidel's childlike perversity. "You can't keep her off the mountain, sir. A lift package is always countersigned. She'll see the signatures."

"But I've locked down all the other Night Hawks. And she can't get through the gates. I'm still commander-in-chief. I need twenty-four hours, Stef."

"Then it really is Blood on the Moon," Stef muttered.

"What's that?" Isaac asked with the same childlike perversity.

"It's kind of the code name to identify unauthorized personnel."

"And I'm the last to hear about it?"

The president seemed in real pain, and Stef was puzzled. POTUS was wild-eyed and wooly on his mountain. "I didn't want you to bring Max," Isaac said. "That's why I excluded you from the package."

Stef usually brought his son along on the lift, and the boy would go back to the District on Dragon if Stef had to linger. Max had a live-in nurse who stayed with him when the colonel disappeared on long lifts. Half the time they all lived in the White House attic and had breakfast with the Big Guy.

"I'm worried," Isaac said. "And I didn't want to add Max to the mix. I'm expecting a visit from Ariel Moss. It seems a lot of folks would be much happier if he didn't make it here alive. And I'd like to know the reason. Do you have a sidearm, son?"

The president's paranoia was beginning to gnaw at Stef. He wondered about all those unfamiliar faces in Oriole caps. Was the mountain overrun with professional body snatchers?

"I left my Beretta back at the base, sir. None of us are sanctioned to carry sidearms on a lift. We're not meant to be Buffalo Bill. We'd only add to the confusion in a firefight." He was disheartened by the president's woeful look. "I could go to the Marine barracks and get a sidearm. I have that privilege."

"No," Isaac said. "It might alert our enemies if you suddenly appear with a sidearm on the mountain."

What enemies? Had the Big Guy gone gray in the head?

"Do you want some company, sir? I could spend the night at Aspen."

"I'll be fine," Isaac said. "But indulge me. Don't make any new friends, not on this mountain."

The colonel had to promise the president, like a Boy Scout making a pledge of honor. Some kind of shit was going down and Stef had to juggle in the dark. But a promise was a promise. He walked out among those body snatchers in Oriole caps and went to the officers' mess at Hickory Lodge. And that's when he saw her, a Marine lieutenant attached to some other detail. She didn't belong to Squadron One. She was wearing rubber boots, tucked into her fatigues. She had dark, curly hair, like Leona, and it filled him with remorse, as he dreamt of his wife. The lady lieutenant was sipping a Dr. Pepper.

They were in a Mickey Mouse canteen, like everything on this mountain. Officers and enlisted men had to suck whiskey on the sly.

She had hazel eyes, and he had to calibrate the contours of her body like a pilot on a presidential mission. Even a widower in his grief had to admit that she was gorgeous. But not a soul in this mess hall was hitting on her, and she was the only female in sight. Then he noticed how lithe she was, how she leaned on the steel toes of her boots, like a night fighter.

She smiled at him, and it wasn't a seductive, slit-eyed smile. He returned her salute, though she didn't have to salute him in the mess hall, not in a company of officers at Camp David. The president's retreat was getting weirder and weirder—it was like tumbling into the rabbit hole with little Alice, but this rabbit hole was on a mountain.

"We're proud of you, Colonel," she said, with a Southern lilt in her voice. "Lieutenant Sarah Rogers, with the camp commander's office. I'm in charge of the commander's books. You know, I count up all the cans of asparagus."

A camp accountant wouldn't have worn steel-tipped boots. But he went along with her play and decided to become POTUS's perimeter detective. What if the Big Guy wasn't paranoid at all, and *Lieutenant* Sarah was some kind of a key? He was drawn to her despite her phony claims. He hadn't expected to discover a siren in a glorified snack bar. Leona had been his high school sweetheart, and he'd never flirted with another gal.

"You're a Southern belle, aren't you?"

Her hazel eyes crinkled a bit, but her smile was genuine. And Stef began to wonder if playacting was as difficult for her as it was for him.

"Lord," she said, "I'm a Texas cowgirl. I rode the bulls at Gilley's, and grew up on a ranch outside Austin. And where are you from, Colonel?"

"Peoria," he said. But it was a bit of a lie. Stef was a military brat, and he'd lived in Peoria just long enough to graduate from high school.

He sensed the same rootless longing in this *lieutenant* with the steel-tipped toes. He'd have bet that Sarah Rogers, the Southern belle, was also a military brat, and that the "ranch" she grew up on was a swarm of airfields and training camps between Okinawa and Stuttgart.

"It's hot in here," she said. "Shall we sit on the verandah?"

The snack bar didn't have anything like a verandah; it had a tiny landing on top of a staircase that led down to the camp garage. Two men in windbreakers wobbled up the stairs, with metal flasks sticking out of their pockets. The colonel couldn't tell if they were soldiers or civilian contractors assigned to the mountain. Both of them had mean whiskey eyes. They doffed their baseball caps at Sarah and pretended to salute Stef.

"Well, well," said the first whiskey man, "if it ain't the celebrity himself? What does it feel like, Mr. Oliver, to ferry the big Jew around in one of your Night Hawks? Does he recite his evening prayers in a yarmulke?"

"I think you had better shut your mouth," the colonel said, "and show a little respect for the commander in chief. You're both standing on his mountain."

"Well, well," said the second whiskey man. "Ain't he gallant? But the big Jew is nothin' but a crook. He stole the election. He doesn't deserve to be at David, unless he's here to clean the garbage bins. Why don't you lend us the young lady, Mr. Oliver? We'll waltz her into the forest and be as gentle with her as Jesus."

Stef moved toward these whiskey boys, ready to "waltz" with them on the landing, in his own way, but Sarah was much too quick for him, leaping out like the Catoctin wind. She battered their kneecaps with her steel toes, and they tumbled down the stairs with the crazy flip-flop of mannequins.

"Those two dirtballs," Sarah said. The Southern lilt was gone. She had that neutral, staccato tone of a military brat who'd spent her childhood hopping from place to place like a gal on an endless circus caravan.

"We could be charged with assault," Stefan said.

"I doubt it."

She had too many puckers around her hazel eyes for a brash young lieutenant. But why would she conceal her true rank?

"You're not the camp's bean counter, are you?"

"No," she said. "I'm a captain with Naval Intel. And this isn't POTUS's mountain. He's a tenant here. Cactus belongs to us."

Stef had to live in a wonderland of code names. *Cactus.* That's what the various intelligence services called this mountain retreat.

"And are you here to protect your property, Captain?"

Sarah smiled. "Sort of," she said. "This lift package was kind of a curveball. It wasn't on our radar. So I came out from Quantico to have a look. But you can call me Sarah."

Naval Intel had its headquarters somewhere in the bowels of the Marine base. It was the most mandarin of all the intelligence services. One or two of the fliers under his command probably belonged to Naval Intel, and Stef would never know. But he had a crazy urge to stroke the auburn hair of this mysterious captain. He wondered if it was the backlash of his own grief. He no longer trusted himself, or his instincts.

It was Sarah who reached out, kissed him, and fondled his hair.

"I couldn't resist," she said with a very soft smile, while the two contractors groaned at the bottom of the stairs. "I guess I'm a groupie. I saw you at Quantico in your flight jacket. You're a legend, you know. The young colonel who ferries POTUS around. I'm sorry about your wife."

Stef clapped his hand over her mouth. Sarah didn't struggle; she nibbled at his hand—they were love bites.

"Please," he said. "I have a headache, and . . ."

He removed his hand, and they stood there in the afterglow of the sinking sun, like dancers in their own invisible, motionless circle. But the two contractors got to their feet and started up the stairs with menace riding on their backs. Sarah plucked a Beretta M9 from her windbreaker without taking her eyes off Stef and pointed it at the two men.

"Don't you dare," she said, and they scuttled into that strange ellipsis from the final scraps of sunlight.

Her eyes were still on Stef. "I'll walk you to your quarters."

It wasn't much of a hike to Walnut. She held his hand. And Stef began to feel that he was tumbling into a dream. Her sleek semiautomatic was the exact replica of his own. Was Sarah the phantom sharpshooter he had seen on the lawn as he hovered over the landing pad on Marine One? It couldn't have been her.

"Would you like a cup of fruit cocktail? That's all I have in the fridge."

She rubbed at his chin with her knuckles. "That's the sweetest invitation I've had in a long time. But I'm still on duty, Stef. I haven't checked the perimeters. And I wouldn't want to lose our chief tenant to some ghost who's wandered in through the wires."

"But this is the most secure facility we have."

"I know," she whispered, and then she vanished into that final scrap of light.

4

He asked to be woken if a stranger appeared on the mountain in the middle of the night—it was four A.M. and Charles, his Seabee chef, who sometimes served as his barber and his bodyguard at Aspen, tugged on his pajama top. "Mr. President, there are two fuzzy white men at the front gate, old geezers, and they don't know any of the call signs."

"*Two* geezers?"

"That's what I get from the gate. And they have no business being there. But one of 'em insists that it's a personal checkpoint between him and you."

"Did he give a name?" Isaac asked, putting his windbreaker on over his pajamas.

"No, but it sounds like he's one mean motherfucker, sir, and he has that awful smell of privilege."

"Like a president—or a prime minister."

Isaac went out into the cold in the same slippers he'd worn at Gracie Mansion—slippers he'd found in an Orchard Street barrel—but Charles made him put on a pair of wool, all-weather socks. Isaac's detail was already outside in a caravan of golf carts, with Matthew Malloy in the lead cart.

"Jesus," Isaac said, "I don't need the whole fucking brigade. You'll scare the pants off the prime minister."

"And what if it isn't him?" Matt asked, in harness with his holster, his hand-held metal detector, his Ray-Bans, and a stun gun.

"Hey, Sherlock Holmes, who else could it be?"

Isaac would have preferred to walk, but he couldn't wait. So he sat in the saddle, while Matt steered the cart, and Charles climbed onto the baggage seat. Matt drove at a maddening speed, and the entire caravan nearly spilled into a ditch. But he got to the gatehouse with his package, Citizen Sidel, and there they were, two geezers in rumpled trench coats and hats with enormous earlaps, like refugees of some long-forgotten winter war.

Isaac recognized Ariel Moss, with his sunken shoulders and that one lazy eye. He looked like a lunatic; his hair hadn't been cut, and he had wild roots at the back of his neck. Isaac also recognized the other man, Mordecai Katz, one of the founders of Shin Bet, whose physique would have rivaled Bull Latham's if he hadn't been so hunched over.

Suddenly Ariel Moss's secret voyage made no sense. Why wouldn't Shin Bet have sponsored him if Mordecai was still at the helm? And then he realized that Mordecai had come as Ariel's bodyguard and not as a spokesman for Shin Bet. No one inside Israeli counterintelligence had sanctioned this move. Mordecai had left the service years ago. He was a retired general and a rogue secret agent. That's why Ariel could come out of his seclusion and go back to robbing banks at will. Shin Bet wouldn't have interfered with their idol, Mordecai Katz. And Ariel couldn't have made it to America without him.

Matt Malloy was about to wave his magic wand—that magnetometer of his—over Mordecai when Isaac started to protest. "Matt, these guys are my guests. You can't do a body search on an ex–prime minister and the former chief of Shin Bet."

But Mordecai intervened in Matt's behalf. "Please, Mr. President, you must allow this young fellow to perform his duties. It's a matter of protocol. Ari and I could be assassins on the run," he said with a grin that revealed a mouth full of battered, broken teeth.

Shit, Isaac mused. *Didn't Israeli generals have a decent dental plan?*

But the Hermit of Haifa and his giant of a companion stood with their paws in the air while Matt probed them with his magic wand. Then the caravan returned to Aspen, with Ariel and Mordecai in separate carts. But a dispute broke out at the bottom of the stairs.

"Mr. President," Mordecai said, "we cannot begin our talk with the Secret Service in the same house."

"That's ridiculous," Matt said.

"Perhaps, but it is *my* protocol."

Matt might have had some violent tango with Mordecai if Isaac hadn't overruled him.

"Charles can protect me."

"Sir," Matt said, "Charles is a cook."

"He's also a Seabee—end of discussion."

Ariel had to hold onto the handrail or he couldn't have climbed the president's stairs. Isaac should have known how fragile he was.

Mordecai stood right behind Ariel, who could have been wandering across some infinite line—that's how long it took him to arrive at the top of the stairs.

Mordecai went into the cabin first. Isaac couldn't imagine what predators Ariel's giant hoped to find. Mordecai went through every room, opening and shutting doors, peering into closets. Then he closed the curtains that surrounded the sun room, and Isaac had a touch of panic as he lost the sweep of the forest that always managed to calm a city boy. Now he couldn't watch the whitetails wander over to the salt lick as the light broke through the trees.

Mordecai could see how unsettled Isaac was. "Mr. President, I assure you, it is absolutely necessary that we are not observed during this discussion. Also, I am a camel. I can survive for days on my own cud. But the prime minister has a special diet. And . . ."

"I know," Isaac said. "*Balanda*. It is already being prepared, General."

Mordecai pulled on the strings of his cap, suspicious of Sidel. "But who could have told you about his diet?"

"Pesh Olinov."

"Ah," Mordecai said, tossing his head back, "that Kremlin gangster."

"He must have been some kind of cutout," Isaac said. "How else would I have known that Ariel was coming?"

"Motke," Ariel said, leaning back on Isaac's sofa, with his lazy eye wandering about in his head. "We shouldn't confuse the president. Yes, I reached out to the gangster. But I wasn't sure how dependable he was. He's too busy buying and selling mountains of toilet paper." Suddenly Ariel grimaced, and his face turned white. "Dear Isaac, I must have something to eat."

Charles arrived from the kitchen with a steaming pot of *balanda*, with Russian rye bread, a jar of kosher pickles, and blackened potatoes that resembled nuggets of coal.

They could have had their *balanda* at the dining room table, but Ariel preferred his own tray. His lazy eye stopped wandering once he slurped his soup. He tore at the Russian rye, bit into a blackened potato. Isaac could hardly believe the metamorphosis. Ariel Moss belched like a Cossack.

Isaac couldn't fathom the healing powers of *balanda*. It tasted like tepid dishwater. But he drank the soup, wondering how the *zeks* could have survived Siberia on such a weak potion. He gobbled the rye bread with a pickle that didn't have the same brine as the pickle barrels along Essex Street.

"Good," Ariel whispered, "I'm refreshed," as Charles vanished into the kitchen and shut the door. Ariel and Mordecai removed their hats and coats; they wore sleeveless sweaters over their winter underwear.

Ariel was silent for a moment, a very sly fox. "It could have been the rumor of a rumor of a rumor," he said with his lazy eye shut. "That's how it started. A drug lord from Medellín sends me a fan letter out of the blue. He admired my raid on Acre Prison, how I had freed my brothers from the Irgun. And this minor drug lord—call him Pepito—met with his banker in Basel. And the banker said that he and his associates all contributed to a lottery."

The sly fox paused again. "Dear Isaac, can you guess what the lottery was about?"

Isaac was no connoisseur of lotteries. "I haven't a clue. What could interest a banker in Basel? The sudden rise of the Swiss franc?"

"Not at all," Ariel said. "The winner had to pick the exact date of your death."

Isaac smiled. "I suppose I should be flattered."

"It's not a joke!" Ariel said. "The lottery had become a fashion—a craze—in certain banking centers. This alone meant nothing to me.

Bankers love to bet. But the lottery spiraled out of control. And whoever won would be a very rich man."

Ariel fell silent again. He puffed on a pipe with a very short stem; there wasn't a pinch of tobacco in the bowl.

Now Isaac was annoyed. It was as if he had to wade through a world of smokeless smoke. He longed to see the forest through his picture window, wait for sunrise, and watch the whitetails assemble under his stairs. He preferred his salt lick to spymasters and a loony ex–prime minister.

"You traveled all the way to America to tell me this?"

"Yes," said Ariel with a deep shiver. "It was imperative."

Mordecai sat with his huge paws on his lap. "Mr. President, you were once a policeman, yes?"

"I still am—I earned my gold shield. I still have it."

"Then you are familiar with our craft. We look for signs, for vectors, really, millions of them traveling in the dark, disappearing into the void, never touching their destination once. But when these vectors collide, you have what is called a smash point."

"That's very poetic," Isaac said. "Are we in the middle of a tennis match? What the heck does it mean?"

Ariel grabbed Isaac's gnarled hand for a moment as his lazy eye wandered again. Lincoln also had a lazy eye, Isaac recalled. You could see it in the portraits, with or without Mary, where the Great Emancipator seemed to squint, or look out into some dark unknown. Isaac was terrified to live in Lincoln's house. No other president haunted him, not even FDR. Roosevelt had his stamp albums, his poker games, his dalliances, and Lincoln had nothing at all to lighten the load of the presidency, nothing perhaps but his little boy Tad.

"Do you trust me?" Ariel asked, and it felt like a religious question, as if Lincoln and the Lord's own better angels were involved.

"With my life," Isaac answered without an instant of hesitation.

"And your soul," Ariel said. "I want that, too. I must have it, or we will never solve this riddle. Do you remember when I was beaten up in the Bronx—mugged, in your American argot. And you visited me at the hospital. The doctors and the nurses were all startled—and impressed. The police commissioner of Manhattan had come to visit some poor, bruised schlemiel, a nobody. I had stature now. The best doctors in that broken-down hospital listened to my heart. And the day before these doctors had left me there to rot. I was a perfect candidate for the icebox in the basement. Isaac, I am in your debt. Do you trust me?"

"Yes, dammit!" Isaac said. "I trust you, heart and soul. You and your emeritus general."

"Then you must listen when we talk of a smash point, of vectors that meet with an explosive force. It was not the bankers' lottery that mattered. There are endless games of chance. It was the mischief and the ferocity of their bet. They weren't gambling, Isaac, they were proselytizing, converting people to their cause. It was well beyond prediction. They were willing your death with their lottery, that's how certain it was to this one banker in Basel, who laundered money for the Colombian cartel."

"But you have Mordecai—Motke," Isaac said. "You could have gone right to Shin Bet."

The two old warriors looked at Isaac as if he had lost his mind. "They're part of the problem," Ariel said. "All the clandestine services are. They're pulled along into the maelstrom."

"Then I suppose I should be frightened of Matt Malloy and my own Secret Service."

Isaac realized that the giant's great paws were as substantial as a pair of catcher's mitts.

"Frightened, no? But they can't protect you with all their gadgets, not the way this lottery is growing."

Isaac had walked into hell houses alone, had sniffed the devil's ass, and walked out alive.

"What's your advice?" he asked with a bitterness in his voice that the two warriors must have noticed.

"Resign," Ariel said. "You don't have any other escape routes. Even I have to admit that you're a catastrophe as a president. That's why we admire you so much. Look, Pepito, the drug lord, is your biggest fan. He can't wait to build schools in the worst barrios of Medellin—just like the *israelita*, he says—but he would kill you in a minute. You're a threat to his narco dollars. The whole banking system could sink with you in the White House, and his numbered account would be washed away with it. The president can't afford to be Robin Hood."

"Why not?" Isaac asked, wounded by this old warrior and his accomplice. "Why not?"

"Because," said Mordecai, "Sherwood Forest wasn't Robin Hood's sanctuary. It was his prison."

Isaac was mortified. The White House had dismantled him, whittled him down to a mess of skin and bone. He'd been a defiant mayor. He could fight the governor and state senators from his perch in City Hall, since he had the realtors under his thumb. He was the ultimate landlord. He owned the lots where all the pharaohs wanted to build their apartment palaces, even owned the little rivers that flowed beneath the lots. He could find revenue for all his pet projects. The Republicans couldn't field a candidate against Sidel. They capitulated, let him play Robin Hood within the five boroughs. But there were fifty Sheriffs of Nottingham he now had to battle, more than fifty. His generals could barely look him in the eye. His cabinet grumbled behind his back. His chief of staff pretended he didn't exist.

"Mr. President," Ariel said, "we can't be the only prophets of doom. Forget the bankers and their morbid bet. You must have had some other sign?"

Isaac showed Ariel and Mordecai the mysterious greeting card on a folded slip of paper he had found under one of the hair driers in the White House's Cosmetology Room. They weren't surprised. They studied the ragged greeting to "Big Balls" from "the Brotherhood" and the imprint of the tattoo, revealing Isaac as a raffish clown with an ice pick in his left eye and his head sewn onto his body.

The slip of paper excited Ariel, woke him from his habitual gloom.

"Motke, didn't I warn you that the White House was compromised? Isaac has enemies under his own roof, or at least the servant of some other master. That's why we had to come here, to this dacha in the wilderness."

Isaac watched the path of that lazy eye. "And to your own tight memories, I assume. This was your Garden of Eden during the Camp David Accords."

Ariel cackled in his winter underwear. "Eden, eh? With Sadat in the next cottage, it was a nest of thorns. We nearly came to blows half a dozen times. But at least I had Motke at my side—and Shin Bet. Sadat was scared of his own security team—and his generals. He was convinced they meant to poison him before he could sign the accords. It was our Motke who watched over Sadat, who had to prepare his food in President Carter's kitchen."

"*Balanda?*" Isaac asked.

"No, no," Ariel said with a frown. "Sadat wasn't a *zek*. That soup would have been worse than poison for a man who'd never been near the gulag. We fed him clear chicken broth, rice, and boiled potatoes. He ate kosher for the first time in his life. It's possible that his own chef may have been peppering his food with arsenic. The fanatics in his country and mine didn't want any pact—no one did. He walked around Shangri-La like a ghost—he was a ghost, and I wasn't far behind. Motke, how many wounds do you have on your body, wounds that were meant for me? Please strip for the president."

Mordecai sulked. "Ari, I'm not a showoff."

"Strip, I said."

Mordecai removed his sweater and his ruffled woolen undershirt. Isaac saw a gallery of punctures along the giant's enormous chest—some looked like indented arrowheads, others like fingers and the imprint of a webbed foot. Mordecai's wounds had all the panorama of cave art.

"See," Ariel said, "now you know how lucky I am to be alive. I returned from Shangri-La to a storm of anger. My own party wanted to scalp me. I would drown in spit every time I walked into the Knesset. And there was Motke at my side."

"But this mountain must have meant *something* to you," Isaac said. "It must have worked its magic, or you wouldn't have traveled this far. You could have sent me a kite."

"Perhaps I did enjoy myself a little in Roosevelt's retreat. Even with all the nasty bargaining, the shuttling between cottages, the meetings with that evangelist, President Carter, I felt outside politics. I wasn't Ari Moss, the reformed terrorist. I was someone else at Shangri-La, a stranger to all the madness. Isaac, you must grow invisible if you want to survive. You can offer the illusion of change, nothing more. That's why you're such a threat. You believe in your own beliefs, or you never would have gotten this kite, as you call it," Ariel said, clutching the slip of paper. "And where did it come from? You spoke to your wizards at the White House . . ."

"I have only one wizard, Bull Latham, and he never saw the card. But he said that a caricature of me with the ice pick in my eye had been floating around, and that it seemed to come from the Aryan Brotherhood."

The ex–prime minister scoffed at the idea. "Amateurs! They could not have conceived such a masterful design in a million years."

"That's what the dwarf said—Olinov."

Ariel's hands were trembling now. "And who were the creators of this art?"

"The *besprizornye*," Isaac said.

"Then it should become clear to you."

"As clear as the broth that Motke made for Sadat. The Sons of Rossiya sent me that kite—a band of orphans who are everywhere and nowhere at the same time, who can strangle stock markets, murder diplomats, and mint money whenever they want. I'm not sure I believe in the mystical powers of the *besprizornye*."

"And did the dwarf tell you about the CEO of the Sons?"

Isaac was getting pissed off. Were the Sons as grandiose as Big Tobacco? The Fortune Five Hundred champions of crime?

"His name is Viktor."

Ariel wouldn't have survived Siberia without the friendship of Viktor's papa, Karl, the patriarch of all the *besprizornye*. Karl grew up in one of the camp orphanages. He had a rare gift. He knew how to draw with a child's crayons, to seize the world around him and his own interior landscape. And the *pakhans* got wind of the boy. They apprenticed him to one of their own drawing masters, a *zek* who had strangled men and women with his powerful hands. He taught this boy the language and ritual of tattoos, a language more sophisticated than a medieval monk's illuminated manuscripts. Each stroke, each color, each animal, each star had meaning in this hierarchy of *urkas* and their *pakhans*. The tattoos marked the history of a *chelovek*'s rebirth in Kolyma, and his ascent within his own pack of werewolves, cat men without whiskers who preyed upon the weak, and those intellectuals who landed in Kolyma for some fabricated political sin.

But this boy, Karl, soon surpassed his own master. No one could instruct him now. He was a prince with his own self-propelled royal line. Karl had learned another art from his drawing master. He strangled whoever stood in his way and welcomed all the *besprizornye* from the orphanages in Kolyma, Moscow, and Kiev.

"But you weren't an orphan," Isaac said. "You were a political prisoner. Why would Karl welcome you into his clan?"

Ariel often wondered himself, but Karl must have looked into Ariel's eyes and seen a werewolf as well as a lover of books. The young *pakhan* had mastered the tattooist's art but was utterly blind to the Russian alphabet. So Ariel read to him all the classics he could find at the camp. Sophocles. Shakespeare. Pushkin. And he would recite in a multitude of voices until the *pakhan* was struck dumb with the modulations and music of words. He cried into a silk handkerchief that had come from the commandant's own laundress. Ariel dined with *pakhan* Karl, had Turkish coffee, and oriental sweets.

Where did such a paradise of treasures come from? It was wartime. The Germans had made their push into Soviet territory. But Karl was also a counterfeiter and the camp's one millionaire—military trucks arrived in the dead of night with stolen goods from as far as Turkey and Iran. And Ariel enjoyed other sweets—Karl's own concubines.

"And still you escaped from Kolyma."

"With Karl's blessings," Ariel said. "He despised the Germans as much as I did, even if he had to do business with them. And he gave me one of his orphans to guide us out of the tundra."

"Pesh Olinov," Isaac whispered.

Karl could have flown off on a magic carpet of money. But he stayed in Kolyma, a werewolf among werewolves. And when the camp closed, he kept his millions and had his own little army of *besprizornye*. They worked all the "gold mines" of the West, went from capital to capital, sucked up what wealth they could, as counterfeiters, contract killers, bankers, real estate barons, black marketeers, and then moved on, leaving behind a ravaged landscape. Karl had a son, born in West Berlin or Basel—nobody knows. The boy's mother is as much of a mystery. Was she one of Karl's concubines from Kolyma? He did not have a Siberian Salome in his baggage train. Was she a baroness or a banker's daughter he had met in the middle of a land deal? Little Viktor couldn't have been attached to his mama. There are no recollections of her at all. But he had an excellent drawing master—his own papa. He went to private schools in Switzerland, learned the art of handling and manufacturing money.

Meanwhile, Karl dodged his rival *pakhans*, eliminated every one. He had many scars from his battles with the *pakhans*, who envied his rise from a tattoo artist to criminal overlord, but their knives couldn't kill Karl. He had too much paté at La Tour d'Argent with his bodyguards. And when Karl died suddenly of a heart attack, Viktor inherited the *besprizornye*.

He didn't repeat his father's mistakes. He dined with his wolf pack on *balanda* and lived out of a suitcase. He could have bought and sold La Tour d'Argent, but it would have been futile to take revenge on a restaurant. Viktor moved about, kept modest apartments in many places, seldom traveling with a bodyguard. Yet his aura was great. He might appear at a Russian nightclub in Tel Aviv, or at Little Odessa in Brighton Beach, while some half-starved minstrel thrummed the balalaika—it must have reminded Viktor of a past he didn't have. His spiritual home was the gulag, even if he'd never been near the tundra. His art had been born in the camps. His tattoos were sought by princes and moguls and movie stars. But he wasn't interested in their money.

Bankers courted this young billionaire. He had no desire for their business. He was a counterfeiter whose "originals" were impossible to find. Even Treasury agents marveled at the details of Grant's beard on one of Viktor's immaculate fifty-dollar bills. His paper was of the purest silk. He could have brought down the U.S. currency—created a blizzard of false fifty-dollar bills—but he had no real argument against the United States. He wouldn't flood the market. Besides, tattoos intrigued him much more than cutting into a soft-steel plate. And he never put a price on his tattoos, never charged a penny for his designs.

People who understood the power and the workmanship of his tattoos began to wonder if he chose his subjects at random. But it wasn't random at all. Most of his subjects were *besprizornye*, the werewolves of his own pack.

"I saw one of his tattoos," Isaac said. "I'm positive—on Olinov. It was a fabulous bird, a griffin that poked right across his chest, with a bunch of claws, and a face that was almost human. I got dizzy looking at such a bird. But why would Viktor pick Pesh?"

The two old warriors winked at one another.

"What kind of policeman are you, Mr. President?" Ariel asked in a rough tone. "Pesh was a *chelovek*. Viktor owed him that tattoo. Pesh had once belonged to his father's clan, probably saved his life. He certainly saved mine. I would never have come back from the taiga without him. He had eyes in both cheeks of his ass. We'd have been devoured by Siberian wolves if he hadn't tossed sticks of fire at them. You cannot imagine a timber wolf with white fur and pale blue eyes that blend right into the dark. Pesh had a way with wolves. He could growl at them, flap his arms like an engine. These wolves would crawl under the wires and rip the throats of guards on the perimeter and attack *cheloveks*. That's why the dwarf was so valuable, and Karl could trust him and only him to get us through the taiga. The griffin you discovered on the dwarf was Viktor's version of a god-man who could scare away the Siberian wolf. And it was a warning to other *cheloveks* that the dwarf was not to be trifled with."

"A winter warning," Isaac said. "It was Viktor who sent the greeting card."

Ariel nodded.

"And he had Pepito write you that letter about the lottery."

Ariel nodded again.

"He might even have invented the lottery to flush those bankers out."

"Yes," Mordecai said, "to bring them closer to the smash point."

The giant began to sniff around him with his enormous nostrils. "Ari, we have to leave. I can smell the snow. We do not want to be trapped on this mountain—it will be worse for us than timber wolves in the taiga."

The two of them put on their trench coats and crazy garrison caps. Isaac had gotten used to these warriors, would miss them now.

"You could stay," he said. "Whatever's out there, Aspen is like a fortress."

But they wouldn't listen, or wait until Charles could prepare a sack of bread and cheese. They were already halfway out the door, and Isaac had to clutch at Ariel.

"You've come this far," he said. "Tell me why Viktor should care whether I live or die."

"Mr. President, he's a businessman as well as an artist. He doesn't want all his assets to go into the toilet. Besides, he has a weakness for Robin Hood."

Isaac didn't catch one fleck of snow as Ariel and Mordecai began to negotiate the stairs. Mordecai was the navigator. Ariel clutched his shoulders as they descended one stair at a time. It was excruciating to watch. Isaac went back inside Aspen, as sad as he had ever been.

He opened the curtains. The light had begun to break, and he could see down into the valley through a narrow cut in the woods. A whitetail arrived, its legs like great jumping sticks, with the picture window serving as a natural screen. A block of salt sat on a stake driven into the ground, but that whitetail never got near the salt lick. It bounded back into the forest in one arcing leap that was both lyrical and violent—the whitetail trembled in midair and was gone. And that's when Isaac saw the gray wolf, with its spindly legs and winter fur. The wolf must have come out of a taiga all its own. Its eyes appeared a brilliant green in the breaking light. It was staring at Isaac with its own timid defiance. Disdaining the salt lick, it loped back into the woods with a lazy motion. Isaac stood against the window, an easy target, and still couldn't find that first snowflake of Mordecai's.

PART TWO

5

There was talk of a winter storm, of air currents rippling off the mountain, but Isaac still hadn't seen a snowflake. And while he gazed out the window, looking for that lost whitetail, Ramona called. "How dare you, Mr. President? Sneaking out like a common criminal. I should be the first to know if you've gone off the track. I could be at Aspen within the hour."

"Then who would watch over the West Wing?"

He hung up on Ramona, and was tempted to call the camp duty officer about the gray wolf. He wanted the wolf driven off his grounds, and then he realized that this renegade had as much right to be here as he did. But finally, after an hour or two, a mob of whitetails appeared on Isaac's lawn, tempted by the salt lick. The leader of the mob, a stag with antlers that pierced the sky like a crooked crown, took short, furtive steps. Isaac had seldom seen whitetails near Aspen this late after early light. The stag stood guard, while its herd hopped around the salt lick with their white throats held high. Isaac longed to go outside and dance with the whitetails, but he knew that a lumbering soul like himself would scare them away.

Then he heard a strange report that couldn't have come from a pistol. It was a riotous beating of wings, as a great scatter of birds flew over his head. Isaac marveled at the pattern, like a series of geometric wheels. The whitetails were frozen for a moment, as if the crack in the air had bewitched them, and then they woke out of their dream and bolted into the forest in one beautiful, whirling line, led by that crooked crown.

Isaac couldn't abandon the window. He was as transfixed as the whitetails had been, mesmerized by that powerful commotion. He was almost surly when his Seabee chef tackled him.

"Mr. President, you'll have to move your ass."

He followed Charles deeper into the sun room as his picture window shattered in a burst of gunfire that sounded like a dull shiver of tin. Both men crept behind a couch. Cushions flew into the air in a second burst of fire, and feathers from the wounded cushions floated across the sun room in a blinding haze. Charles wore a tin plug in his ear.

"Tango One," he whispered into his chest, "this is the Dancer . . ."

Isaac didn't hear the crackling spit of a radio. Charles removed his ear plug.

"Mr. President, we can't raise the dead. All the channels have been scrambled—as a precaution, sir. We're under attack."

Pepito—the sage of Medellin—had been right. Sidel was a damn sitting duck. Some money-laundering son of a bitch of a banker would win all the marbles, millions perhaps in a fanciful lottery over the president's last breath. Isaac shouldn't have complained about that spindly lone wolf. The attackers, whoever they were, had driven the wolf onto Isaac's lawn—that wolf was a warning sign, so was the herd's late arrival. The whitetails were having their last lick.

It was some kind of bewildering Armageddon. Circuits had been cut. There were flashes of brilliant light. For a moment he thought the compound was ablaze. And then the fire vanished with the same stubborn, irrational pull, and he tumbled into a world of silence, broken by an occasional cry and the sullen crack of a pistol. Separated from the Secret Service, Isaac was a commander in chief suddenly adrift. Ramona Dazzle must have been rejoicing that POTUS was hidden somewhere in the ether. Had she installed Bull Latham in the Oval Office as president pro tem, with his own nuclear football and "biscuit," the little plastic card that carried all the codes of destruction? He and the Bull were the only ones who had the football and the biscuit. Isaac had lost sight of his own military aide and football. But nothing could be launched without him, not yet. Isaac still had his biscuit. And he still had his Glock.

"Charles," he said to his Seabee, "let's shoot it out with the cocksuckers. We'll join the *razzia*."

"What's a *razzia*, Mr. President?"

"A raid, a romp, a surprise attack. The Bedouins would arrive in the middle of a dust storm, steal another tribe's horses and drinking water, and disappear into the dust—a perfect *razzia*."

But when Isaac tried to get up with his Glock and move toward the sun porch, the Seabee tackled him again.

"I could have you court-martialed," Isaac said.

"Maybe so. But I have one mission, sir, and that's to keep you alive. You can't move from Aspen. We're in lockdown."

"How do you know?"

"It's protocol once we have unfriendly fire. No one can get in or out of Cactus until our boys fine-comb the facility."

"That could take a year," Isaac said with a growl. He inspected the scars around Charles' eyes, souvenirs from Nam. "You're not really a chef, are you? Who the hell placed you here?"

Charles must have had some Seabee code of honor. Isaac had to stare at him for five minutes flat until Charles finally relented.

"Captain Sarah Rogers, sir. She kind of oversees this mountain from some office in Quantico."

"You tricked me, Charles. All that jazz about the Polo Grounds. You're with Navy Intel."

"Yes and no," Charles said. "I am the chef attached to Aspen. But Cap'n Sarah put me on special assignment—to watch over your dumb ass. Forgive my informality. Those were Cap'n Sarah's exact words."

"And how come I never met this hidden sleuth from Quantico?"

"Sleuth, sir? She considers herself the landlord of Camp David, and you're her prize tenant. She don't like to interfere."

"That's lovely of her," Isaac muttered. He'd send this captain of intelligence to the coal mines once the *razzia* was over. Meanwhile he sat there while Charles crawled into the kitchen and returned with a thermos of coffee and egg salad sandwiches on Italian whole wheat bread imported from a bakery on Long Island. Isaac felt ridiculous having a picnic in the midst of an assault on the mountain. But he ate his sandwich dutifully, drank his mug of coffee with low-fat milk. The president, with his doomsday codes on a little card, was everybody's child. He was pampered, protected, bullied, buffeted around. Charles had tackled him twice.

The Seabee began to sniff around him. "I can smell the snow, sir. The storm should be coming."

"That's ridiculous—a farmer's tale. I haven't seen one fucking snowflake."

"She'll come," Charles said. And within ten minutes the air outside Isaac's shattered window was clotted with flakes, as if Charles himself had summoned the snow, like a mass of ragged white dots in a modernist painting. And then the dots whirled faster and faster.

Charles didn't have time to play the farmer-philosopher. "The storm will blow right through the cabin like a choo-choo train and wreck everything in sight. You sit where you are, sir—don't move."

Charles stacked the furniture in a great pile, and then he took the drapes from the picture window, battened them down, and stapled them to the valence above the window and to the wall. He built his own cluster of sandbags with all the blankets, sheets, and pillows he could find, wedging this cluster close to the battened drapes until he had his own little fort.

The little fort didn't last. The snarling wind tore into the drapes, and chairs flew across the sun room like murderous missiles. Charles thrust a blanket over Isaac, and covered him with pillows, while he swatted at the flying chairs like Willie Mays—with a broom. Then the wind died down. Isaac crept out from under the blanket, and realized that he sat in a blinding white tomb of snow. The cabin had become a burial ground for the living. Charles had to brush him off with the broom.

They survived the storm, engulfed in that white glare, while Isaac suffered the humiliation of being utterly out of the loop on a mountain that was no longer his. He'd almost forgotten the *razzia* when Bull Latham burst through the door in a bulletproof vest and a snow cap that covered his ears. Behind him was his aide, carrying the football. Isaac could hear the crackle of flashbulbs, see a cornucopia of television cameras. The press rarely set foot inside the citadel of Camp David, but the Bull had come as Isaac's savior, and the Bull had to shine. With him was a luscious lady officer with hazel eyes, dark curls, and steel-tipped boots. The Big Guy didn't have to guess who it was—Cap'n Sarah of Navy Intel.

"Lo, Bull," he said. "I hope your rescue will be on all the networks. Did you enjoy sitting in the catbird seat? How many pictures did you take with Barbara Walters inside the Oval Office?"

The Bull's lower lip was trembling. He would have liked to hurl Isaac down the stairs at Aspen and into the arms of the press corps. "I never went near the Oval Office."

"Come on, didn't Ramona ask you to stage a coup d'état in front of the television cameras?"

Isaac had a curious affliction—he loved to taunt his vice president. But the Bull had to bite down hard on his lip and swallow his own venom. He couldn't afford a wrestling match in front of reporters from all over the planet. It was Miss Steel Toes who answered him, protecting her eyes from all that glare.

"Forgive me, Mr. President, but don't be such a prick. We've had a very rough day. It wasn't that easy to neutralize the mountain. The unfriendlies seemed to come out of nowhere. We had little warning. Not a single one of them should have been able to infiltrate the facility. I'm Captain Sarah Rogers, sir."

"Ah," Isaac said, "I know. You're my landlady on the mountain."

The Big Guy was beginning to enjoy himself. He liked this young captain with the curly hair.

"Was there any collateral damage?" he asked.

"Very little, sir. These mothers were professionals, mercs of some kind. A couple of our guys had superficial wounds. I suspect we're dealing with a paramilitary unit that had some training right on the mountain."

"How is that possible?"

"Beats the shit out of me," Sarah said. "But we did have some suspicion. The supply orders from the electrical shop didn't sound right, sir—power plugs strong enough to break every circuit at the facility, and enough high-voltage wire to wrap itself around the Great Wall of China. I couldn't interrogate the chief electrician; he'd already scattered, and he didn't leave much of a forwarding address. Some dude must have paid him a whole lot of cash."

Suddenly Isaac was involved in his first caper as commander in chief. He felt much more comfortable as the nation's policeman-president, though Teddy Roosevelt had also been a police commissioner, and Isaac had inherited his desk at police headquarters in Manhattan.

"Did we take any prisoners?"

"That's the problem, Mr. President. The mercs were in and out with the storm. They didn't leave many footprints in the snow."

The Big Guy had been right. *A perfect* razzia. Phantoms with their own flair.

"Do you think they were trying to kidnap me, put out my lights?"

"I'm not sure," Sarah said. "I had my Marines stationed on Aspen's perimeter once I discovered that the chief electrician was compromised."

"The fuckers still shot out my picture window and scared away the whitetails."

"Mr. President," the Bull said, "that could have all been for show. They proved their point—that they could infiltrate the mountain despite all our damn security details. They weren't after the football, or they would have swiped your biscuit. And even then, I can override any order once you're outside the safety zone. I agree with Sarah. They've been here before, on this mountain. And this hit was a trial run."

"Or a kite," Isaac said. "*Hey, Big Balls, we can get to you anytime and anywhere.*"

Sarah and the Bull wanted to know about the two visitors Isaac had—Ariel Moss and Motke Katz—just before the attack on the mountain. But Isaac wasn't prepared to discuss the Sons of Rossiya and that bankers' lottery on his life, not while he was at Shangri-La. Ari and Motke must have gotten off the mountain, or else they were lying in some grave.

There was a great deal of clamor on Isaac's patio; reporters hovered around like beetles in fur-lined coats.

"Isaac," the Bull said, "sooner or later you'll have to talk to the press, and it might as well be now."

"What do they know?"

"Not that much," Sarah said. "No one alerted them about your ride up the mountain on Marine One. And it's pretty isolated up here. Some locals might have heard the gunfire. But they've heard gunfire before. They figured it was a Marine drill."

"Then why is the press parked on my porch?"

"That's Ramona's mischief," the Bull said. "She started making a few calls. I stopped her in time. You can make up your own song, Mr. President. The attackers didn't even leave any of their shell casings."

"A surgical strike," Isaac said, "and the only thing that's missing is a motive."

Isaac went outside onto the patio in his windbreaker. He stood with the Bull and the beautiful captain; the wind nearly knocked him off the rails. He was still wearing his slippers. He had bits of glass in his scalp, like hard, biting dandruff. He mentioned a power shortage in the blizzard, a president who was cut off from the rest of the world.

"Sir," one of the reporters asked, "what if there had been a nuclear attack?"

"We're still covered," Isaac said. "The Bull has his own biscuit—all the nuclear codes and keys."

Then he saw them; the whitetails had come back, the entire mob, led by that stag with its crown of thorns. They must have been hungry, starving, to risk this avalanche of human animals on *their* lawn, and satisfy their craving for salt. Isaac wanted to approach the stag in his slippers, touch its antlers, and he dreamt up his own little ballet while he was with the press. It was well past the mating season, and this stag should have shed its antlers, but it still had its crown of thorns, as if to defy all the gods of winter. And in his dream Isaac did touch the different branches of bone. The antlers had a slight envelope of fuzz, with a greenish tint. And then he was jostled out of his dream, as one of the cameramen approached the mob of whitetails at the salt lick.

"Don't," Isaac cried, "don't." But the cameraman didn't heed Isaac. The stag seemed to charge the cameraman with its antlers; the snowstorm must have maddened it a little. Isaac hopped about and hurled his slipper at the cameraman—it struck the side of his head. The cameraman toppled into the snow with all his cargo. And the mob of whitetails, with the stag in the lead, bounded back into the forest. Isaac watched their leaps in midair, and the beauty of it just about broke his heart.

That's what the press picked up, not a *razzia* that few people noticed, or a president who was out of touch with a nation during a blizzard, but a president who tossed his slipper at a rogue cameraman about to interrupt the feeding ritual of winter whitetails.

6

The Night Hawk wandered across Maryland and returned to the White House as if it were part of a funeral procession. The Big Guy barely breathed a word. He sat in his king's chair, reliving the raid on the mountain moment by moment and recovering nothing at all—some army of werewolves might as well have been behind that *razzia*. He didn't come into the cockpit once to schmooze. But he whispered to Colonel Oliver just before he disembarked. "Need you, Stef. I'd like you to spend the night."

The colonel hadn't been with his little boy in five fucking days, couldn't even phone Max during the lockdown at Cactus, find out if Max had any problems at school.

So he was in a rotten mood until he looked outside his cockpit and saw Maximilian standing on the South Lawn. He wouldn't even have to pilot the Night Hawk to Quantico and bed her down. His second in command was also on the lawn in full gear. The Big Guy must have arranged the switch. As uncomfortable as he was in the White House, Isaac was still a master of detail, a strategist in hibernation.

Stef climbed down, saluted his second in command, and watched the Night Hawk float back into the sky like a ghostly gondola.

The Secret Service let him and Max through the gate without a call sign. He was the president's pilot, Colonel Stefan Oliver, commander of Marine Squadron One, and didn't require any identification marks. He wove through the labyrinth of the West Wing, shunned the elevator, and hiked up to the attic with his boy. Stef was prince of the third floor, a kind of heir apparent, even though he wasn't Isaac's actual heir. The Big Guy had an estranged wife and a daughter who hadn't visited him at the White House yet.

The attic had its own peculiar feel, filled with ironing boards and maids' paraphernalia. It also had its own tiny kitchen. And there were usually no other guests; Ramona liked to park her favorite cousins on the second floor, in one of the historic bedrooms. But Stef didn't want to be surrounded by the stink of history. He preferred the randomness of the attic, where he had his own separate suite.

He scooped up Max and carried him on his shoulder across the threshold like some abandoned bride. The boy was so damn thin. He'd mourn his mother for the rest of his days.

"Problems at school?"

"No, Pa."

"Has Karina been strict with you, huh?"

Karina was their live-in maid.

"Missed you, Pa," the boy said, looking at Stef with skeletal eyes. "All that snow. I dreamed you were lost."

Max was as wise as a witch doctor. Stef had felt disoriented during the lockdown, helpless and abandoned in a nondescript cabin at Camp David, without the least bit of connection, not even to the gunfire outside his own walls. And now his button mike crackled.

"Tango One to Rio, the Citizen would like to see you."

"Jesus, Tango One, I'm with my little boy."

"Citizen says you should bring him along to the meet. He's in the dollhouse."

The "dollhouse" was the beauty salon on the second floor, the Cosmetology Room that seemed to be Isaac's favorite haunt in the entire residence. He didn't have to deal with Ramona in the dollhouse.

"Copy that," the colonel said, unloosening the button mike while he combed the boy's hair.

But Max was excited, almost feverish. "Pa, am I gonna wrestle with the Big Guy again?"

The boy loved Isaac, worshipped him. They often played together like a pair of orphans. That was the secret of Sidel. No matter what mantle he happened to wear at the time—president, mayor, or police chief—he still behaved like an orphan, with an essential sadness in his eyes.

They went down one flight, past the Secret Service, and into the Cosmetology Room, and it startled Stef. Captain Rogers sat in one of the salon chairs, like some cosmic beautician in an officer's blouse. She was still flirting with him, right in front of the Big Guy.

"You've both met, I believe—on the mountain," Isaac said.

"Yeah," Sarah said. "He's almost as handsome as his little boy—what's your name, son?"

"Maximilian," Max said. "I go to a special school. I can't spell or recite poetry. And I stutter sometimes."

"Well, Lincoln's little boy, Tad, was also a stutterer," Isaac said. "And he ruled the White House."

"Perhaps Maximilian doesn't care to rule," Sarah sang in a gentle voice, and it troubled Stef, the way she seemed to caress the boy with her hazel eyes. Isaac could sense the discomfort in his helicopter pilot. He hugged Max and delivered him to a pair of Secret Service men, whose assignment was to play hide and seek with the boy on the second floor. Stef was still pissed off. He didn't want his privileges with the boy usurped by Isaac's ruffians. But he kept his mouth shut. Sidel, it seems, had absconded with Sarah, plucked her out of Quantico, and made her his liaison to the White House. The admirals at Navy Intel must have been ripping mad, but they couldn't go to war with the commander in chief. If a single one of them complained to the Secretary of Defense, all these cloak-and-dagger admirals might lose their perks.

"Stef," the Big Guy said, with a delirious fire in his eyes, "I'm gonna turn this room into a command post. We can get around Ramona and bypass the Bull and the rest of my national security mavens. They can't help us here. This will be our very own caper."

Stef was still morose. "Mr. President, I don't get it. I'm a pilot, not an intelligence officer."

"Ah," Isaac said, like a chess wizard, "but you have information in your skull that's indispensable. You were an eyewitness."

"Witness to what?" Stef had to ask, more flustered than ever.

"The Camp David Accords."

"I told you, sir. I wasn't in command. I was a pick-up pilot, the mascot of the pack."

"But you took Ariel Moss on a ride across the mountain, and it's Ariel who interests me right now."

Isaac told Stef the details of Ariel's mysterious visit to Aspen Lodge with the former chief of Shin Bet as his bodyguard and companion. Ariel had insisted on meeting Isaac at Camp David, but kept referring to the mountain as Shangri-La, and seemed obsessed with FDR—Roosevelt's retreat, Ariel called it. But there was hardly a trace of Roosevelt on the mountain—the rustic cabins were gone, so were the outhouses, the water troughs, and the fishing holes. There hadn't even been a high-wire fence or a gate, just a deserted road, a sentry, and a shack full of Marines. Yet Ariel kept harping back to this earlier time. Someone must have talked to him about Roosevelt's days and nights on the mountain, and summoned up Shangri-La.

"Who could have talked to Ariel Moss about FDR?"

"I don't know," Stef shouted at the Big Guy, with a merciless thumping in his brain.

"Sure you do," Sarah said. "He was in the archives. I went through all the manifests. He was right there with you, and he was also at Warm Springs with FDR—or Mr. Frank, as he called him. He was one of the rare polio victims who was ever cured."

Raymond Tollhouse, Stefan Oliver muttered to himself. He was the fool of fools. Tollhouse was commander of Squadron One while Ariel Moss and Sadat were at Shangri-La, and had singled Stef out from the raw recruits, shepherded him right into the squadron. Stef would have remained in Stuttgart, with a remote, forgotten crew, if it hadn't been for Colonel Ray, who was promoted to general right after his tour with Squadron One. And yet, for some unfathomable reason, Colonel Ray had fallen out of Stef's universe. Tollhouse had been one of his instructors at Quantico, had first introduced him to the intricacies of the Night Hawk. Now he had to conjure up the same secretive man for Sidel and Sarah.

"Tollhouse," he said. "Colonel Ray was the only one of us who'd actually visited the mountain with FDR. He was the president's mascot—in 1942."

"Like a batboy, but without a baseball team," Isaac said.

"So he knew the landscape by heart," Sarah said.

"Every inch of the terrain."

And suddenly the words flew out of him with all the intricate magic of a musical score.

"He would have remained a cripple if it hadn't been for Warm Springs."

Roosevelt himself had contracted infantile paralysis as an adult, and had come to this tiny rural retreat in Georgia with its bubbling spring water, a politician exiled from his own career. He had this insane belief that he could find a miraculous cure in warm mountain water. He stayed at the Meriwether Inn, a run-down hotel for rich people who wanted to escape the infectious summers of Savannah. FDR had his own ambitious plan. He started a little clinic at the Meriwether, a rehabilitation center for polio victims, and invested half his fortune in the clinic. His mother thought he was insane. But Mr. Frank won her over with that patrician charm of his. He also won over the nation and was elected president in 1932. He still visited Warm Springs whenever he could, swam with all the other "polios," and didn't have to hide his crippled legs. Warm Springs had become his winter retreat.

And that's how Tollhouse entered the tale. Polio victims had to travel in the baggage car if they wanted to go anywhere by train. Tollhouse had come all by himself from Savannah, a ten-year-old cripple, to enroll in Mr. Frank's rehabilitation center. And the president, who couldn't take a single step on his own, met Tollhouse at the station. Two of his handlers lifted up his wheelchair, and Mr. Frank plucked that boy out of the baggage car with the powerful arms of a swimmer. Tollhouse had been locked in the dark without food or water. Suddenly there was a blaze of light, as the porter opened the baggage car door. And the first thing he discovered was Mr. Frank, biting into his cigarette holder, smiling with all the warmth in the world at a frightened, sickly boy.

"Colonel Ray would have done anything for FDR—strangled a widow, drowned a kitten, anything."

"Raymond was his poster child, his own big success story," Sarah said.

"No, no," Stef insisted. "It wasn't anything like that. FDR was generous to all the kids at the polio clinic. But he couldn't visit Warm Springs much after the war began. That's why he had Shangri-La. It was his mountain retreat in Maryland. And he liked having Raymond around."

"As his batboy," Isaac said. "The kid couldn't have been more than fifteen in '42. Raymond must have been fixated on Shangri-La—and Warm Springs—most of his life."

"I suppose," Stefan said.

Tollhouse had a couple of tours in Nam, where he was on loan to an Air Cav medivac unit; he rescued Marines from every sort of hellhole. He returned to the States a war hero and was assigned to Squadron One. But he developed a mysterious limp, almost a vestige of the polio he'd had as a boy, as if his own body had become a haunted house. He left the Marines and started his own security firm.

"Called it Wildwater," Stefan said. "He was a sentimental son of a bitch. And he had to name his new company after the wild mountain water he remembered as a boy—at the clinic. He couldn't bear leaving Roosevelt country. His training grounds are on Pine Mountain, in the hills above Warm Springs."

Sarah's smile seemed elliptical; all her flirting was gone. Stef could have been some stranger. "It was a kind of calculated sentiment, Colonel," she said. "Tollhouse was the helicopter pilot to three presidents—a perfect calling card. He had access to the biggest corporations and banks. Did he try to lure you to Wildwater?"

"Yes, but I didn't bite."

"Even so," she said, "he could rely on your logistics. You were a known item, inside his domain."

"Then you're telling me it was a Wildwater strike?"

The colonel felt trapped in the middle of a cockeyed caper in the Cosmetology Room. Did they really think he had conspired with his former commander to harm the president?

"Doesn't it make sense?" she asked. "That mad mercenary from Warm Springs has access to all the power lines. He bribes the chief electrician—and *boom*, his men disappear into the storm without harming a soul."

Stef began to see blood spots in his eyes. This captain with the raven hair had become his nemesis now. "Are you saying that I was his spotter? We were in lockdown, dammit."

She was sparring with Stef as if he were a child.

"You wouldn't have to be a communications wizard to override our codes," she said. "Isn't it a little too *strategic*, Mr. President, that the colonel here developed a sudden amnesia about General Tollhouse?"

"Stop it!" Isaac said. "You're squabbling like a couple of brats. This is the only team we have. If we unravel, we'll have nothing. And Ramona wins. She'll send the Bull and his ninjas from the Bureau to Wildwater. We'll have a bloodbath and won't learn a thing about Tollhouse's staged destruction. I'm his one casualty. He caught me with my pants down."

Stef was more confused than ever. He preferred an ex-cop who stumbled about in a snowstorm rather than a president who played spymaster in a beauty salon.

"Am I gonna go undercover?" Stef asked with a curl of his lip. "Do I make a pilgrimage to Tollhouse on Pine Mountain?"

"No, no," Isaac said. "We leave Wildwater alone. What matters now is who the hell hired him? We'll all have to dig."

"Fine," Stefan said, feeling like a pilot and a navigator again. "Boss, are we all equals here?"

Isaac mused for a moment. "Sure—we're equals. Forget that I'm commander in chief."

"Then you shouldn't bring any software up to this salon. Ramona will find out, and she'll shut us down. You ceded this mansion to her, and you can't take it back. Rogers should do all her digging at Quantico, where she won't be compromised by a chief of staff who's a ballbuster."

"And you?"

"I'm going to collect my little boy from the Secret Service."

And Stefan Oliver fled this lunatic salon without looking back at Isaac or the captain from Quantico.

He thought of resigning, but he'd miss that white-topped gondola, and he'd miss Sidel, a president who seemed to wear a wound as palpable as the damn Glock in his pants. He had considered joining Wildwater after his last tour, but Stef was a bit naïve. He hadn't realized that Tollhouse ran a bunch of mercs. He thought he'd be guarding bank presidents on some fancy loop and earning a $100k a year, with his pension as a maraschino cherry. Instead, he'd be carrying mercs on commando raids for South American dictators and drug lords. His $100k would be choked with blood. Tollhouse had lied to him. Stef fell for that tale of a security firm rising out of Roosevelt's waters. But

FDR had died in 1945 of a cerebral hemorrhage at the Little White House in Warm Springs, and there was very little trace of him on Pine Mountain.

Tollhouse was the new manor lord of the mountain springs, and he milked money for his own cause.

The colonel read to his little boy. He wasn't that inventive. He'd borrowed the same books that his own father had read to him—*Bambi, Pinocchio,* and *The Three Musketeers,* stories inherited from generation after generation of military brats. Max loved *Pinocchio* the best, and his eyes would gleam with terror and delight every time Pinocchio was swallowed by Monstro the whale. Stef had forgotten that there was no whale in the book, just a mile-long shark; Monstro was Uncle Walt Disney's creation. Perhaps Stef had seen the film too many times, and his own father had also been confused, but Max loved to imagine the boy with the pointy nose, who was as disabled as himself—a bundle of wires and wood—flopping around in Monstro's belly.

"Aw, Pa, doesn't Monstro have a heart, like you and me?"

And that's when Stef heard the double click from the White House operator, who told him that a Mr. Wildwater of Warm Springs was on the line.

"Are you available, Colonel?"

Stef took the call. "You motherfucker," he said, "why are you pestering me here?"

He recognized the guttural laugh of Raymond Tollhouse.

"Stef, who else can I talk strategy with, huh? You were on the mountain with Big Balls. I would have liked to play a little ping-pong. But I forgot my paddle, and you were in lockdown."

"Do you want to be in permanent lockdown? Half a dozen agencies must be listening to this call."

"And I probably do business with every single one of them," Toll-house said, with all the cockiness of a retired Marine general. "I'm untouchable, kid. You'll have to come to terms with that. I broke into the president's most guarded facility—Shangri-La—and could have tapped him on the shoulder. What does that tell you, huh? His life isn't worth shit."

Stefan Oliver felt abused; he'd been Tollhouse's protégé, had followed right behind him as the president's pilot and commander of Squadron One, had worshipped his warrior's unselfish devotion. Tollhouse had bolted from his squadron and attached himself to Air Cav, because the Marines didn't have a medivac unit in Nam. He didn't care about rank or prestige; he went deep into Indian country to save the lives of wounded jarheads, carrying Marines for miles across rice fields and mountainous terrain—he was pilot, nurse, marksman, and fairy god-mother. He never grandstanded, never even sought recognition for him-self and his unit. And here he was with all his hoopla. It sickened Stef.

"Go away," he said. "You proved your point, General. How many millions did you make on this op?"

"More than you and I could ever spend in our lifetimes. Tell your president that he should come to Pine Mountain. He might have a real revelation."

"He's not interested in your mountain, General, only in who hired you."

"Tell him it was the United States," Tollhouse said and hung up on his protégé.

Stef considered running downstairs to the beauty salon, but he realized that the Secret Service had tapped into the line and was probably preparing a transcript of the conversation for the presi-dent. So he went back to Monstro the whale. Max fell asleep in his pajamas, and Stef couldn't sit still. He wandered from room to room, his mind ablaze. What could have tempted a war hero like Tollhouse to become such a renegade? Not money alone. He'd never been that interested in loot.

The president's pilot heard footsteps in the corridor. It couldn't have been a maid at her ironing board, not at this hour. He stepped out and saw the captain from Quantico, wearing one of Sidel's fluffy flannel robes. She looked like a transient from the far side of Lafayette Park.

"The Big Guy wants me here," she said. "It wasn't my idea."

His boss was playing Cupid, and Stef was angry at the idea. Isaac could be his own fucking matchmaker. "Did you listen to my conversation with Tollhouse?"

"Of course."

"He said the United States hired him. What the hell does it mean?"

She had the same damn elliptical smile. "That's above your pay grade, Colonel."

He wanted to slap the smugness out of her, teach her a lesson.

She searched his eyes and her face softened a bit. "I'm sorry, Stef. When I realized it was a Wildwater op, I thought you had given away our codes and was steering him from inside the facility. I was wrong."

She was standing close to Stef, her body like a magnificent furnace in the winter iciness of the attic. Her pungent bouquet of sweat and perfume aroused him. She put one of her arms around his neck. He undid her robe with one flip of his finger. She was wearing a bra and silkies. They leapt at one another like big, strong cats and crashed into an ironing board. Stef hadn't been near a woman ever since he lost Leona. He delivered a mourner's kiss, tender and a little cruel. He sucked on her navel like an embalmer, as if he meant to drain her blood. He felt like a captive all of a sudden, overwhelmed by this captain from Quantico.

7

The colonel's conversation with "Mr. Wildwater" hopped across Washington's intelligence circuits like a sizzling wire. It seemed that half the planet had listened in, and now Isaac had to meet with his national security mavens in the lower dungeon of the West Wing. He had little faith in these wise men. So he sat with Sarah and Stef.

Tim Vail, Isaac's national security advisor, was the magician here with his monitors and electronic maps; he could create and destroy entire universes on a side wall with his silver wand, but he couldn't conjure up a single glimpse of the *razzia* at Cactus. Some mischievous troll must have pulled the plug—all the surveillance cameras had been shut off.

Tim still had his sense of majesty; he balked at Colonel Oliver's sudden appearance in the Situation Room.

"Mr. President, your helicopter pilot lacks the clearance to powwow with us."

"Well, Tim, put on your blinders and pretend he isn't here. But be a good fellah and explain to me why General Tollhouse has the notion in his head that the United States hired him to shoot up Camp David?"

Isaac's resident boy genius had graduated summa cum laude from Harvard at nineteen and felt superior to everyone in the room, including his own boss.

"It's not that simple, sir. We did hire Wildwater to test our security at David and review whatever fault lines we had in our system. His record was impeccable. He's a war hero, for Christ's sake."

"And you gave him our call signs?" Isaac asked, while he swiped away Tim's silver wand. Tim seemed a little lost. "We had to, sir—it was part of the security package."

"So he shut his eyes, said 'Open Sesame,' and marched right into Ali Baba's den."

Tim slumped in his leather chair. "We couldn't anticipate that—"

"He would make fools of you all and mount a raid on a facility he was supposed to monitor. Why don't you shut him down?"

Tim fell silent and slumped deeper into his chair, impotent without his silver stick. The Bull had to pinch hit for him. "We can't, Mr. President. We'd cause a national crisis if it ever got out. He's still under contract to us. He's been invaluable. He comes through in all the tight spots."

"And you couldn't gallop to Warm Springs and slap the shit out of him—for starters?"

"The *Washington Post* would have a field day," Ramona said. "They'd pronounce it a civil war within the president's closet."

"Why? Mr. Wildwater doesn't work for me."

Ramona wouldn't slink into her chair like Tim. "I'm afraid he does, sir."

"That's grand," Isaac said. "So Wildwater fucked me and sent us the bill." He brooded in his chair. "That's why you wanted to stop Ari Moss in his tracks. It wasn't about K Street and the Jewish lobby. It wasn't about politics at all. He sensed that some bad stuff was going down. Ramona darling, was I the very last to learn about the raid? Did Tollhouse warn you of his little exercise in advance?"

Bull Latham broke through that silent wall of static in the Situation Room. "He gave us a few hints."

"And nobody thought to tell me?"

"It was too late," the Bull said. "You rushed off to Cactus without giving *anyone* advance notice. Colonel Oliver couldn't even prepare the lift package."

"You're a fine one, Bull. You left me there to sit in the dark."

Bull Latham, who wasn't a cautious man, measured his words. "You were never in harm's way, Mr. President—not really. Tollhouse was taunting us. He made us squirm, I'll admit."

Isaac couldn't contain his captain from Quantico, who bristled in her chair. "You cunts," Sarah said, with both her elbows on the table, "you worthless cunts. You abandoned your own president. If Mr. Wildwater hadn't gotten Colonel Oliver on the horn, it would have been business as usual, and you would have left every single one of us at Cactus to take the fall."

"Mr. President," Tim rasped, rocketing out of his chair, "she can't talk to us in that tone of voice. We have admirals and generals in this room—we'll resign."

"I doubt that, Tim," Isaac said with a touch of pure silk. "What think tank would hire a security wizard who can't even protect his own commander in chief? Sit down and shut up."

There wasn't even a thin stripe of mutiny in the Situation Room.

"Did you pay Tollhouse any ransom money?" Isaac had to ask his mavens.

"We did," the Bull said, hesitating a bit. "We had to, boss. He'd turned the tables on us. Tollhouse had all the keys to the kingdom, and we had none. We couldn't risk a battle royal on the mountain. You might have gotten hurt in the crossfire."

"So I was the hostage, huh? And you're the president's wise men. Did you ever stop to think that someone might have hired him to pull off that stunt? It's not the first time he's shown his bravura. Didn't he shadow the Viet Cong and drag wounded grunts and jarheads out of enemy camps? That fucker has no fear. And suppose someone wanted to embarrass us and warn me at the same time. Wildwater would have been the perfect vehicle."

Isaac snapped Tim's silver wand like a twig and walked out of the Situation Room.

The general was a ghost rider, Isaac grasped. He'd lived among ghosts in that baggage car as a little boy until Mr. Frank plucked him out of the dark, a savior with spindly legs. He'd lived among ghosts at the clinic—"polios" who'd never walk again—while he rode the parallel bars until his muscles grew lithe and he taught himself to walk like an acrobat. He'd lived among ghosts at Shangri-La, the ghosts of war, and watched Mr. Frank's face turn white as chalk under his old gray hat. He was a ghost rider in Nam, swirling around the enemy, carrying the wounded in a cradle across his shoulder. And he was a ghost rider at Cactus, walking in and out of his own gunfire. Isaac had misjudged him, seen him as a clever lunatic. But Mr. Wildwater was a man to be reckoned with. Ari had intuited this without ever recalling his presence at the Camp David Accords. The ghost rider danced within an invisible cloak.

Isaac could push back against national security experts who had failed him so. He could push back against the Secret Service. He was going to Pine Mountain to meet with the ghost rider, and he didn't want Warm Springs neutralized, turned into a risk-free zone. "There are always risks," he told Matt Malloy.

"But we'll have to sweep the roads, Mr. President, and place sharp-shooters on the mountain."

"And have every citizen in Georgia hate us? This is sacred ground. FDR would never have returned to politics without Warm Springs. It was his haven. He could be a polio among other polios here, not the president of the United States. You can't have your sharpshooters, Matt, and Tollhouse might not let you into his camp. He's the lord of the mountain in pine country. It's his fiefdom, not yours. I'll wear a bulletproof vest. And you can keep his camp under surveillance, but that's my only concession. I don't want to get into a turf war with him. I need to make the general purr, or he'll never open up."

Matt was disturbed by Isaac's intransigence. "And what if you walk into a trap?"

"Come on, Matt. I'm a ghost rider like the general, living on bor-rowed time. He had a hundred chances to finish me off. But he kept me alive, and I want to know why. You'll have to trust my instincts."

"And what if I remove myself from the detail?"

"You wouldn't do that," Isaac said. "You're as curious about the general as I am. Let's be bravos, Matt. It can't hurt."

And so the lift package was arranged by the colonel. Isaac could have flown to Atlanta on Air Force One. But his private quarters at the front of the plane reminded him too much of a five-star hotel. And he'd have to travel with the press and a whole retinue of retainers, like a little king. No, he preferred the colonel's White Top. He'd have a tiny caravan of two Night Hawks, while Matt flew down to Warm Springs with his own retinue and swept whatever he could sweep.

The Bull wanted in, and Isaac had a hard time fending him off.

"We can't risk having both footballs and both biscuits on the same hostile ground."

"What hostile ground?" the Bull asked.

"Tollhouse's camp could be the heart of darkness. He must have returned from Indian country like a crazy guy. How else could he have survived Nam? I looked at his record. He was a medic and an angel of death. I'll meet with him on my own."

And so he left from the South Lawn in Colonel Oliver's White Top with Sarah and his own Secret Service detail, minus Matt Malloy. Isaac's heart was thumping with all the excitement of a man in love—in a windbreaker and a bulletproof vest. They had to hover over barren fields and refuel at three local facilities. The colonel wore his Beretta on this trip.

They didn't land at Roosevelt Memorial Airport and ride up the mountain in Isaac's armored car. They rose above the pines in Marine One until the colonel finally spotted a tiny crack among the winter trees. Isaac couldn't have caught that camouflaged airstrip. Still, he wasn't utterly blind. He knew that they had come to the general's own memorial to FDR—Shangri-La on another mountain. Isaac could recognize the rustic cabins, the water troughs, the outhouses, the tents, the old barracks, just as he had imagined them. There wasn't a soul to greet him or make any hostile noises as they climbed out of the Night Hawks. But they could hear the purl of water from some mountain stream that wasn't visible from this hump of ground—it was a sweet, intoxicating sound. Isaac felt hypnotized. He shut his eyes for a moment.

And the general appeared out of the pines. He walked with a slight limp. He wasn't wearing fatigues and a military cap. He had the same windbreaker as Isaac Sidel and a Baltimore Orioles cap with a torn bill. Isaac didn't see any foot soldiers around, or Indian fighters. Tollhouse must have hid his army somewhere. He had deep fissures on his face and the skin was discolored—souvenirs from Nam. The Viet Cong must have set fire to their own rice fields, looking for a demonic angel with a medicine bag. And Mr. Wildwater must have come walking right out of these fires . . .

Tollhouse welcomed Isaac's war party. He winked at Stefan Oliver, but gave him no other sign of recognition. Isaac wouldn't let the Secret Service near Tollhouse with a magnetometer. He looked under the torn bill of the general's cap. Tollhouse didn't avoid Isaac's glance. There was nothing shifty or evasive about his pale blue eyes. *At last*, Isaac thought. He wouldn't have to feint and fool around with this man.

"It's Shangri-La, isn't it?" Isaac asked, his eyes wandering across the camp.

"Congratulations, Mr. President. I had to reconstruct it from memory—I was still a boy when I visited Shangri-La, with a boy's fascination for detail. I stayed with Mr. Frank at his own cottage. The Bear's Den, he called it. I'd have been a deadbeat without him. My papa got rid of me with a railroad ticket, a ten-year-old boy in a wheelchair. I was never invited to Warm Springs, but Mr. Frank took me in, paid all my bills, settled accounts with my papa, had one of the docs become my legal guardian . . ."

The general was still that boy in the baggage car, still Roosevelt's fellow invalid at Warm Springs, with magical visits to Shangri-La that had given him a taste of immortality. Shangri-La was his survival kit and shield.

The Big Guy and his war party entered a cottage that was like a bear cave. It was lit with electrical torches. There was a small mountain of turkey sandwiches on a crooked table, with a huge canteen of coffee, and a supply of tin cups—a mercenary's meal. But Tollhouse went off with Isaac into another room, which must have been his own quarters. It had a military cot and a reading lamp; there were no pictures on the walls, no clues of the general's past. Its tiny window was covered with a black shade. Isaac and the general both sat on the cot in the room's own diminishing twilight. The general's burn marks had a queer glow, like the heat coming off a lantern.

Isaac wasn't offered any liquor or condiments. They sat like two monks with a flask of water and two tin cups.

"I apologize, Mr. President. I should have stopped off at Aspen Lodge and said hello."

"In the middle of that *razzia?*"

"It was nothing of the kind," Tollhouse said. "A training exercise—a maneuver."

"But you frightened the whitetails and shot out my picture window."

"It couldn't be helped. I had my own checklist."

"But that wasn't your real mission. You were paid to kill me."

Tollhouse smiled, and the fissures leapt across his face. "Yes."

Isaac sucked in that last bit of twilight. "And you didn't finish the job."

"I would have dishonored Mr. Frank."

"Why?" Isaac asked, as Tollhouse sat like a shimmering idol in that little lost land of shadows. "I have none of FDR's aura. I'm a cop who arrived here by accident."

"Still," Tollhouse said, "it would have been like fratricide."

Isaac laughed bitterly to himself. "General, are we brothers now?"

"Mr. President, your own handlers failed you. They knew I have many clients, each one contradicting the other, and yet these handlers played Russian roulette with your life."

"Are you surprised? They haven't walked through fire, like you have. They're accountants and clerks."

"Not Bull Latham," Tollhouse said.

"Ah, the Bull's a special case. He admires me and also wants my chair."

They sat in silence. But Tollhouse seemed to tear right into the dark, like a vivid wound. Isaac heard him sigh.

"It's not certain who hired me to wax you and wind your clock, Mr. President, and it will never be. My clients have lawyers, who have their own lawyers."

"Then you know about that bankers' lottery in Basel?"

"The lottery has a double bind," Tollhouse said. "The longer you're alive, the bigger the payoff. You're like a whirling money ball. But I was going to wind your clock. I didn't want another president sitting at Shangri-La."

Now Isaac had to wonder if this rescuer of jarheads and grunts had gone off his rocker. "Jesus, you piloted *three* presidents. You trained Colonel Oliver."

"And should I tell you how many times I went to bed swearing I would crash Marine One on my next lift package?"

"We all dream of murder," Isaac said. "That's built into our fabric. Do ya know how many bad guys I had to whack to get where I am?

I climbed right up the golden ladder. So tell me, general—whisper in my ear. Who's my fucking savior?"

"The tin man."

"Jesus," Isaac said, "are we riding all the way back to *The Wizard of Oz*?"

"No. Our tin man doesn't come out of a children's book. He and his associates have cornered the market in tungsten and tin. But I believe you've heard of him as a tattoo artist."

"Viktor and his *besprizornye*. The Sons of Rossiya."

"Not the *besprizornye*. They never had Viktor's romantic streak. You're poison to their interests, and they'd love to see you in your grave. But the tin man is another matter."

The general rolled up the sleeve of his windbreaker and revealed a tattoo of a dragon with many eyes and many tails and one shortened hind leg; the dragon belched a blue fire from its mouth; the "tat" was streaked in blue and red, with a dagger coiled around one of the dragon's tails.

"Viktor says my autobiography is engraved in the *tat* somewhere."

"It looks like the mark of an executioner—how can I meet the tin man? Does he use that Soviet gangster-politician, Pesh Olinov, as his calling card?"

Pesh, it seems, wasn't really in the picture, except as a bagman or delivery boy.

Viktor depended on that Washington Cave Dweller, Renata Swallow, as his blind. That's why Isaac had met her in Pesh's hotel room. She hadn't come to admire Pesh's tattoo, but to leave instructions. Why was a blueblood like Renata involved with the *besprizornye?* Was she laundering money? Had the tin man become her private banker, or had her own fortunes crumbled? Was she in love with the tattoo artist? Isaac would never understand the irrationality of romance.

The tin man had appeared suddenly one afternoon on Pine Mountain with a child's wooden paint box and not a single bodyguard. He walked into Shangri-La right in the middle of maneuvers. Tollhouse's mercs looked like ghouls in their black night-fighter paint. Viktor ignored their ferocious grimaces. He sat down with the general in this monk's closet and removed his works from the paint box—the dyes, the nipples, the ointments, the electric needles. And he engraved the dragon, wiping off the blood and bleeding colors with alcohol dipped in cotton balls.

"He had no uncertainty," the general said. "None."

The tin man didn't bargain or cajole.

"But what did he look like?" Isaac asked with a beggar's smile.

"Ordinary. Without menace. He didn't have the arrogance of a billionaire, but of a great artist. 'Big Balls is not to be touched,' Viktor said. That's what he called you—not Mr. President, not Sidel . . .

"But these were not my orders, I told him. And my orders were very specific—eliminate Sidel, and I would never have to work again. I could disband my army. 'Your own people were persistent,' I said. The price of tungsten was fluctuating because of a president who did not listen to the markets, who talked of redeeming the poor.

"Viktor sipped a little water from a cup. 'But it is my pleasure that he stays alive.' So I listened. And I asked him about the dragon he had carved into my skin.

"This dragon with many eyes was a werewolf, he said. Only a werewolf could have survived Vietnam the way I did—or a dragon high on drugs. I felt no pain. I walked through fields of fire. I was shot in the shoulder, ripped across the face with a knife. My legs were swollen with bruises and bites. The docs wanted to ship me home. 'It's Stateside for you, Colonel. A little hula dancin' in Hawaii.' But I went back into Indian country. Perhaps I was a werewolf."

The general took a swallow of water from his own tin cup and then he called Stefan Oliver into the room. He hugged his protégé.

"You take care of this man, sonny. You check that White Top of yours every time you're on a mission. Don't trust your maintenance people."

"General Ray, I picked them myself."

The general rolled his eyes like a banjo player. "That's the whole point. The closer they are to your ribs, the less you can rely on them. Didn't I teach you that? They'll come at Big Balls from every direction. A little girl with flowers for the president could be carrying a bomb."

"But we're a long way from Nam. I've never seen a little girl wired up with a bomb."

The general rinsed his throat and hawked up some phlegm. "She doesn't have to be a local. They could import her from Turkistan, build a mud shack for her ma and pa, and train her to be a martyr. You're still living in an age of chivalry, but it's gone, all gone. They'll hack him to pieces the first chance they get."

"But where the hell is this omnipotent gray army?"

The general lit a torch, and his eyebrows twitched within a halo of gloom.

"It includes all the fuckers who would profit from his death—the file clerks and double agents who want to land on the easy side of the dollar."

"General, how can I prepare a lift package when I can't trust my own mechanics? We'd be stranded forever on the ground. POTUS couldn't go anywhere and he couldn't govern."

"I suspect that's what they prefer—ultimate immobility."

Isaac felt caught in a maze, living in that tangled world inside Tollhouse's head. He had to get out of the bear's den. He rushed through the rooms and out into the winter air, with his own retainers and the general right behind him.

There was a satanic gleam in Tollhouse's pale eyes. "Mr. President," he whispered, "it isn't safe."

"Where's your own gray army?" Isaac asked. "Where are those mercs who raced through Cactus with mischief on their minds?"

"I hid them," Tollhouse said, "hid them from you. There's murder right behind your baggy pants."

"Ah," Isaac said, "I'm the master of mayhem now."

Isaac had asked too much from this poor general, who'd gambled his own blood and bones in Indian country. That romp through Cactus had been his very last maneuver. He was all alone on this mountain. His gray army had deserted him. And then Isaac saw why. Tollhouse hadn't been wrong. Isaac had brought the angel of death with him. Bull Latham broke into this solitary camp with his ninjas from the Bureau and Matt Malloy.

He must have arrived at Roosevelt Memorial on a transport filled with field agents of every stripe. The Bull had been feuding with Tollhouse all along, and had lied to Sidel. That meeting in the Situation Room was a managed affair.

The Bull strode up to the general with his military aide right behind him, carrying the football. He didn't even acknowledge his own commander in chief.

"Bull," Isaac said, "you can't arrest him. You're not a peace officer. You're my vice president."

"I was deputized," the Bull said. "And I have a warrant for his arrest. He can't fuck us over like that. He raided a federal facility."

"But it's futile," Isaac said. "I'll pardon him."

"Not until he's been arraigned. You can't interrupt due process."

"Yes, I can," Isaac said.

He walloped the Bull as hard as he could with his bare knuckles. Bull Latham shook off the blow, wiping the blood from his mouth with the back of his hand, while his eyes darted with a fierce agility.

His ninjas stood there utterly frozen.

"Bull," Isaac muttered, "I'm the general's guest. I won't dishonor him."

And then he realized something. If mortality had to be measured, Isaac was a safer bet. Tollhouse wouldn't survive on this mountain. His own mercs might have already been recruited to kill him. So he decided to let Bull Latham have his moment of glory and grab the renegade general. But he shouldn't have been so magnanimous with the general's skin. He'd been concentrating on his own navel and had missed the sheen in Tollhouse's pale eyes. There was no sign of surrender in the ruts on his face. He didn't have to move about like a leaping candle. Isaac hadn't seen past Tollhouse's magnificent camouflage, and neither had the Bull.

The camp wasn't deserted at all. The doors of the cabins and outhouses opened with their own quiet steel, and Tollhouse's mercs appeared. They weren't dressed as ninjas, like the Bull's circus soldiers. They looked wild and mean in their windbreakers, men on their last mission. Their faces were marked—they were all wearing tattoos. Had Viktor gone across the entire camp with his wooden box, initiating these soldiers into the rituals of some surreal Siberia? These weren't common mercenaries, soldiers for hire. They were werewolves in war paint, with machine pistols and sticks of dynamite.

The Bull must have grasped their heartlessness, and glimpsed his own human frailty.

"Stand down," he told his ninjas and Matt Malloy's company of Secret Service agents. "We'll catch you another time, General," he said with a sneer. "You can't make war on the United States."

"I just did," Tollhouse said.

"Mr. President," the Bull muttered, "are you coming down with us?"

"No, Bull. I'll leave you to make your own grand exit. You're damn good at it."

And the Bull went away with his armed caravan.

"General," Isaac said, "you just lost your sanctuary. You can't stop the Bull once he has a stick up his ass. He'll be back."

"Maybe—maybe not."

The general kissed Isaac on the cheek, kissed the Big Guy's entire retinue. He'd find some other hinterland, or remain on this mountain. He wouldn't starve. He belonged to the Sons of Rossiya.

Isaac felt gloomy as he marched away from the cabins. He could hear that purl of water again. And that's when he stumbled upon a geyser at the base of Shangri-La, shooting jets of bubbly water into the air in a curtain of steam, like a smoke bomb. He cupped his hands and drank from the geyser; the water tasted sulfurous yet sweet. He grew giddy as he approached the colonel's gondola. He could have sworn that a whitetail had come prancing out of the woods. Isaac blinked, and the whitetail was gone. The wind blew across the winter pines; the trees swayed with their own somber call. He boarded Marine One with his retinue. He sat in his king's chair and fell into a clotted sleep, dreamt of his own destruction. Sarah had to wake him with a forceful tug of her arm.

"You were crying, Mr. President. I was worried."

Could he tell her that he was reciting "cafeteria kaddish"—a secular prayer—for his own ragged residency at the White House? Who would have believed him? Not one damn soul.

8

Renata Swallow, the doyenne of Washington's Cave Dwellers, who was still in her thirties and much more voluptuous than the other Queen Bees, was having lunch with her Swiss banker at the Salamander Club near Dupont Circle. Her late husband, Arthur Swallow, she would sadly learn upon his death, was something of a swindler and had systematically looted her inheritance and emptied their joint accounts. Renata was left with very little—a mansion in Georgetown with a lien on it, a Florentine villa in disrepair, a farm in the South of France that was bleeding cash, servants whose salaries hadn't been paid, a yacht that sank into the Potomac, etc. The Swiss banker, Pierre, assured her that she had enough liquid assets to keep her afloat for another sixteen months. It was Pierre's bank that looked after all her bills.

"And what then, Pierrot?"

"Ah, Renata darling, we downsize and sell, sell, sell."

"Will I lose my house on Orchard Lane?"

"We'll finesse," the banker said. "It's a duelist's art, you know. We thrust and parry and see where the blood lies."

"Whose blood?" she asked.

And Pierre laughed, stroking his silver cufflinks. "There's always the *maître*."

"I wouldn't want to borrow from him."

"We're all in his debt," the banker said.

"I won't be his mule again—it's undignified. I'm a Republican Party princess."

"But you wear his tattoo," the banker said.

"That doesn't mean he owns me."

"But he asks nothing of you," the banker said.

"He asks—with his big eyes."

"Well, have creditors been knocking at your door?"

"Pierrot, if he threatens the locals, I'll be erased from the Green Book and lose my table at this club."

"He never threatens, Renata. That's not his style."

"Yes," she said. "He cuts your throat with a silk cord, and it doesn't leave a mark."

"Don't exaggerate," the banker said. "There have been no mortalities—none that I know of."

"But I could be the first one. My body will be found in the C&O Canal, stuffed with the *maître*'s little ink bottles."

"You're being morbid, darling. Viktor's asked a few favors of you."

Pierre was as adroit as a professional pickpocket. He handed her an envelope stuffed with cash. The envelope slid like a fat glove into Renata's purse. There must have been ten thousand in that sack. She could neigh like a high-strung horse, but Renata was getting a regular allowance from the *besprizornye*, with Pierrot as the conduit.

"I can't sink the Republican Party for Viktor's sake," she said.

"But you've done nothing wrong. He's contributed millions to the National Committee."

"That's the problem. His millions are in my name. I sign the checks, and all the while I'm unraveling."

"But he'll save you," the banker said, "one stitch at a time."

And she'd have to pay for each stitch with her blood. Yet she was attached to the *maître*, even if he undermined all her traditions and values. Renata wouldn't have been surprised if he ended up owning shares in the Salamander Club. He infiltrated, perverted, possessed. Viktor grew out of his own whirlwind. Werewolves, that's what they called themselves, these *besprizornye*, rootless boys and men who smothered everything Renata believed in. She was old-line, and the *besprizornye* had no line at all. They dressed in silken suits from some Jewish tailor along the Arbat. They probably owned half of Moscow. They sucked up Paris and London like a colony of anteaters. Nothing was ever written in their own name. There were Swiss banks and holding companies, even publishing houses. Their emblem was an upside down rose. It must have had every sort of meaning in the tundra, in the ghostly prison camps that had given birth to them. But their *pakhan* was a pauper on paper. His sole possessions were that silken suit—velvet, really—and a paint box with his medieval instruments and inks.

Yet he must have had a mind for numbers, carried his great fortune around in his head. But why was he suddenly interested in old-line

Washington? What could the Cave Dwellers mean to an artist who had to shed your blood, slice into your skin, to create his master-pieces? He was a vulture—or a vampire, with his dark Russian eyes. He was the most delicate lover she'd ever had. No one had Viktor's touch, despite the blood, ink, and pigment imbedded in his finger-nails. Still, death hovered over him somehow—death was his constant companion and pal.

"Pierrot," she said, "he can't crash into the Republican Party like a safecracker. It's immoral."

"He asks nothing," the banker said.

"But Viktor's *nothing* has its own weight. *Nothing* doesn't exist for him."

"Darling," the banker said, "your own husband bankrupted you. And the *maître* is helping you crawl out of that hole."

She should have been more attentive to her surroundings. The one thing the *maître* had taught her was vigilance—and paranoia. He couldn't afford to advertise wherever he was. That's why he had a half dozen pieds-à-terre and no permanent address.

Why didn't she recognize a single creature at the tables around her? Renata knew *everyone* at the Salamander Club. Had her own little descent into crime crippled her, robbed Renata of all her intuition? And then this stranger had the nerve to cop a chair and sit down next to the Republican princess and her banker. This stranger was Sidel.

"Sorry, Renata. You wouldn't answer any of my calls. And so I had to find you at your favorite canteen."

And he introduced himself to Pierre.

"Hello. I'm the president of the United States."

"Stop showing off," Renata said. "This is Pierrot, my Swiss banker."

"From Basel?" Isaac asked.

Pierre nodded, and Isaac knew in his own heart's blood that this was the banker who had started the lottery, or at least had conspired to start it. This fuck wished him dead and was also keeping him alive. That was the double edge of currency, if the rate of exchange was measured in spoons of blood—Isaac's blood.

He looked at the banker's silver cufflinks.

"Are you carrying your passport, Monsieur?"

The banker nodded again.

"Give," Isaac said. He scrutinized the passport—Pierre François Marie de Robespierre, born in Basel. Isaac could have pinched it, but why bother? Sarah Rogers was at the next table, and she could prepare a composite of the banker from her computers at Quantico. So he returned the passport and said, "Please, Monsieur, I have important business to discuss with Madam Swallow."

"This is outrageous," Renata said. "Pierrot hasn't finished his avocado salad. We're drinking Pinot Noir. I'll have the manager chuck you and your entire menagerie out on your heels. Wendell—"

"Please," Isaac said. "Wendell is in the closet."

"You're a bunch of hooligans," Renata said.

"Indeed, we are. And it feels nice. We've captured the Salamander Club. It's our little fort."

He glared once at Pierrot, who got up, pecked Renata once on the cheek, and walked out. Isaac sat down in the banker's chair and picked at his avocado salad.

"You're vile," Renata said.

"I want to see your tattoo."

She laughed in Isaac's face. "It's on my bottom. And we're not that intimate. Or are you planning to play the Neanderthal, Mr. President—and carry me upstairs to one of the private rooms? I've heard about your Bronx brutality."

"I'm from the Lower East Side," Isaac said. "And I couldn't carry you very far, not at my age. I'd get a hernia."

Her laughter was less harsh. She almost felt sorry for that bumbling bear of a man. The Cave Dwellers had rubbed him out of their vocabulary long before he arrived in Washington. He had no political grace. He walked around with a pistol in his pants. He had no friends. He was feuding with the Democrats. He was isolated, all alone, in a town that still traded on its Southern elegance. Lincoln had been an outcast with his mad wife. And Sidel was even more of an outcast.

"You're the Queen Bee," Isaac said. "You have Viktor's stamp of approval—a rose or something else on your ass. How can I meet him?"

"Well, you just ruined your chances," she said. "You shouldn't have insulted Pierrot. He's been handing me packets of money from the *maître*. You and your little bloodhounds should be following him. Why did you lock Wendell in the closet?"

"Because he said I had no business being here. I could have declared this club a firetrap and kidnapped you."

"You're not the mayor of Washington—not yet."

But she was warming to the clumsy bear despite herself. He was as madcap and whimsical as the *maître*, who always seemed to arrive out of nowhere, with some tiny gift—a trinket from a toyshop in Sochi, a tin lantern from Cracow, a Gypsy heirloom made of marled glass.

"Did you know that Pierre and his banker friends in Basel have taken out a lottery on your life? I hold six or seven lottery tickets. Pierrot says it's a very good investment. I have an excellent chance to collect."

She had a sudden urge to undress for this *besprizoryne* from the wilds of Manhattan, display the upside down rose that Viktor had painted on her bottom, and reveal it to Sidel before he croaked.

"You'll miss me, Renata. Bull Latham will push much harder into Republican country. He'll bring down the Cave Dwellers in his wake. Tell me, does Viktor talk about Balanchine with you, is he a balletomane?"

Isaac should never have broached this subject with the Queen Bee. Her face softened in the pearly light of the Salamander Club.

"My poor Mr. President," she said in the subtle glow of the Salamander's chandeliers. "The *maître* saw Balanchine in his last performance—as Don Quixote. Balanchine wore a full suit of armor. He hopped around his Dulcinea for three hours, and died on stage—in the performance."

Isaac panicked. He had never heard of the ballet master performing in his own ballet. Don Quixote, in a suit of armor, like Isaac's armored vest.

"Balanchine was in love with the ballerina. You couldn't possibly recall her name. And I won't soil it by mentioning who she was. He worked on *Don Quixote* for years, but no matter how much he shortened it, the ballet was still three hours. Viktor was enthralled. He couldn't take his eyes off the old man with a wisp of a beard glued on tight, and shivering in front of his Dulcinea . . . but you couldn't comprehend the pathos of it with your policeman's mentality."

She got up from the table, but she glued herself to Sidel for another moment. "I never bet against you with those tickets. I didn't want you to disappear like that—with a puff. But Pierrot said my little piece of the pie was worth a small fortune. And I'm a widow in serious debt."

She walked right past Isaac and couldn't find Wendell or any of the waiters. That wild boy had stripped the Salamander clean. She stepped out onto Massachusetts Avenue a bit forlorn as she watched the Lincoln Continentals drive along Embassy Row. She'd lost her chauffeur in the big money spill after her husband's fatal heart attack.

She lost her servants one by one, even her skeletal staff on Orchard Lane, and had seen the last of her own trusted laundress.

Another chauffeur suddenly appeared in a Lincoln Continental. It puzzled her until she saw a tattoo on the chauffeur's knuckles and realized that this bounty had come from Viktor, her own wild boy.

He was wearing a silken suit, like the other *besprizoryne*, and some kind of a military cap, like a general who'd rid himself of his army.

"Please, Little Mother, get into car."

She didn't argue. She was still a Republican princess, after all. When she opened her eyes, she was on Orchard Lane. She couldn't even tell if her key would fit the lock. Her husband's creditors had put a lien on Orchard Lane, with a notice from the county clerk stuck to the front door. But the chauffeur, who was called Arkady, scraped off the notice and all its stubborn glue with a chisel. He had his own key and let Renata in. But she shouldn't have been startled. Her husband's bankers had all abandoned her.

Pierrot had been a gift from Viktor, with all the little "liens" that went with her own private banker in Basel. There was a rose on the foyer table, turned upside down, like the tattoo on her rump. She opened the closet, and inside was a rust-colored velvet suit and a black shirt. She realized that Orchard Lane was now one more of Viktor's pieds-à-terre.

She dialed a number that Viktor had given her. She couldn't recognize the area and country codes. It was her only way to get in touch with him. The message on the answering machine was always in a woman's throaty voice.

This is Siberian Apparel Company. Please leave name and number and brief message.

"Hello," she said, feeling like a secret agent, or a high-class whore. "This is the Widow. Please have the kindness to tell the Apparel

Company"—Viktor—"that the Bald Man"—Sidel—"would like to see him . . ."

She hung up the phone with a dizzying sense of triumph and defeat. She'd become addicted to this strange new life, as the Queen Bee of the *besprizornye*. A penniless Cave Dweller with clumps of cash, she could bribe Republican politicos to build a vast wall around the White House, neutralize what little power Sidel had left, devour him one toe at a time. That was a *besprizornye* trademark. But Renata didn't believe in it somehow. Viktor could never understand these politicos, who would nod yes, yes, yes, and disappear with the money stuffed in their shoes.

What if she were wrong? Perhaps Viktor knew he was lulling Republican lawmakers to sleep with the magical aroma of money. Who could really read his mind?

9

This was a very different Sidel. The Big Guy was vetoing bill after bill, and Congress couldn't seem to override his vetoes. He lambasted Republicans and Democrats alike and revealed a political savvy he didn't have before. "Ladies and gents, either you put back provisions for food stamps and public housing, or I won't sign shit." The Big Guy also watched as Soviet borders began to crumble. His generals wanted him to rattle his sabers at the Soviets.

"They're imploding, Mr. President," said his chairman of the Joint Chiefs of Staff. "We can catch Gorby with his dick in his hand."

"That will send a wonderful message to his generals and the KGB. If the hardliners come back, we'll have to start counting warheads again. We help Gorby wherever we can. We stabilize the ruble, because we can't afford a currency meltdown. Our own markets will crash."

"Sir," said Isaac's chief economic maven, "the ruble is beyond repair."

Isaac looked into his maven's eyes like a gunslinger, Wild Bill Hickok of the West Wing. "Come on, Felix. We've manipulated currencies many a time, you and our miracle boys at the CIA. We can have our *ghosts* buy up rubles."

"But they're worthless," said Felix Mandel, who had just won the Nobel Prize in Economics with his treatise on phantom currencies that could destroy nations like malicious worms.

"So what? We buy, we sell. You've never lost a dime, Felix, in any of our currency deals. The rubles will be our bargaining chip."

Who the hell was advising Sidel? He hadn't turned to Ramona Dazzle once. She no longer held sway over his agenda. He'd managed to box her out, keep her contained in her corner office. His press secretary didn't have to confide in her. His speechwriters went directly to Sidel. The Big Guy had found another guru. A certain Dr. Genevieve Robinson of the State Department visited him once a week. She wore dark glasses and a long mantle of brown hair that covered most of her face. The Big Guy himself had initialed her ticket. No one had bothered to check that this stout woman in dark glasses wasn't the Genevieve Robinson who worked at State. Isaac had smuggled Brenda Brown, his former chief of staff, back into the White House, with an elaborate subterfuge.

It was Brenda who rewrote his speeches and helped him strike down the legislation that irked him. She was smarter than his generals and she understood Felix Mandel's notion about the peculiar warp of phantom currencies. Brenda was coming out of her breakdown. But Isaac preferred to keep Brenda where reporters couldn't find her and harp on her love affairs with Isaac's female ushers. He pulled money from his pension plan to pay her a little *gelt*. And she was the one who suggested how the Big Guy could have much greater mobility.

"We create a fictitious persona who happens to be real—a foreign diplomat, with epaulettes and other embellishments."

"But where will we find such a fellah?" Isaac groaned. "I'm surrounded by spooks and every sort of policeman. They'll see through that disguise."

Brenda's younger brother played the diplomat. And Sarah Rogers, his own liaison to Navy Intel, provided him with a convenient persona right off her computer screen. Colonel Alfonso Borges, Argentina's air attaché.

Now all Isaac needed was the perfect occasion to disappear for a few hours, and not be tied to the Secret Service. He found the occasion—another greeting card left under a hair drier in the beauty salon, with the same stamped tattoo of Isaac's wandering, headless head and a cryptic note.

THE DUMMY SCHOOL.

LOOK FOR THE WORKMAN'S SHACK ON FLORIDA AVENUE.

TONIGHT AT NINE.

BIG BALLS, DON'T BRING THE BULL.

Isaac was pretty clear about the destination. Gallaudet University, Washington's own college for the deaf. Isaac wouldn't be the first president to visit that school.

Lincoln had gone there in 1862, when it wasn't a college, but a grammar school for the deaf and blind, funded with federal money. It wasn't called Gallaudet then, but the Columbia Institute for the Deaf and Dumb and the Blind. Lincoln sat with the school children, read to them, played with them in the school's tiny yard. The blind children felt his face, plucked gently on his beard, while Lincoln could hear the rumblings of war across the Potomac.

Isaac could visualize that scene, imagine the president arriving with Tad, who had his own speech impediment, and he could sense the grief on Lincoln's grieving face. It embarrassed Isaac, who hadn't bothered to visit Gallaudet on his own—but was summoned there for some monkeyshines. Lincoln had carried a divided nation on his crooked back and prevented it from utterly unraveling. And he took the time to visit a little school for the deaf. What had Isaac done except follow the irregular arc of his own demise? All he had was a bizarre portrait of himself—a winter warning—and a brief encounter with Mrs. Swallow, doyenne of the Cave Dwellers, who wore a tattoo on her ass. The elusive tattoo artist, Viktor, was a lad without a surname.

Captain Alfonso Borges appeared at the West Gate around seven P.M. and was ushered upstairs to Isaac's residence. Isaac already had a duplicate of the captain's fanciful uniform. Brenda's brother, who was an amateur makeup artist, stuffed cotton balls into Isaac's cheeks—a bit like Brando in *The Godfather*—and made him wear his military cap at a steep angle, severing half his nose. And while Brenda's brother waited in Isaac's private sitting room on the second floor, the Big Guy marched out of the White House as Argentina's air attaché. A limousine was waiting for him on New York Avenue, with Stefan Oliver behind the wheel and Sarah Rogers in the back seat, both of them carrying Berettas.

"Boss," Stefan said, "I could barely recognize you."

"That's not what bothers me," Sarah said. "The colonel and I could be court-martialed, Mr. President. This isn't exactly legal."

"Come on. The president can't commit an illegal act. Not while he's in office."

"Isn't that what Nixon said? And look what happened to him."

"Ah, Tricky Dick should have toughed it out."

"So now you're a believer in Watergate," Sarah said.

"I'll bet Lyndon did much worse. But he was never caught."

"Oh, my God," Sarah said. "I must be mental. I mean, the colonel here is a babe in the woods—Stef, have you ever fired that Beretta of yours at a human target?"

Stefan hunkered down into his seat. "I'll be fine."

"And now we're desperadoes in search of a man who doesn't even exist. I can't find the Sons of Rossiya in any of our data banks. And we have a tattoo artist with the shady name of Viktor, who's the king of a criminal enterprise that's so enormous it doesn't have a beginning or an end. Then there's the Baron Pierre François Marie de Robespierre—he is a baron, you know, a very minor one, without family connections. He launders money for South American drug lords and has his own private bank in Basel—without a legitimate address."

"That's a start," Isaac said.

And the Big Guy seemed so pathetic and foolish in his epaulettes that Sarah sat back and decided she would come along for the ride and see what happened next. She knew that the admirals at Quantico were waiting to pounce. All she had to do was slip once and fall off her trapeze. Yet she was an analyst, and the raid on Cactus—without a single casualty—was like a sportive dance, or hunt, with a seraglio of veils. And she had to crawl under those veils. Besides, she liked the Big Guy and she was drawn to this quiet colonel with his slightly damaged son.

They got to Gallaudet—a miscellany of Gothic mansions with turrets and spires and burnt brick walls on a vast campus that could have been the City of God. Even Isaac was intimidated by the dynamic proportions of this college for the deaf. Frederick Law Olmstead, the father of Manhattan's Central Park, had designed the current campus in 1866, less than a year after the Civil War. The college that Olmstead envisioned had a greensward, a meadow, a chapel, and academic buildings, all connected by a subterranean tunnel system that would protect students, provide them with refuge and an escape route into the Washington woods in the event of another war.

Isaac wondered if the subterranean route still existed under the campus. He would have loved to explore Gallaudet. The winding road into the campus enticed him, but the workman's shack was outside the front gate, on Florida Avenue. Isaac didn't see a light inside the shack.

"Boss," Stefan said, "you shouldn't go in there alone. It could be a trap."

"If we wanted to announce ourselves," Sarah said, "we could have brought the Secret Service. We'll never be more than a step or two away—don't pester him. He's a big boy, even if he can't tie his own shoelaces."

And Isaac stepped out of the limo with his laces untied. He was in his element now, on a deserted street, beside a campus with very few lights in the windows. The shack had a dented door with a missing hinge. The door wasn't locked. He went inside, stood in the darkened doorway. He was wearing a button mike and could have signaled Sarah and Stef. A hurricane lamp was switched on, and there was the tattoo artist as Isaac had imagined him, sitting on a workbench in a velvet suit with a bandanna around his throat. His face had the brutal twist of a man who had been in many fights. His eyes, which had a liquid calm, were very dark, almost black in the light of the hurricane lamp. His mouth had once been ripped by a razor and still bore several scars. His chin had puncture marks. And yet, even with that brutal twist and all the wounds, he didn't seem unkind.

"I haven't come alone," Isaac said.

"Yes, you have two babysitters across the road—your helicopter pilot and his sweetheart, an intel officer who has annoyed her superiors because of her allegiance to you. Both of them are armed, and they can probably hear every word we say. But I have nothing to hide, Big Balls."

"Have we ever met before, Monsieur?"

The man laughed, and his wounds leapt about in the glare of the lamp. "Why are you so formal with me? I'm Viktor Danzig."

"Ah," Isaac said. "So you do have a surname."

"It was my mother's," he said. "And I use it sometimes, in her honor, and sometimes not. No, we have never met—until now."

One thing rubbed at Isaac. "Why am I Big Balls if we haven't met?"

"Because that's how you are known in penitentiaries around the country. And I admire convicts . . . their fortitude, their endurance under the duress of a prison system that has robbed them of all dignity."

"Then you're familiar with the Aryan Nation?"

"I despise their beliefs," Viktor said, "but I visited them at a penitentiary in Illinois, taught them a few tricks with pen and ink, since they knew about my talents and had asked for me."

Isaac was suspicious. "How come such lowlife bastards knew more about you than I ever did? And I have half the government's spooks behind me."

"It's the curious propaganda of prisons," Viktor said. "And your spooks have never seen the inside of a jail."

"Neither have you," Isaac said.

"But I still have the stink of Kolyma on me. It's in my blood. And we do business with the Brotherhood. They peddle drugs for us. And they get rid of FBI rats—sit down, Big Balls, we have a lot to discuss."

Isaac sat on a workbench a few feet away from Viktor, who wore a Beretta of his own in a little leather cup attached to his belt. "Little Brother, this is not a town for you. It does not welcome mavericks from Manhattan. You had a perfect laboratory—New York. You could break into restaurants, visit abandoned children at Rikers, knock your own police commissioner senseless. Who would dare challenge you? The Republicans didn't even bother to come up with a candidate. And then you allowed the Democrats to put you on the national ticket. They had to prop up that crook, Michael Storm, and who better than a mayor with a cop's credentials? The DNC planned to hide you in the Naval Observatory and have you go around the country from time to time to shoot at bottles with your Glock."

"Like Buffalo Bill."

"But Michael exploded, and then there was you, only you, with your democratic vistas and ideals. But you were outside your own candy store. The Pink Commish who would have lowered the subway fare if his own City Council hadn't threatened to lock him inside Bellevue."

Isaac squinted into the splashes of light and dark in that somber shack. "You started the lottery, didn't you? Baron Robespierre is one of your clerks."

"The baron was my father's banker. But I admit—the lottery was my idea. I had to find the means of capturing the imagination of all the business moguls who recognized you as an immediate threat—a Stalinist in the White House."

And the Big Guy would have to explain himself all over again. Stalin had murdered millions and sent millions more into the gulag. All the poets mocked his oily fingers and cockroach mustache, but he still kept the Germans out of Moscow. He never had a kopeck in his pockets, wore the same sweaty uniform summer and winter. He was as poor as Isaac Sidel.

"A Stalinist couldn't have been elected," Isaac had to say in his own defense.

"But you weren't elected," Viktor said. "You're the accidental president. You can't be manipulated or massaged. You're not interested in money and power—you're a very dangerous man."

"So were Lincoln and FDR," Isaac said, incensed. "Who taught you so much about American politics?"

"I spent half my summers here with my mother—in a cold-water flat."

Ariel had implied that Viktor's mother was no more important to him than a spool of thread, that Karl, the *pakhan* prince of Kolyma, had carried the boy from capital to capital, sent him to private schools in Switzerland. But Isaac discovered otherwise. The boy hadn't despised his mother—it was the *pakhan* who had cast her out of his domain. She was a seamstress from Danzig he had dallied with. She meant no more to the *pakhan* than a mote of dust in his eye. He might have given her a wad of dollars or Deutsche Marks for his moment of delight. But when he uncovered that this seamstress, Pauline, had given birth to a child in a charity ward—a boy with eyes as black as his—he was furious. He stole the boy from her, had his lawyers bribe officials to make the little boy's birth certificate disappear and mark Pauline as a whore. She was tossed out of Danzig, and the *pakhan* himself paid for her passage to America.

Groomed by Jewish butlers on the Place des Vosges, in the same house where Alexandre Dumas had once lived, Viktor didn't believe his father's story of a cruel, careless mother who had abandoned him at birth. He was a resilient, artful boy who searched for her traces. She was still a seamstress.

"Where?" Isaac asked, touched by Viktor's tale.

"In your kingdom," Viktor said. "On the Lower East Side."

"And she never got married?"

"No," Viktor said. "She was still in love with that gangster from Siberia."

"But how the devil did you find her? You couldn't have had any help from your father."

"But I'm my father's son," he said. "I had some capital of my own. I sought out several retired homicide detectives. They located her in a month. And that's when I heard of the mythical Pink Commish. They were frightened to death of you, that you might catch them in some corruption scheme."

"I hate corrupt cops," Isaac said.

"That's not the point," Viktor said, leaning into the hurricane lamp. "They would have been guilty no matter what they did. But my mother worshipped you. She said you were out on patrol every night, even escorted her once to a class at the Educational Alliance."

"You see," Isaac said, with a sudden excitement. "We have met—through your mother."

Viktor was also wearing a button mike. He whispered into the mike, then turned to Isaac. "Big Balls, we have to cut this conversation. Bull Latham is two blocks from Gallaudet."

"Fuck Bull Latham," Isaac said. "Where's my tattoo?"

"You haven't earned it yet."

The Big Guy panicked. He didn't want Viktor to leave on such short notice, just when he was warming up.

"Why should the Bull give a damn about you and the Sons of Rossiya? You're a bunch of ghosts. You're name doesn't even appear on the computer screens at Quantico."

"That's because you haven't punched in the right codes. I'm the most feared counterfeiter in the business. My fifties are without a flaw. Speak to your man at Treasury—Felix Mandel; he's the only one with half a brain. Your advisors have served themselves. They sit you down in the president's seat, call you POTUS, and give you blinders to wear. Big Balls, you never had a chance. I'm the biggest informant Bull ever had, and also his biggest pain in the ass. He doesn't own me. I do special favors for the CIA from time to time, me and my band."

"The *besprizornye*," Isaac said.

"Goodbye, Big Balls. I have to run. My mother survived because of you. You wouldn't let the governor and his cronies ruin rent control."

"Jesus," Isaac said, "you could have bought her a penthouse with all your loot."

"She wouldn't take a nickel from me—called it blood money. Said she was ashamed of my credentials. I had to buy a plot for her in Woodlawn, near Herman Melville's grave, or she might have ended up in Potter's Field. You're familiar with Herman, yes. He lived underground, like my *besprizornye*. Goodbye."

And Viktor bolted out of the shack with all the exuberance and grace of a whitetail buck. He didn't disappear into some dark street. He raced right into Gallaudet. And Isaac realized that Viktor must have memorized the hidden tunnels of Frederick Law Olmstead. Perhaps he was one of Gallaudet's donors, a patron of the school, and had seen Olmstead's original plans—a school that would have been ready for another catastrophic war. He was twice as clever as the Bull, who wouldn't have known about the tunnels and didn't have the least idea of where to look.

Isaac waited outside the shack with his arms folded as the sirens blared and the Bull arrived with his armada.

"Mr. President, where's that little cocksucker with the scars on his lip?"

"The tattoo artist? I thought he doesn't exist. Is Viktor Danzig in some kind of witness protection program meant for kings? You shouldn't have lied to me, you son of a bitch, and played me for a sap."

"I had to lie," the Bull said, whispering in front of his own men. "He's diabolic, damn you—no one can forge Ulysses Grant like him. His paper was priceless. He could have destroyed us with his fucking fifty-dollar bills. Ask the people at Treasury. We had to pamper him."

"And were you ever planning to tell me, Bull?"

"No," the Bull said. "It was for your own protection, your own good. He's been betting heavy dollars that you won't last. That's why we put you in a cocoon. Matt Malloy shits a brick every time you leave the White House. That rumpus at your dacha was some kind of foreplay, a first act. The little bastard hired General Tollhouse to mock us. He might have finished you off tonight if we hadn't wised up to your masquerade. You look wonderful in your epaulettes. We let him listen into our frequencies."

"And you still couldn't grab him," Isaac said, walking away from the Bull. He was caught in some merciless web. The people paid to protect him were always a few paces behind someone else's curve. And the culprits, the killers in waiting, sat on angelic wings and rescued him at the last minute. It wasn't fair. Isaac should have had more involvement in his own fate.

It was a fool's paradise. He held on to Brenda Brown as his virtual chief of staff since she wasn't on any government payroll and couldn't be fired. He held on to Colonel Oliver as his helicopter pilot because it would have been complicated to remove the commander of Marine Squadron One without the president's approval. Stef was too damn visible, but Sarah Rogers had never really been assigned to the Big Guy. The chiefs of Naval Intel were fierce about guarding their own entitlements, yet they still pulled Sarah from the White House and hid her deep within Quantico. These admirals dared Sidel to do something about it. He went to Quantico in a presidential caravan, with sharpshooters and a medical team, and was stopped at the gate. The facility was in lockdown, the admirals had declared—no personnel, authorized or not, could enter or leave until the lockdown was lifted. Marine Base Quantico was a sprawling, secretive site that also housed the FBI Academy and half a dozen covert combat schools.

Isaac returned to Pennsylvania Avenue with his tail tucked between his legs. He couldn't get near Captain Rogers. She was incommunicado as far as the president was concerned. Brenda Brown advised him to look for another intelligence harpy who wasn't stuck so far up some admiral's ass. But Isaac wanted Sarah. He summoned Felix Mandel, chief assistant to the Secretary of the Treasury. They sat on a couch in the Oval Office, Felix in a rumpled tie. He could have sunk the Soviet Union by substituting the ruble with one of his phantom currencies. He was the Darth Vader of the currency markets. Economic ministers from all over the planet paid homage to Felix. His Nobel Prize was like an open wound for these ministers, who waited in line to sit with Felix and beg him not to tinker with their currencies. Felix Mandel was a native son of Manhattan, and Isaac had inherited him as assistant manager of the budget in the first year of his mayoralty. Felix worked out of a cavernous closet in the Municipal Building, like some modern Bartleby who was a numbers cruncher rather than a scribe. It was before his Nobel and Felix was utterly unrecognized. But Isaac cherished him. Felix never lied about the budget.

"Mr. Mayor, I can't tell you how many teachers we have in the public school system. Firemen, yes. But teachers come and go. None of us can keep track. The city payroll is a behemoth that feeds on its own flesh. And our revenue is beyond anyone's crystal ball. One week we're bankrupt and the next we're a fatted calf."

"Then how can I plan, Felix, how can I take the homeless out of city shelters and put them into public housing?"

"You can't. The housing might disappear tomorrow."

"Then were all my campaign promises a lie?"

"Mayor Sidel, that's the black hole of politics—promises, promises."

Felix was soon whisked away to Washington, and Isaac was left with a swollen cadre of jesters and clowns. He never solved the housing crisis. The homeless multiplied. He blustered and finagled, walked in and out of Rikers with his Glock. He was visible and beloved. One morning a deranged man at a city shelter tried to carve him up with a kitchen knife. That's the closest he ever got to a mayor's immortality. He soothed the man, and they ended up playing pinochle together. But now he'd crept down the rabbit hole and stumbled into the fourth dimension. There was nothing random about the assault on his life.

He drank coffee with Felix Mandel and shared a piece of carrot cake from a local farmers' market. "Felix, can't you put some heat on the budget director and cancel the paychecks of certain admirals who are in revolt?"

"You can pension them off for dereliction of duty. But the provost marshal will eat you alive. And God forbid if there's ever a court-martial. You'll have to testify, Mr. President."

"All I want to do is stop their paychecks."

"Then you'll have to run up to the Hill and argue in front of Appropriations. Do you want Congress to declare that you're having a secret vendetta against the admirals of Navy Intel? Get off that track. Your numbers are down. You'll go into free fall."

Isaac brooded a bit and summoned up his conversation with Viktor outside Gallaudet. "Why is that tattoo artist such a no-no? His name doesn't appear on any list."

Isaac's maven was silent for a moment. The mention of the tattoo artist had made him ill at ease. He could barely look at Isaac. "You have no idea of that man's genius, and his power to destroy whatever he has in mind. It's not just the artistry of his plates. He has half a dozen apprentices, men—and women—who can perform miracles with soft steel. They're master engravers, every one; and they seem to replicate like rabbits."

"So how do you deal with Viktor Danzig?"

"We bargain—and we beg. We pay him not to circulate that soft metal of his."

"Then he holds us at ransom."

"Worse," said Felix. "He commits atrocious deeds, sometimes in our behalf, sometimes not. He and his aging orphans are an army within an army."

"And who's responsible for keeping him in line? It can't be the Bull. He tried to capture Viktor."

"Ah, it's a game of cat and mouse. But Viktor's the cat, and we are all his many mice."

"Viktor said I should ask you about my own slim chance for survival."

Felix's face was twitching. "We shouldn't get onto that subject."

"What are my chances?"

"Almost none."

"But the Dow has risen a hundred points since I was sworn in."

Felix smiled like Bartleby in his old municipal cavern. "There are much better indicators than the Dow. The managers of the biggest hedge funds are all betting you won't survive your maiden year."

Isaac suddenly felt as if he'd lost his own language. Perhaps that's why the tattoo artist had called Gallaudet a dummy school. He hadn't meant to be cruel. Isaac had become a man without his own proper signals. "Ariel Moss said I should resign."

"It's too late for that," Felix said.

"Then what should I do? This mansion is no safer than my dacha. And I'm not a guy who likes to sit at home. I imagine the Bull can't wait to inherit my chair, with Ramona right next to him, as the solitary Witch of the West Wing."

"You're wrong," Felix said. "The Bull is as much a policeman as you are. He couldn't bear to preside over the death of a sitting president."

Isaac started to laugh. "Then I suppose I'll have to sit shiva for myself while I'm still alive."

PART THREE

10

They could have met in Geneva's Old Town, with its fairyland flavor, or in Amsterdam, where he would have had a perfect escape route along the canals, but he picked Paris to meet with all these money launderers, maniacs, crypto-bankers, and ministers of crime. They had billions at their disposal in hard cash. Viktor had found a nondescript hotel in the thirteenth arrondissement, near Chinatown, with its vast plain of high-rises. He'd booked every room in the hotel. He was wary of his own partners, but the waiters and laundresses at the Hotel des Artisans worked for him. They all carried silencers under their blouses and bibs. He might have to turn the hotel into a killing ground, so he sent the manager on a month's vacation. He was aware that his partners had their own accomplices and also plotted among themselves, but he couldn't operate without such risks. There was too much wealth at stake. His partners were angry at him because he refused to initiate measures that would have favored them. They could have made a killing in Mother Russia, but Viktor hesitated, Viktor stalled. So they sank their talons into America's soft underbelly, but Viktor wouldn't share his paper with these princes, wouldn't give them access to his prize plates. Their own paper was crude, and couldn't have weakened the American economy. Half their associates were already in prison, and they didn't want T-men on their tail.

"But you, Viktor, you are our Rembrandt," said Rainer Wolff of West Berlin. Rainer owned newspapers, publishing houses, and nightclubs. But he couldn't expand his holdings without Viktor and his apprentices, with their little sacks of engravers' tools. "You must give us these children—or share them with us."

The others *seemed* to agree, or perhaps they wanted to give the impression that they were within Rainer's reach. There was Pesh Olinov, who'd just come from Moscow, and who worked for and against Gorbachev at the same time, crippling him while he held him aloft; there was Michael Davit from Manchester, who'd made his fortune with a string of tobacco shops and had his own snug little school for assassins who were almost as invisible as the *besprizornye*, and Viktor was convinced that Davit had brought some of these thugs from Manchester and had put them at Rainer's disposal; there was Pavel Lind from Poland, a publisher of pornography who owned a fleet of truckers in a collapsing communist empire; Pavel also controlled the Eastern Bloc's black market in dollars and had the most to gain from Viktor's magical paper.

Pavel was desperate for dollars, and half crazed. He watched Viktor like an embattled hawk.

Then there was Pierrot, the Baron de Robespierre, who was one of Viktor's messengers and confidants, but the baron had his own allegiances, and Viktor's other partners kept their money in the baron's invisible vaults inside a bomb shelter in Basel. Thus it was hard to tell where the baron's real allegiances lay, and at what price he would sell out. And then there was Rosa Malamud, who had her own line of fashion shops on the Left Bank; she'd done a bit of freelancing for Shin Bet and MI6; her weapon of choice was a sharpened knitting needle that she would dig between a man's eyes. Viktor wasn't frightened of her violence or her volatility. She was quicker on her feet than Viktor's partner-princes. She was fifty years old and had all the cash she would ever need, yet she sat in the darkened dining room at the Hotel des Artisans. It wasn't greed that had brought her here, or adventure. She was curious about this *pakhan* with the wooden box. Perhaps she'd slept with Viktor's father once upon a time and her maternal instincts had turned deadly. Viktor watched for any signs of the knitting needle.

They must have elected Rainer Wolff as their spokesman. Viktor had avoided West Berlin, because Rainer had enough punch to bribe every single border guard, and Viktor might have ended up in some Stasi cell in East Berlin without his passport. He was more comfortable in Paris, even if it was Rosa's roost, and he had a lot to fear, but his father had settled in Paris, as much as a *pakhan* could settle in any one place, and he felt nimble in its streets. He loved the odors of each Metro station, loved the little parks with their ping-pong tables topped with marble and mosaics. Paris was his *bled*, his personal canteen, his wanderer's home, and he wouldn't allow a clever maniac like Rosa to ruin it for him. So he listened to his partners' grievances.

"*Mensch*," Rainer said, "you cannot have a monopoly on those dollars of yours. You must share."

"I have shared," Viktor said. "Rainer, you have a very short memory. When you were in a hole and needed my paper to settle your debts with some gangster from MI6, I did not hesitate for a second. I prepared a special plate."

Rainer whistled through his teeth. "A masterpiece! And I am forever grateful. But gratitude can only go so far. We have to stop the Yankee invasion. Their spooks are everywhere. We cannot conduct our business."

"And you think my paper will end your problems."

"Yes," Rainer said. "They'll pull their bloodhounds from our territories if their own market is flooded."

Viktor stared into the heat of those hostile faces. "They'll come at you more and more. They'll close your shops. Pavel, they'll arrest all your traders. You won't be able to move the paper you have. And they'll whack you in the head out of pure spite. We've seen it happen before."

"Ah," Michael Davit said, "but we never had paper of your quality—we have our own atom bomb and you tell us we can't use it."

"Stop that," Viktor said, "I've given you enough to make you all rich."

"What about Sidel?" Rosa asked, looking like a delirious spider in a designer dress. "We paid Tollhouse a fortune to get rid of him. You contributed to the pot. And I thought we had the whole Republican Party in our pocket. Didn't we bribe those bastards?"

"Ah, the good old Republican Party," Viktor said. "It's like bribing a sea of sand."

"So what? Sidel's a dreamer. He'll turn Yankee Land into one big welfare state. All our holdings will be flushed into the toilet. We can't afford him, Viktor. People will riot. I'll lose all my shops. Tollhouse has killed for us. Why did you stop him now?"

"Because," Viktor said. "I did not fancy killing Sidel."

"Is that how we conduct business?" asked Pesh Olinov, the dwarf. Pesh was the only one at this table who had been with the *besprizornye*, who'd risen up from the ranks, and he was the only one with the mark of a werewolf on his chest. The others weren't werewolves. They were ruthless entrepreneurs, but they hadn't been reborn in a prison camp.

"Brother," Pesh said, "it is out of your hands. Assassins have been sent."

And Viktor knew in his bones that this meeting would end badly. But he had to make one last attempt to avoid a bloodbath in a hotel that didn't have a decent view—the high-rises that flashed in the sun could have been a land of graves above the ground. He would have liked one final stroll along the Place des Vosges.

"Assassins can be recalled," Viktor said.

Rainer chortled to himself; he'd been a young captain in the Abwehr during World War II, a master spy involved in the Abwehr's gigantic counterfeit racket. It was their last desperate fling; they hoped to flood the world market with American dollars and bring down the currency. But their engravings were rushed, and the thieves they hired were no better than amateurish louts. The paper these men produced would have been rejected at every bank and couldn't have fooled the simplest of shopkeepers. The entire operation was botched. Rainer was demoted and sent to the Eastern Front. But he never lost that desire to bring down America and its currency.

"I will recall no one," Rainer said. "You cannot stop us this time, Viktor. Even if none of us leaves this hotel alive, it will not change a thing. Come, we'll all do our little dance of death. I don't mind. But you have your proof, Viktor. Isaac the Pure will never change. Didn't we woo him while he was mayor? We buttered up his lieutenants, but we couldn't get near him. He was too busy visiting shelters for the homeless. We wanted to rebuild the Lower East Side and all its crumbling *dreck*, turn it into a shopping center and an amusement park for foreign tourists. We spent millions in lawyers' fees, and what did Sidel say? He'd rather have his pickle barrels than our amusement park."

"It wasn't out of malice," Viktor said. "He's like a child with this enormous toy at his disposal—the presidency."

"A preposterous child, a child we can't afford."

Rainer stared at Michael Davit with a kind of crushing omniscience. Viktor had to prepare himself for the worst; his partners had met without him and planned this escapade. "And now you want revenge, Rainer, because he wouldn't let you invade Manhattan."

It was the spider lady who answered him. "Don't belittle us, Viktor. We're not in the revenge business. Sidel should have stayed in Manhattan where he belongs. He threatens all our enterprises. He's a disaster as a president. You know this. His secret services run rampant around him. We could deal with Bull Latham. He understands the truth of your paper, but Sidel tilts at windmills while our profits go down and down. He must be replaced. You agreed with us. What changed your mind?"

Viktor had no reasonable answer. Perhaps it had something to do with his waiflike mother and Isaac's battles to preserve rent control. He saw Sidel as some kind of *zek*, entombed in his own spiritual prison camp—the first werewolf to inhabit the White House. Viktor didn't have the will to launch him into eternity. That was not his gift. He knew now that his partners had bribed the waiters and laundresses who were meant to ensure his own safety. The Hotel des Artisans had turned into a trap. He shouldn't have been that naïve. Paris was as much a graveyard as Geneva or West Berlin.

"Tell me, Little Brothers and Sister Rosa, how do you mean to flourish without my paper?"

"We have reckoned with that possibility," Rainer said. "One of your own apprentices now works for us."

"*Mensch,* even if you had them all, you would still have nothing. They are wonderful engravers—I taught them all my strokes—but they still lack the final touch. A crooked line in Grant's bowtie, a missing curlicue in his beard. I have to improve upon their artistry. Bull Latham would spot these errors even without his loupe."

"Ah," said Rainer, "then we will keep you here as our guest until you are in a more negotiable mood."

One thing in this conspiracy enraged Viktor. "And you, Pierrot, my littlest brother, who was my father's pet, why did you join these plotters? You have all the wealth in the world, and I have made you even wealthier."

The baron didn't apologize. "My dear Viktor, your *besprizornye* are now middle-aged, some are old men. They've lost their teeth. And many of them grumble about you. They worry about their *pakhan.*"

"Still," Viktor said, "I trusted you with my life. And you, Brother Olinov, you were one of my *cheloveks.* You carry the tattoo of a werewolf. I painted your chest."

"I am a werewolf," said Pesh, "and proud to be one. I was born in the prison camps. But you have betrayed us with this sentimental attachment to Sidel—a policeman who probably pisses in his pants. You must share your art with us—you must."

"Don't appeal to him," Rosa said. "We will have his paper."

Viktor noticed her knitting needle, as it glistened like an elongated ice pick. She lunged at him with all the art of an MI6 assassin, perhaps to graze his cheek as a warning, or to stop him in his tracks with a hole in the head. Did his erstwhile partners have their own magic, their own Talmudic engraver? Why should Viktor care? He stepped outside the arc of her lunge like a matador, or a *chelovek* in the middle of a knife fight in Kolyma, and watched her crash into a wall. She sat there in a perfect daze.

A laundress appeared with a silencer and a lunatic smile on her face. That smile cost her, that moment of arrogance. She was rejoicing in her act of betrayal. Viktor seized an ashtray from the table and hurled it at her. It bounced off her forehead and sent her flying. But he couldn't defeat the entire staff. Waiters arrived with their own silencers.

"Slow," Rainer said. "We want to taste his agony. He might relent and allow us a little pinch of his paper. If not, we'll bury him in the cellar, and who will mourn a werewolf?"

"Not me," Michael Davit said. "Not me."

"We'll inherit his *besprizornye*," said the dwarf who wasn't a dwarf.

Michael Davit was amused. "Those tits? We're better off without them."

Viktor watched the merriment in the waiters' eyes, that sense of their own sadistic pleasure, as if they were about to take target practice on a scarecrow. And that's when he heard the sirens. He'd phoned the Sûreté just before the meeting began. He knew a certain chief inspector, had done him some favors. Told him to arrive at noon with a little fleet.

"Bravo," Rainer said. "You've walked your way out of this, Viktor, but how will you survive on your own, even with your band of aging orphans?"

"You're the ones who should worry," Viktor said. "Rosa, you won't have your shops very long. I will ask your landlords to have another look at all your leases. And the rue du Cherche-Midi will become a labyrinth. Deliveries will be impossible, customers will be scarce. Your little clothing empire will be without a clientele."

Rosa sat calmly on the floor, awakening from her little nap, but the princes started to panic. "It's silly to declare war," said Rainer. "We will find a solution, but it must be without Sidel. His heartbeat is not negotiable."

Viktor shoved past Pesh and Michael Davit, slapped a laundress and two waiters as he left the dining room, and marched out onto the tiny, hidden boulevard near the riverbank. There was a blaze of white from the high-rises that nearly cut into Viktor's eyes. He saluted the police cars in front of the hotel. The chief inspector stepped out of his own sedan to greet him. They spoke French, a language Viktor had explored as a little boy on the Place des Vosges. With his father and the other *pakhans* he was perfectly fluent in English and Russian. But he couldn't find much melody in his voice with the chief inspector. He was stuttering, in fact. He could have had the entire troupe at the Hotel des Artisans taken into custody, yet what would he have accomplished? There were no corpses inside the hotel, no signs of conflict. Yes, the waiters and laundresses had their silencers and might have sat six months inside La Santé. But Rainer and the rest would have snaked out of reach of the Sûreté. Rainer's million-dollar lawyers could have outwitted any magistrate.

The problem's been solved, he said, and slipped a packet of money into the chief inspector's sleeve.

"Impeccable, Monsieur Viktor."

The cars drove off, leaving Viktor with that slash of sunlight off the high-rises. He'd had a very bitter revelation at the hotel. He could trust no one—not his apprentices, not his associates, not even Sidel.

11

The baron was sitting with his two bodyguards in a mini compartment on board the bullet train to Basel. He'd already cut off Renata Swallow's monthly allowance. He'd closed Viktor's accounts, and he was warehousing whatever paper "Rembrandt" had left with him—immaculate fifties that could have been hung on the walls of museums as works of art. He had to side with Rainer and his other partners. Viktor had become as temperamental—and reckless—as a prima donna. He was a *pakhan* who had lost his touch. He spent half his time marking the skin of random people—soldiers or convicts and high-class whores like Renata Swallow—with little memorials. What did it all mean? He carried around his wooden box of ink and tools rather than his engraver's kit. The baron couldn't afford that luxury, not in the winter of '89 when the Soviet Union was caving in and the economies of Eastern Europe were up for grabs—it was like stealing into a barnyard with a bunch of sacks and shovels. The loot was everywhere.

His mobile rang, but there was very poor reception on the bullet train. He fiddled with the antenna, and a voice came through like the echo of some familiar ghost. It was Rainer Wolff from West Berlin, as if he were speaking from the netherworld.

"Rainer, I cannot hear you."

"Your bodyguards," the ghost said.

"They're tip-top. The best in the business. They come from Michael Davit's crew."

They had to be careful, since they weren't on a landline, and the baron couldn't tell who was listening. "Yes, yes, I am disposing of Rembrandt's assets—he must be submerged somewhere, like a submarine. Davit's lads will find him. It is a great pity. But we never asked him to self-destruct . . . indeed, it is time to cash in on our lottery. And we'll start another—for Rembrandt. Goodbye, Rainer."

The first bodyguard was gone. "Where is he?" the baron asked his second bodyguard, who sat across from him.

"Ian?" the bodyguard said. "He's in the loo, love. He'll be back. Ian's a good lad."

But Ian didn't return after ten minutes. And the baron snapped at the second bodyguard. "Find him. I don't want to be here alone."

"Right you are."

And the second bodyguard left. Viktor sat down in his place, and the baron could feel his bowels twist.

"I'll scream," he said. "This is an exclusive train. And there are many more conductors in first class."

"Scream your head off," Viktor said. "I bought out every ticket in this car—it's empty."

"But I have two bodyguards. The best in the business. Michael Davit's lads."

"They won't be back."

"But they're incorruptible," the baron said. "Ian and his partner can't be bought."

"They won't be back."

The baron started to cry. "They threatened me, Viktor. Michael Davit put a gun to my head, and Rainer was behind that gun."

"Pierrot, please. I let you in close, and you saw how indecisive I was about Sidel. You read that as weakness. It wasn't. We can't *always* kill. Sometimes it's a question of civility."

He slit the baron's throat with a razor. The baron didn't scream—it was a gentle stroke, without effort, it seemed. Bubbles appeared in the baron's mouth. He started to say something and stopped. Viktor laid his head back, as he would have done with a sleeping child. He sat there. Not a single conductor came. He got off at the next stop with his *besprizornye*, millionaires in their fifties, with scars on their faces, like Viktor.

Pierrot had been right. Michael Davit's men couldn't be bought. Viktor and his *besprizornye* had to strangle them in the corridor, with a wire. They had to wear leather gloves, or the wire would have cut deep into their own hands. They'd hurled both bodyguards out a broken window of the bullet train. Michael Davit's men should have been more attentive, should have noticed the empty seats, some of them filled by the *besprizornye*. They had covered Pierrot with the latest copy of *Paris Match* and wiped off the surplus blood.

The conductors wouldn't discover him until the bullet train arrived in Switzerland. They would talk about the banker from Basel for days. A corpse in a first-class car. It would remind them of an unsolved murder they had read about in *Paris Match*. Italian gangsters from the Riviera, no doubt. Or a feud among Corsican cutthroats.

PART FOUR

12

I t was all confusing to Stefan Oliver. The Marine commandant at Quantico avoided him; the admirals at Navy Intel whispered in his presence; the FBI instructors and recruits stared at him as if he were some idol touched with leprosy or the plague. His fellow pilots and crew were careful around him; that pure sense of play was gone. He couldn't even set up a ping-pong match with any of his rivals. He had to race around the gym all alone in his silkies. Stef had become the pariah of his own squadron; as the president's pilot, he was caught in the middle of a feud between the admirals and his boss. He had problems with every lift package on account of his mechanics, who were loyal to the admirals at the base. Stef was living permanently at the White House with Max and their Serbian maid, Karina, while the FBI harassed her with background checks that never seemed to end. He was a Marine at odds with his own service. The duty officer at Quantico was very blunt with him.

"Wildfire to Rio, how's life in the attic? Are they fattening you up with peanut butter pie?"

"Rio to Wildfire, it's none of your fucking business."

"Well, homeboy, you're getting back your roommate."

Stef wasn't even listening. "Roger that," and he tuned out the frequency.

But Wildfire wasn't wrong. Sarah Rogers returned to the attic, in Isaac's bathrobe and all. Her eyes couldn't focus. All her flintiness was gone, that rough edge he admired. Her skin was very sallow. She looked like a wraith in curly black hair. The bastards must have kept her in deep cover at Quantico. She began to weep like a child. He'd never seen Sarah cry. It tore at him, and for a moment he wasn't a widower and could grasp beyond his own grief.

"What's wrong? I'll never hurt you. I promise."

"Stef, I'm their spy. I have to report back to them—Navy Intel. All our intimate acts. Every time you eat me out I have to describe it in detail. They're gunning after you and the president."

"Does the boss know?"

"He says he still wants me around, even if I have to wear a wire—I missed you, Stef. All the while they kept me in the freezer at Quantico, I missed you more and more. I could feel my hand slide down the fur on your chest."

They kissed in one of the attic's utility closets. She never bothered to take off Isaac's robe. He was tender and fierce with her, as fierce as any satyr. It excited Stef that she was tattling on him about their sexual exploits to her bosses at Quantico. He felt like a porn star.

The daily briefings grew more and more urgent. Secretary of State Colin Fremont had just returned from a whirlwind tour of Moscow, Warsaw, Prague, and East Berlin. Fremont was elegant, brash, and brittle as sandpaper. He never wore a necktie, not even at an embassy dinner. He replaced it with a red scarf and a black silk shirt with a soft collar. That was Colin's uniform. He spent more time in the air than he did at his bachelor pad near Dupont Circle or his ancestral home in Boise. Isaac didn't give a damn that there had been rumors of a love affair with a male professor while Colin was a student at Swarthmore.

"Isaac," said the chief counsel of his selection committee, "this gay business could come back and bite you on the ass."

"I still want Colin Fremont," Isaac said. And here he was, arrogant as always, and the shrewdest member of Isaac's court.

"They did a dance at the Kremlin, Mr. President. We fed on wild boar and drowned in Veuve Clicquot. The Russkies are all curious about you. The Pink Commish—Stalin with a Glock. But I could see the terror in their eyes. The Veuve Clicquot tasted like piss. They're running out of dollars. And they print their rubles on toilet paper."

"What are you driving at, Mr. Secretary?" Tim Vail asked in that superior tone of his.

"They're desperate. We don't dare make a hostile move. But the Bolshoi goes on with five-hour performances and their ice-cream factories hum with new flavors. I learned more in Prague from a junior finance minister than I did in Moscow. The Russkies can't buy dollars, so they're trying to kidnap some master engraver and print their own product, but they can't afford high-quality silk. Whatever they touch is atrocious."

Isaac muscled his way in. "Tell us about Prague."

"The president's castle is filled with mousetraps. The maids can't afford panties and bras. They have to settle for military underwear. Half of them are whores and all of them are members of the StB—the secret police. The whole country trades in counterfeit dollars. I think we ought to help. A high-quality product of their own would make them less dependent on the Soviets. We'd be the first ones in Prague Castle, Mr. President, ready to pounce when the shit begins to fly, and it will."

"Are you suggesting that we give those Czech gangsters a fortune of fake fifties?" Ramona asked with a growl.

"Yes."

Isaac was falling in love with his Secretary of State. "Bull, do we have any of Viktor's paper on hand to show Mr. Fremont?"

Bull Latham removed a fifty-dollar bill from a plastic case in his pocket and handed the bill and a jeweler's loupe to Colin Fremont.

Fremont peered at Ulysses Grant through the loupe. "This stuff is priceless—pure gold. We'll put the Kremlin out of the business. Who's the engraver?"

"He uses many names, Mr. Secretary. We call him Rembrandt. He's one of my prize informants. I have enough of his product on hand to supply the Czechs—if POTUS approves."

"What will it do to our economy with queer fifties floating around?" asked Tim Vail, who liked to serve as the Cromwell of Isaac's court.

"It won't leave a dent," said Felix Mandel. "As Mr. Fremont says, the product is pure gold. And if we control the supply, where's the harm?"

The Secretary of State rubbed his hands together as a sign of his appetite for the deal. "That will make Karel Ludvik a happy man." Karel was current occupant of the Castle. The Soviets had put him into power after the Prague Spring of '68, with its quiet revolution that was crushed by Soviet tanks and artillery. He was a minor poet, novelist, and diplomat with sterling communist credentials. He'd also been a colonel in the StB. But Colin Fremont found him "a man of culture" who rebelled against the atrocities of the secret police. "Karel's eyes have turned toward Washington rather than Moscow, Mr. President. He's one of your biggest fans—in camera, of course. But he would welcome a visit."

"So would London, Paris, and Bonn," said Bull Latham. "But POTUS can't travel. There's a price on his head."

"Indeed," said Colin Fremont. "We've heard rumbles about some mysterious raffle that predicts the president's demise. What does it mean?"

"A lot," said Tim Vail. "There are rogue agents everywhere—in the Kremlin, in the StB. They'd all like to collect."

"That's what Karel told me," said Colin Fremont. "Can't even trust his own men. 'It's open season on Isaac Sidel,' he said."

"*Kafka*," Isaac muttered to himself. His mavens pricked their ears and listened to the president. "I want to walk the streets where Kafka walked, sit in the cafés and coffeehouses where he sat."

Tim was exasperated with Sidel. "That Prague is long gone. You can't go on a sentimental journey, sir. You're the prince of West—"

"I'm no prince," Isaac snapped at his Oliver Cromwell. "I'm a cop who landed in the White House."

"Still a prince in the eyes of the world," said Tim, "and this is hard-nosed politics. We have to catch Karel at his own game, bend him to our will with a bargaining chip—Rembrandt's paper."

"No, no, no," said the Secretary of State with his own flair for drama. "POTUS is right. We take politics out of the picture, at least as an appetizer. The president isn't visiting Prague to cause problems for the Russkies. He's recapturing his own literary past. That will play, but there's a slight dampener—President Ludvik says Prague isn't safe. We can't mount every spire with sharpshooters. And the Castle itself is compromised; it's filled with so many palaces and gardens, you could wander around for days and never find yourself; it's like a souk for secret agents, a clearinghouse, and everyone has murder on his mind."

"Then what's our strategy for the president?" Ramona asked.

"We accept Karel's invitation," Colin said. "We make it strictly a cultural tour—POTUS is making a pilgrimage to Franz Kafka's birthplace. But he can't go to Prague, not in public, at least. Karel has his own dacha about fifty clicks northwest of Prague Castle. It's an old hunting lodge, a haven once upon a time for Czech noblemen and their mistresses. It's isolated and impenetrable. Very few people know its whereabouts."

Ramona grinned. "That was the word on Cactus—impenetrable. And look what happened."

"I don't give a crap," Isaac said. "Get back to Karel. We're going to Prague."

He had to see Kafka's birthplace, suck up the atmosphere and vanish for a moment within the famous Czech fog, even if the fog itself was an American fairy tale. He didn't care what the communist regime thought of Kafka, a Prague Yid who left around unfinished manuscripts in crystalline German prose, a tubercular werewolf who told about miraculous transformations and hunger artists. Isaac was mystified when he discovered that Kafka had been six feet tall. He'd always imagined him as a tiny man in a bowler hat who could have walked into a cafeteria on East Broadway and asked for a bowl of barley soup.

13

Ah, Air Force One. It was a traveling media circus where Isaac had to play juggler, wise man, and magician-clown. The press had its own compartment at the back of the plane, but reporters wandered about like petty cannibals prepared to devour the skin and bones of presidential advisors who had tagged along on the flight. Their favorite was Colin Fremont, who sat in his red scarf and black silk shirt and served as the president's portmanteau. Colin had his own spies at State, and he was aware of what these reporters knew.

He was like a dentist in the middle of a probe, revealing what he wanted to reveal.

"Of course it's political. Every time POTUS gets on a plane it's a political act. We're bailing out the Czech president. His tenure at the Castle is a bit shaky. But he's smiling now, as well he should. Karel's the beneficiary of POTUS's first trip abroad. And we're not brandishing missiles or challenging the Soviets."

"Why not?" asked a political correspondent from *Time* who'd been invited aboard by the Secretary of State.

"Because we're the USA, and POTUS is making a spiritual mission. That's our policy. It's a cultural package. The president's going to revisit the cobblestones of Prague's greatest writer."

"Sir," said one of the bureau chiefs at the *Washington Post*, "Prague isn't even on our agenda."

"That's a bit of a wrinkle," said Colin Fremont. "But it will be resolved before we touch down."

"Isn't it true, sir," asked the same bureau chief, "that there's a price on the president's head, and we have to hide out at some half-pint castle miles from Prague?"

"That half-pint castle is President Ludvik's country estate," Colin declared, but Isaac had to wander into this hornets' nest.

"There've been threats, and we have to take precautions, but I will cross the Charles Bridge and retrace Franz Kafka's steps."

"Why is Kafka so important to you?" asked a correspondent from Atlanta. "He's not an American author. He didn't invent Gatsby's green light. He writes about cockroaches and castles that cannot be penetrated."

A fury began to build in Isaac. He could have been back at Columbia College, during his one season of classics, sitting somewhere at the back of Hamilton Hall, in a freshman humanities seminar.

"Well, isn't Air Force One some kind of a castle? And Kafka didn't write about cockroaches. Haven't we all woken up from a bad dream and felt a sudden metamorphosis?"

"Mr. President," answered the most sympathetic member of the press pool, "what do you mean?"

"Metamorphosis," Isaac repeated, wearing his Camp David windbreaker on Air Force One. "That your whole life had changed, that you weren't even human—that you could have become a pathetic creature with spindly legs."

"Oh," said the same reporter, "we've all had the blues like that."

And Isaac trundled off to POTUS's suite with Captain Sarah and Colonel Oliver, who should have flown ahead to Prague on a military transport to reassemble the presidential package of Night Hawks. But Isaac wanted Stef with him on Air Force One.

"I can feel it," he said, once they were all alone in his private compartment. "Somehow, somewhere, I'm going to get fucked. What's the word on Karel Ludvik?"

He knew that Sarah was sharing her secrets with the admirals at Quantico, but she was still the intelligence maven he trusted the most.

"He might be the genuine article, sir," she said. "He climbed the usual commie ladder, but Moscow is imploding. And you may have a much better lifeline to him than the Kremlin and the KGB."

"He's still a thug—he's had people tortured and killed."

Sarah perused the Prince of the Western World. "Give him a little credit. He managed to survive a police state. No one has toppled him—not yet."

"Does he have a family?"

"He did. A wife and two daughters. But they were killed in front of his eyes—in a car bombing."

Isaac brooded for a moment. "And it's impossible to identify the perps, I suppose."

"Oh, there are the usual suspects," Sarah said. "Rogue bankers, or a rival in the StB. Karel owes millions to his handlers, whoever they are."

"And was there a lottery out on his life?"

"I have no idea, Mr. President, but I wouldn't walk around without your vest. We can't tell what company we might meet at the hunting lodge. I'm not as sanguine about it as the Secret Service. They might have sharpshooters on the battlements, but it's in the middle of nowhere. I'd have taken my chances in Prague, sir."

"So would I, but Karel was against it. And we're his guests. Stef, I hope you brought a sidearm or two with your Night Hawks?"

"Roger that, sir. I managed to smuggle a Beretta on board the lift package."

And Isaac laughed for the first time in his flying fortress.

There was too much politics involved in every one of his sorties. He preferred a landscape of Berettas and Glocks.

It was an airstrip, a secret military base, used by the Russkies, Isaac imagined, whenever they wanted to drop in on Prague. He saw the meanest looking soldiers.

But the Night Hawks were there, in enormous barns. Isaac had to endure a military salute, since the Czechoslovak Socialist Republic couldn't allow the Prince of the Western World to enter its domain unnoticed. He returned the salute as he descended the air stairs.

There was even a military band, a ragtag troupe that swayed like drunken men. They missed half the notes of "The Star-Spangled Banner," and the national anthem sounded like an aria out of Looney Tunes.

He'd only traveled to Eastern Europe once, when he was mayor of New York. He'd gone through Checkpoint Charlie into East Berlin with a little gang of other mayors and some mid-career viceroy at the State Department. He had to exchange his Yankee dollars for eastern marks, which looked like Monopoly money to Isaac; the paper was pathetically thin. They crossed the border into some no-man's-land of gigantic murals, revealing the wonders of the worker state; behind the murals were mounds of rubble. The State Department viceroy was very smug. "It's all one big façade," he said. But Isaac felt a crippling sadness. He mourned something he didn't quite understand. Perhaps this violent pull into East Berlin was the finale of his socialist dream. He saw goose-stepping soldiers in front of monuments celebrating some Russian victory in the late world war. He was ushered into an enormous restaurant replete with chandeliers and marble walls. The headwaiter wore spotless white gloves. There must have been a hundred tables. But only two were in service, where the mayors sat with the viceroy. The rest of this food palace was an enormous, silent cavern with its own odd celestial music. Isaac tried to strike up a conversation with one of the waitresses, a plump woman with blue eyelashes, a natural flirt. The other waitresses stared at the ceiling, never looked once into Isaac's eyes.

"*Guten Morgen,*" Isaac said in a guttural growl he'd picked up from German Jews at the Garden Cafeteria. The viceroy frowned at him. And the plump woman disappeared into the kitchen.

"Sidel," said the viceroy, "no intimacy is allowed."

"Jesus, how will I learn anything if I can't talk?"

"You'll meet scientists and poets, Mr. Mayor. You'll be more in your own arena."

But the scientists and poets must have been plucked right out of those murals on the far side of Checkpoint Charlie. They all babbled about their freedom to create.

"We feel so sorry, Herr Sidel, for the problems you have in the West. Will you ever get rid of Rikers Island?"

Sidel tumbled back into silence. The poets had all been rehearsed. But one scientist in a ragged collar did manage to tease Isaac out of his surly mood. "How is the Pink Commish? You're famous in these circles, Herr Sidel, as the proletarian *Bürgermeister*, the one mayor in America who has helped the poor."

Isaac didn't argue. He couldn't win. He met with a bunch of police chiefs who tried to convince him that all crime had been erased from the German Democratic Republic. Isaac nodded his head. But he must have gotten into trouble with the viceroy. After he arrived back at the Kempinski in West Berlin, he discovered that his room had been ransacked . . .

The airstrip outside Prague reminded him of the gigantic murals hiding mounds of rubble; half the hangars were made of cardboard, and many of the Czech planes were wooden replicas of the latest Soviet aircraft. Isaac was glad when the soldiers and musicians vanished from the parade grounds, and he was left with these strange wooden toys.

He climbed aboard Marine One with his White House staff and the Secretary of State, while the Secret Service and Colin's staff rode in the second Night Hawk, and the third was a decoy. The three White Tops must have looked like ships from another planet to farmers in the Czech countryside. They swerved north across hilly terrain, past gardenless gardens and orchards where nothing seemed to grow, and hovered near Karel Ludvik's dacha, a hunting lodge that resembled a miniature castle. The castle overlooked the fortified town of Terezín, which had been a transit station for Jews during the war, a kind of model camp. Terezín was the most diabolic of all the death camps. It had its own children's chorus, an opera house, its own philharmonic orchestra, a theater troupe, and an artists' colony. Many of its inmates had come from Prague—musicians, actors, poets. They performed for the Red Cross at Terezín, for German generals on leave, for Czech industrialists. The Germans made propaganda films about this Jewish utopia. But the children's chorus went right from one of these idyllic performances and propaganda films to Auschwitz. Ottla Kafka, Franz's youngest sister, who had been an inmate at Terezín, looked after these children, and accompanied them to Auschwitz as their companion and "nurse."

And when Isaac looked into the heart of Terezín, which was now a sleepy garrison with many of the same barracks, he felt a rage he could barely control.

The Czechs had built a helipad on the battlements for Marine One. And Colonel Oliver landed his White Top on two red markers with all the precision of a gigantic metal glove. Isaac could see Matt Malloy and his coterie of sharpshooters on the ramparts like medieval warriors with sniper scopes. Matt had been the first of Isaac's crew to arrive and had made a sweep of the hunting lodge and Ludvik's grounds with his metal detectors and bomb-sniffing dogs; the dogs had come in their own kennel.

The Czech president stood alone on the ramparts to greet this Jewish prince of the West. He wore a blue blazer with silver buttons, a white shirt with a soft collar, and a brilliant red tie. The president had tiny feet. He was slightly stooped and had unruly brows and the crisp gray eyes of a hunter. Isaac felt an immediate kinship with him.

He's a werewolf.

"Mr. President," Karel Ludvik said, "I'm most grateful that you have honored us with your visit."

"The honor is mine. Call me Isaac."

"And you shall call me Karel."

From the battlements Isaac could see inside the walls of Terezín, with its orange rooftops, and it irritated him that Karel Ludvik would select a dacha near one of the Nazis' model camps. But he kept his own counsel and descended the winding, windy stairs to Ludvik's living quarters. He'd left his Secretary of State to deal with Ludvik's own diplomats, and he sat alone in the president's study. He found a rocking horse in the corner.

The two presidents drank some wine and shared a poppy seed cake.

"I'm sorry about your loss," Isaac said, as he looked at the rocking horse.

Karel scratched his cheek. "Mr. President, I would rather mourn alone."

"I'm sorry. I didn't . . ."

"Forgive me," Ludvik said. "I was told that the Americans might have been involved."

"I don't understand," Isaac said.

"The trigger mechanism, it was of an American design. We are not fools, Mr. President. I would not allow my wife and little girls to wander about. We have our own tracking devices. And this bomb was beyond our abilities."

"And you think people around me . . ."

"No. But perhaps the people *around* the people around you. I tried to reform the banking regulations in my country. I did not want farmers squeezed out of their own small farms. The bankers allied themselves with the StB. There were battles in parliament, fistfights. I was stabbed twice in the halls of Prague Castle. I put down a rebellion of StB colonels—had them shot. That's why I could not invite you for an official visit to the Castle. There would have been chaos. And in the confusion . . ."

"But I wanted to see the house where Kafka was born."

Karel laughed bitterly to himself.

"The bankers can't wait for this regime to fall. They will build their own Disneyland devoted to Kafka—with cafés, gift shops, and a museum. They count up all the Western tourists and salivate like mad dogs whenever his name is mentioned. Don't talk to me of Franz Kafka."

"Have you read a single line of his?" Isaac asked with a growl, aware that Karel was a novelist *and* a poet.

"I could recite *A Hunger Artist* by heart. But I do not want Prague to become a theme park—a toy town."

"And yet you have your country estate on the hills above another theme park."

Karel's cunning gray eyes narrowed with a hunter's alarm. "What theme park?"

"Terezín," Isaac hissed. "The devil's own Disneyland, a Jewish menagerie with deportation as the very next stop. Did you know that Ottla Kafka was a volunteer nurse at—"

"Kafka," Karel muttered, "always Kafka." And he strode toward Isaac as if he meant to harm him. "Terezín was a transit camp with lace curtains, a lavish second act. I felt all the fury, the hot air— violinists and dramaturges fighting for the last crumbs of bread. Isaac, I was an eyewitness."

Seems Karel Ludvik had spent his childhood in Terezín. His father was one of the "essentials," shopkeepers who were permitted to remain when the town was converted into a camp. He was a shoemaker with a little shop next to the main square and served the SS and other officers and journalists who were always in transit, preparing reports about this strange Jewish utopia. Karel was seven or eight when the camp opened, in 1942. He had his pick of tutors among the doctors and professors of law who were "pensioners" at Terezín. And he had a special task. He met once or twice a week with the camp commandant, who was half blind and hid his worsening eyesight from fellow officers in the SS. The commandant was a bibliophile, and he would rave to Karel about a Yid from Bohemia who could scribble *Deutsch* like a Teutonic demon. Karel's task was to read *A Hunger Artist* and other tales to the commandant. They were like conspirators, the SS commandant and the shoemaker's boy.

"Isaac, I was no innocent," Karel said. "I made a profit from the camp. But I wasn't cruel. I found bread and cheese—at a price. I repaired shoes with my own hands. I fell in love with a little Jewess. I kept her and her family from starving. I removed their names from the deportation list. I had that power. I told you—the commandant was nearly blind. He was in my power. I served as his little secretary . . . and yes, yes, I know you're dying to ask. I was well aware of Ottla. The commandant wanted to meet the little sister of his favorite Jewish demon."

"What did she look like?"

"I can't recall," Karel said. "I think she had curly hair, cut very short."

Isaac was like a guilty boy confronting a parable that couldn't be penetrated without some magic fist. "Do you remember what Ottla said about Franz?"

Karel whistled to himself. "Isaac, it was almost fifty years ago."

"Lie. Make something up. I don't care."

There was a craftiness in Karel's smile—he had found a flaw in this Jewish prince. And that flaw was Franz Kafka.

"She said he sang out his sentences sometimes."

Isaac savored the words. "Sang out his sentences? Like an aria?"

There was a knock on the door. A bodyguard entered with the majordomo of the dacha.

"Excellency, dinner is being served."

Karel removed one of his dainty leather shoes and tossed it at the majordomo's skull. "Why do you interrupt us with mundanities? Can't you see that I'm in conference with the president of the United States?"

"I beg your pardon, Excellency," the majordomo said, bowing twice. The bodyguard was wearing a Beretta in his waistband. Both of them vanished.

"Karel, why couldn't your precious commandant save Ottla?"

"He tried, he tried. She wouldn't leave the children. She went right on board the train with them to Auschwitz."

"But he could have removed the children from the deportation list—or you could have done it for him."

"Impossible," Karel said. "The order came from Himmler himself: *Children who sing like angels should be treated like angels—at Auschwitz.*"

"But why have your kept up this little castle near Terezín? You could have easily found another refuge."

Karel shut his eyes. "The commandant lived here, on this hill. And this is where I had my happiest moments as a child. Not because he fed me sweets, not because his Czech mistress pampered the shoemaker's boy and showed me her tits. It was the moments we shared, reading the words of that Bohemian in the bowler hat."

His eyes twitched, like a man coming out of a coma. "Forgive me, Mr. President. I'm selfish. I've kidnapped you all to myself." He shouted into an intercom on his desk. "Ivo, come back. Accompany the president to his quarters."

Isaac picked up that dainty little shoe and returned it to his Czech counterpart, who must have crafted it himself. Karel would always be a shoemaker.

14

omething bothered the Big Guy. There were bodyguards galore, with pistols in their waistbands, but they pretended to be drowsy, and that wasn't a good sign. They were either fed up, or waiting for some signal. They wore blue wristbands, as if they belonged to the same fraternity of brutes. Isaac didn't trust them for a minute. Matt Malloy was there with his own detail. But his special agents seemed like Boy Scouts compared to these brutes.

Isaac wouldn't dress for dinner. He arrived at the table in his windbreaker, with his Glock. They were in the dacha's main dining

JEROME CHARYN

hall. Isaac was startled to see pictures of Terezín on the walls—the
children's chorus, an acting troupe, a soccer match among starving
Jewish athletes and the SS, as if it comforted Karel to revisit his own
childhood, or perhaps these images had been put up as souvenirs
for Sidel. He'd never unravel all the riddles. He was surrounded by
Czech diplomats, members of his own court, including Bull Latham
and Colin Fremont, colonels from the secret police who hovered over
Karel like hawks, communist party officials, and a blond woman in
a blue dinner dress.

The doyenne of Georgetown had arrived at this dacha before Isaac
ever had a chance. Renata wasn't here to see the sights. She was Viktor
Danzig's courier. And Isaac realized that all the counterfeit currency
Bull Latham had grabbed from Rembrandt didn't matter now. Karel
had made his own deal with Viktor. And suddenly the Big Guy was
enjoying himself. His mavens in the Situation Room didn't know shit
about Karel. This president of Czechoslovakia, who was still under
Soviet scrutiny, had made idiots of them all. Isaac's visit was hardly
more than a smokescreen, a chance to puff up Karel's stature in the
West, and hide his money deals.

Isaac could imagine Czechoslovakia as one big Monopoly board.
And Karel was in league with the bankers who may have tried to murder
him. Yes, he wanted to help the local farmers, but he also wanted Prague
revitalized and revamped, turned into a tourist's paradise, with cafés
and museums that would re-create the ambience, the aromas, and the
vitality of Franz Kafka's Bohemian village. If the Jews were gone from
the old Jewish Quarter, he would replace them with young artists and
rebels, once the Soviets withdrew inside the walls of the Kremlin. Karel
must have been banking on that, and even if he lost his seat at the Castle
and had to give up the president's dacha, he would still be the virtual
ruler of Prague. The *besprizornye* must have been behind this deal. If

Isaac couldn't congratulate Viktor, he still had Viktor's courier with the clipped blond hair.

She sat next to Karel, across from Sidel. Bull Latham was in full bloom, in a bowtie and shirt with ruffles as befit a vice president. He was drinking *pivo*, amber Czech beer, and toasting everyone at the table. Renata Swallow meant little to him. She was a Republican Queen Bee, and the Bull had crossed party lines and joined Isaac's Democratic ticket. It no longer mattered who ran the CIA or the FBI and the Secret Service; Bull had a stranglehold on all the agencies. But he hadn't grasped that Rembrandt was running rings around him and Isaac Sidel.

The waitresses wore peasant blouses with full bodices, and they weren't like the zombies of East Berlin. They stared into Isaac's eyes with a lasciviousness that almost made him blush. Had they come from an StB bordello in Prague? Their mascara was as thick as a mask. They slid from table to table with bowls of potato soup and baskets of dark rye bread with caraway seeds. They could have been StB agents themselves, prowling the tables like lusty she-wolves. They had little cords behind their ears, and they whispered into button mikes as they served the soup.

Everyone drank mineral water—*minerálka*—and dark or light beer. The president of Czechoslovakia stood up, tapped his pilsner glass with a spoon, and toasted Isaac Sidel.

"To the president of the United States, a child of Manhattan, who has come here as a pilgrim, paying homage to one of Bohemia's favorite sons. And I would like to honor Sidel with a tale of my own, composed for him on the occasion of his visit."

Isaac's sleuths and spymasters should have studied modern lit rather than the political contours of a communist state. Then they might have understood Karel's real predicament. His persona had shattered—the werewolf poet was devouring the politician. Karel held up a blinding mirror to Terezín. He didn't spare himself or the commandant. He told of the commandant's lust for Jewish girls, how he would take a starving young woman from the barracks, picked by the boy himself, declare her as his housekeeper, and fondle her in front of Karel's eyes.

I told her not to weep. The commandant is blind and he will give you bread.

A communist party official cleared his throat and tried to interrupt Karel.

"Mr. President, I beg you to stop. Is this the picture you want to give of us to our American guests? Select another story, please, in a lighter vein. We were victims, not vultures."

But the Czech president ignored this official, sang above his complaints.

There was one woman who would never have been sent to Terezín if she hadn't divorced her husband—a Gentile—in 1942. After the divorce, she put on her rucksack, kissed her two daughters goodbye, walked the streets of Prague for the last time, stopped at the central police station, declared herself a Jew, and got on the bus to Terezín. Her face revealed nothing at all. She could have been going on a picnic in the woods . . .

It was Kafka's sister, of course. She was no great beauty, yet the commandant and the little boy were entranced. She would not touch the bread and cheese the commandant had served her. She was a hunger artist who saved the tiny parcel of food for the children in her care.

The little boy watched her board the train to Auschwitz. Her hair shone in the sunlight. Her shoulders had a marvelous sweep. Another picnic, the boy thought. A picnic in the East.

"We will not tolerate such an indignity," said the same party official. All the party members rose, hurled their napkins onto the table, and left the dining hall. Karel sat down again. He tore into the dumplings and breaded mushrooms on his plate like a wild animal. "Eat, Mr. President," he shouted with a fanatical joy, "this may be our last supper together."

One of the waitresses whispered in his ear. Karel ripped the cord of her button mike and sent her into the kitchen. The other waitresses mumbled while the president had his compote. Bull Latham got up from his chair and stood behind Isaac, cupped his hand, and muttered, "I don't like it, Mr. President. There are too many tricksters at the table. I think it's time to leave Dodge."

"Finish your compote, Bull. Wouldn't want to abandon Karel."

"It's imperative, sir."

"Finish your compote."

The Bull returned to his chair, while Isaac reached across the table and clasped Renata's hands.

"Are you gonna be the next queen of the winter festival in Prague, Renata dear? Is that why you've come to Czech Land?"

"You'll never see Prague," Renata said. Isaac wanted to stroke her clipped blond hair. If he couldn't have Kafka's streets, he still wanted to step inside the Staranová Synagogue with its medieval pitched roof. He loved the tale of the Golem that he'd heard as a boy on the Lower East Side. Near the end of the sixteenth century, it seems, there were rumors that the King of Bohemia wanted to raid the Prague ghetto and burn it to the ground. And to protect the Jews of Prague, the illustrious Rabbi Judah Loew fashioned a creature of clay from the banks of the Vltava River. He worked in secret for six moonless nights. He blessed a stone with the word of God and dug this *sem* under the Golem's tongue; the monster's eyes blinked, and the Golem came to life. The Golem guarded the ghetto from the king and his troops. But the rabbi always removed the *sem* from the Golem's mouth on Friday nights to preserve the ritual of the Sabbath—even a Golem had to have a day of rest.

The rabbi forgot to retrieve the *sem* one Friday night, and the monster went on a *razzia*, attacking Jews and Gentiles alike. Rabbi Loew was able to lure the Golem into the attic of the Staranová Synagogue. The rabbi reached into the monster's mouth and removed the *sem*, whereby the Golem reverted to a dumb creature of clay. And the rabbi locked this lifeless clay man inside the attic and kept him there. Isaac would have loved to reconnoiter in that old, medieval synagogue and look for the iron ladder that led to the attic . . .

He found himself standing next to Karel. "Isaac, this castle isn't safe. You must leave as soon as you can."

"Why? You have a whole garrison of troops at the bottom of the hill, inside Terezín."

"These soldiers have been sent out on war games. They can't help us—we're isolated, alone. I can't even recognize my own bodyguards. And the women who served us are pirates from an StB unit in Prague."

Isaac was amused. "I never saw pirates with such deep chests."

"They're runaways, rogues," the Bull said, clutching a mobile phone with the biggest antenna Isaac had ever seen. "Mr. President, there's a NATO base within five hundred clicks of here. I suggest we saddle up in twenty minutes and evacuate. I checked with Colonel Oliver. He can assemble the lift package. What choice do we have, sir? We're a walking nuclear arsenal, with a pair of fucking footballs and biscuits in our possession."

"We're not moving," Isaac said.

"Matt," Bull Latham shouted, "talk to the Big Guy, will ya?"

"Sir," said Matt Malloy," I'm not certain we can protect you here."

"Then where can you protect me, Matt? You went through this castle with all your devices. Do we have a secure perimeter?"

"Not if Ludvik's own team is compromised. The White Top on the ramparts is secure at the moment, with all our sharpshooters guarding the perimeter. But the situation could deteriorate in a matter of seconds. This isn't our terrain. Mr. Latham is correct, sir. We should evacuate."

"We're not moving until I have a couple of minutes with Karel—alone."

"Impossible, sir," Matt said. "You have to have at least one baby-sitter at your side."

"Then let me have Captain Sarah."

"Negative, sir. She's not part of our detail."

The Bull nodded once with that monstrous phone in his fist, like a torch with an antenna, and Matt Malloy backed away. Isaac stood in a tiny alcove of the dining hall with Karel and Captain Sarah.

"Now you tell me what the fuck Ramona Swallow is doing here on the same exact day of my trip? A lovely coincidence."

"Roger that, sir," Captain Sarah said.

All of Karel's bravura was gone. He was neither the poet nor the politician, but a hapless shoemaker's boy. Isaac had missed the mark. Karel had never been a werewolf, not even inside Terezín.

"We're bankrupt. There's no point printing any more currency. The Czech crown is almost as worthless as the ruble. An entire tank corps is on strike. Several garrisons have gone home. The mayor of Prague hasn't collected his salary in months. Our policemen are out of ammunition. That's why I couldn't have you come to Prague—it's utter madness."

"And yet you angled to have me visit Czechoslovakia."

"It was a great coup for us. The prince—"

"Enough," Isaac said. "I was your currency. I was your bait. That's how you lured Ramona, the Queen Bee. My appearance makes Viktor Danzig's paper more valuable. Rembrandt is helping you stay afloat. I'll bet he and his *besprizornye* are among the biggest investors in Prague."

"They're buying up whatever real estate they can," Karel said.

"Then where's the glitch? You're the new King of Bohemia with all those fifty-dollar bills. You can bribe the young Turks in the StB and fill up your garrisons again. Where's the glitch?"

"Viktor isn't immortal. He has his enemies. And you've become a hazard, an endangered species."

And that's when Isaac noticed her out of the corner of his eye. One of the "pirates" was prancing toward him with a snarl on her face and the snout of a machine pistol rising from the folds of her skirt, like a metallic infant in its own soft cradle. Sarah shoved Isaac and Karel aside, charged into the lady pirate, knocked the machine pistol out of her hand, and walloped her so hard, her teeth rattled as she flopped into a chair.

"Five unfriendlies—no, six, at five o'clock," Sarah said, with her right hand turned into an arrow.

Karel's bodyguards appeared with their Berettas; they didn't seem so sinister, as Isaac's detail stared them down with .357 Magnums.

Matt Malloy disposed of the renegade bodyguards without firing a shot. He had them drop their Berettas inside a sack. Isaac had never seen Matt with so much zeal. He had them sit with their noses touching the floor, while his agents mummified each bodyguard in a roll of plastic tape.

Was this a palace coup? Isaac was disappointed in the assassins that the anonymous Swiss bankers had sent. Or were these bums just disenchanted members of the StB?

"Sir," Matt said, "it's time to roll."

"What about Karel?" Isaac asked. "We can't leave him in this mess."

"Mr. President, we'll create an international incident," the Bull said, holstering his hand cannon. "You can't grab the leader of a

Warsaw Pact nation. He could have staged this little drama to get our sympathy."

"I don't care," Isaac said. "I'm not leaving without him. And that's final."

Isaac didn't have a chance to continue his chat. His own body betrayed him, as his feet collapsed first in a roar that rang in his ears, and he flew right over a table. He heard groans all around him as the dining hall went dark. Isaac's head was spinning. He danced around in the debris.

15

I t was beyond Isaac's control. A medivac team had come from the U.S. military hospital in Wiesbaden, two hundred clicks away. A doc in fatigues nearly poked a pencil-thin flashlight into Isaac's eye.

"It's protocol, Mr. President. Please state your name and place of birth."

"Sidel," Isaac said. "I was born on the Lower East Side of Manhattan. Jesus, Doc, how many of us are hurt?"

"I'm not prepared to answer that, sir. We haven't assessed the situation. You're my immediate concern. I haven't felt any broken bones. Could be some internal bleeding, and we have to get you off this site. I noticed a lot of nasty gas in the air—poison, sir, could be part of the device."

A team of medics carried Isaac through the blinding dust in a gurney, and up to the battlements. Isaac didn't remember much after that. He flew over the bombed castle in a gondola that did its own curious ballet, as if it had an angel's whirring wings.

He woke in a palatial room that overlooked a long garden, with the reek of overripe flowers in his nostrils. Isaac hadn't come out of some miasma. He was as alert as a lion on the lam. There were no tubes attached to him, no monitors, no machines. He stood up in his hospital gown. He was still wearing his socks. He wandered into the hall, which was cluttered with gurneys.

"Where are we?" Isaac asked a medic.

"Wiesbaden, sir, but you're not supposed to get out of bed."

"Do you have a casualty list?"

"Negative, sir."

"But where are the wounded?" he had to ask.

The medic gave him a sly look. "All over the facility."

A general arrived, saluted Isaac, and made him return to his own little palace overlooking the gardens—it didn't even have a TV monitor on the wall. The Big Guy was kept in some kind of quarantine. There were no casualty reports.

"I want some fucking news," he shouted. But he might as well have been talking to the wind. He got rid of his gown and was given a military uniform to wear without any insignias. An MP arrived and drove him to some airport that wasn't on the map, with his football and a military aide he had never met. He flew to Washington on Air Force One. He didn't recognize any of the stewards. He was the only real passenger on board, except for his aide—it felt like a ghost ship.

There was still no news from Wiesbaden. Then he got an oceanic call from Ramona Dazzle, and Isaac realized that she was the one who had choreographed this return trip, had kept him in her own isolation ward. She gave the Big Guy his new itinerary. He'd land at Andrews in the middle of the night. The Secret Service would be waiting to whisk him to Walter Reed, where he'd have to endure a battery of tests. He should have gone to Bethesda, the hospital of presidents, but Ramona wanted to dodge any reporters who might be on Isaac's trail. So she put him into cold storage, told his family and his aides where he was, but she wouldn't issue a press release. And Ramona was an amnesiac when it came to Karel Ludvik's castle.

"Welcome home, Mr. President."

He was closeted at Walter Reed. Doctors in surgical caps loomed over him and then disappeared. Matt Malloy and the Bull stood in their wake, wearing bandages on their skulls. The Bull had a patch over one eye.

"Thank God you're here," Isaac said. "I've been living among doctors and lunatics."

"Colin didn't make it," the Bull said. "An artery burst and the medics couldn't stop the bleeding. He died on the way to Wiesbaden."

"It's my fault," Isaac muttered. "I shouldn't have gone hunting for Kafka's footsteps. Does Colin have much of a family? Brothers, sisters?"

"No one," Matt said.

"What about a live-in lover?"

"Mr. President," the Bull whispered, "we can't get involved in that. It would sully Colin's reputation if word ever got out, and consider the collateral damage to State."

"Fuck collateral damage. I want Colin's live-in notified. Pronto. And what about the others, damn it? Colonel Oliver, Captain Sarah, and the whole White House detail?"

"I'm not sure about Sarah. She's with Naval Intel right now, and Stef's still in Wiesbaden, but I hear he'll be fine. The detail took a lot of hits."

Isaac couldn't hold back his rage. "You had your bomb-sniffing dogs, Matt. How come the castle was compromised?"

"It's not that simple. The device came from inside Terezín."

"But it's a military garrison," Isaac insisted.

"It was once, sir—the soldiers are gone. There's a tunnel that leads from Terezín to Karel Ludvik's castle. That's how the bomber got in. I'm told the device was standard fare—plastic explosives with a time switch. Forgive me, sir, but luck was on your side, or you wouldn't be here. The bomber might have been in a hurry, and he didn't have a chance to mold his gel. But you were the main target. The blast pattern proves that. He was tracking your movements with a very sophisticated stethoscope—the kind that burglars use."

"Burglars and assassins. It's their magic tit. What happened to Karel?"

"Karel's contained," the Bull said with a diabolic grin. "We brought him with us. He's in protective custody. He blubbers about political asylum, but he has to be debriefed before we send him back."

"You're not sending him anywhere. You'll grant him whatever asylum he wants and you'll move him into my attic. I don't care if he has a Marine stationed outside his door, but Karel stays with me."

The Bull had a murderous look in his eye. He left with Matt Malloy, and Isaac had to endure a lecture from the physicians at Walter Reed about the calcium deposits in his heart. He wore a hospital gown like some sick crusader and was wheeled from lab to lab with the Secret Service at his tail. It was midnight before he returned to his room. The telephone console near his bed lit up. His daughter was on the line.

"Isaac, we were worried sick. The papers mentioned a massive detonation. No one could tell me if you were alive or dead. We're coming to DC tomorrow."

"That's out of the question, sweetheart. The docs say I can't have any guests."

Isaac didn't enjoy lying to his own daughter. But he'd been reluctant to have her here even before his coronation. He was ashamed of the presidency and all its pomp. He felt like a fraud who had put others at great risk. Marilyn was married to one of Isaac's own troopers, Vietnam Joe Barbarossa, the most decorated cop in the history of the NYPD, but the contradictions were always there. Barbarossa had dealt drugs in Nam, had murdered other dealers, and continued the drug war while he was a cop. Vietnam Joe still had his citations. He survived firefights with the worst Mafiosi in Manhattan. He jumped off a burning roof with two children in his arms and landed in a cavalcade of clotheslines. Isaac wished he had Barbarossa at his side. He wouldn't have needed a White House detail. But he would have involved Marilyn in his own *mishegas*.

"Sweetheart, I'll visit soon as I can. Put Joey on the line."

"Dad, Dad," Barbarossa said, "the city's a wasteland without ya. The correction officers can't control Rikers. And the streets have become a shooting gallery."

"Yeah, and I can't get a decent half sour pickle. Keep in touch, Joey. I may call upon your services—soon."

"You bet, Dad. I'll be there in a zip."

Isaac began to cry the second he got off the phone. He missed Manhattan, but it was more than loneliness. He felt betrayed by his own impulses. He could have rounded up his Modern Library collection of Kafka. He didn't have to drag his court to Czech Land on a sentimental journey to relive a classic at Columbia College—his humanities instructor, a young man with a frayed collar and dandruff in his scalp, had refined the rabbinical art of excavating *The Metamorphosis*. "It's not really Gregor's tale. It's Greta's." Gregor Samsa was the guy who woke one day as an insect. He was a traveling salesman who could no longer travel. His father was an unsuccessful businessman who had lost his business. Gregor had become the mainstay of his family. His little sister, Greta, was seventeen, and loved to play the violin—she was the artist, not Gregor, who had hoped to send her to the conservatory. Greta cleaned his room and fed her insect brother scraps of spoiled food. But she soon turned away from Gregor, repelled by him. Greta didn't feel remorse after the insect died—she bloomed. She had her own metamorphosis—a sexual awakening—and she walked with the vitality of a panther.

It was Greta who had remained in Isaac's mind all these years, not the insect trapped in his bedroom. And that's why he was drawn to Ottla. Perhaps she, too, played the violin, and had walked with a panther's step. And that's what the half-blind commandant at Terezín must have noticed as darkness descended upon him—a Jewish panther in the shadows, a panther prepared to pounce.

Isaac's console lit up again. This time it was the head of security at Walter Reed.

"Mr. President, we have two vagabonds outside the gate. They're pretty insistent, sir, about knowing you."

"Are they wearing trench coats and forage caps? If so, send 'em up."

Soon Isaac had his old winter warriors, Ariel Moss and Mordecai Katz.

"How did you guys get here? This isn't even the president's hospital. My own chief of staff is hiding me. Can you beat that?"

"We're not idiots," Ariel said. "We have our spies."

"Jesus, where have you both been hibernating?"

"At a cheap motel near the White House," said Mordecai.

"Are you my godfathers now?"

"How could we leave you all alone? You're like a baby who's lost his diapers, *Itzik*," Ariel said, purring Isaac's Yiddish name. No one called him Itzik except a few renegade rabbis and religious gangsters at the Garden Cafeteria. Isaac didn't realize how much he mourned that lit dungeon on East Broadway—the Garden had vanished with most of the pickle barrels.

"What possessed you to run to Prague? Are you an imbecile? Prague is a haven for every gangster in Europe. It's as bad as Palermo."

"But I never got to Prague," Isaac said.

"Sure you did," said Ariel.

"Come on, I didn't even get to see the Staranová Synagogue. I wanted to look for the Golem in the attic."

Ariel laughed. "You are the Golem, Isaac, with an attic of your own. That's why people are so frightened of you. A Golem made for Manhattan—it's a perfect fit. You could ride above the streets with your giant steps. You could rule with or without God's stone under your tongue. But a Golem in the White House is another matter. You can't sleep in the capital with a stone in your mouth. You'll choke on God's words. Such a character! A bomb explodes under your feet and yet you manage to survive. Isaac, a Golem like you brings the smell of death."

"I'm not a Golem," Isaac had to whisper. "No magic rabbi created me."

"That's because you created yourself," Mordecai said.

But Isaac was adamant. "Tell me, comrades, will the Manhattan Golem survive the Swiss bankers and their lottery?"

Ariel began to ponder with a knuckle in his mouth. "Itzik, that's a good question—that utterly erases the smash point. But Golems can be killed, certainly."

"No, Arik, not at all," Mordecai said. "You can deactivate a Golem, put him in a coma by removing the *sem* from under his tongue. But kill him—never!"

They argued well into the morning like three Talmudists, while doctors came and went, checking the Golem's blood pressure, putting a thermometer into his mouth. And Ariel concluded that a Golem couldn't be destroyed but could be retired.

"You can't stay at some fleabag motel," Isaac said. "That's final. Your new address is 1600 Pennsylvania Avenue. You'll be living in my attic."

"And how many Golems will we discover, dear Itzik?"

"As many as you can manage," Isaac said. And suddenly his sadness slipped away. He'd follow in Roosevelt's footsteps, surround himself with friends. FDR had turned the White House into a Washington resort hotel. His speechwriter and confidant, Robert Sherwood, had his own bedroom. And Crown Princess Martha of Norway lived at the White House with her royal retinue during the war. FDR loved to go riding with Martha in the Maryland countryside. FDR's aides considered the sultry crown princess his "girlfriend," even if she had a husband of her own, Crown Prince Olav. This was the kind of intrigue that Isaac enjoyed. He'd never have FDR's flair or his political savvy. But he would bring a little of Manhattan to the White House, with as many guests as could fit into the attic.

PART FIVE

16

eneral Sol Ben-Zion, current chief of Shin Bet, had come all the way from Tel Aviv. He had an ominous presence, because his face was scarred from a dozen skirmishes and wars, battles with his own officers, and bombings in Beirut. He looked a bit like Boris Karloff in full bloom—hangman, soldier, and Frankenstein monster. He'd been whisked into the West Wing from a little private gate, a "ghost" who didn't appear in any logs. There was no hard evidence that Sol had even been let into the United States. He sat in the regal office of Ramona Dazzle. It was Ramona who had summoned him.

Sidel, it seems, had fallen off the face of the moon after a disastrous trip to Czechoslovakia and was hidden somewhere within the walls of Walter Reed.

Sol wasn't alone. With him were the vice president and a female officer from Naval Intelligence, Sarah Rogers, a thoroughbred beauty with hazel eyes and curls in her hair. Sol was already lusting after her. She had a delicious bruise on her cheek that Sol would have loved to touch with one of his knotted hands. He was a widower with several rich widows in the wings.

Ramona served as her own self-styled grand inquisitor at this clandestine briefing. She invited the female captain to talk first. Sarah was uncomfortable. The admirals at Quantico had ordered her to the inquisition. She wasn't Ramona's little spy. She felt a sudden fury and wanted to lash out at Ramona.

"It was after dinner and—"

Ramona interrupted her. "What dinner and where?"

"At the Czech president's dacha—his version of Cactus."

Ramona interrupted her again. "The captain means Camp David, General."

"Yes," Sol Ben-Zion said. "I'm familiar with Cactus Land. I was there, you know, at the Camp David Accords. I think I saved Sadat's life more than once. But this is not the right time to boast of such exploits. Continue, Captain, please."

Ben-Zion wanted to brush against her hair, fondle her right in front of the vice president and Sidel's chief of staff. Ramona was clever enough to sniff his sudden desire, and she didn't like it at all. She would have preferred to bury Captain Rogers in the caverns of Quantico, but the admirals had sent her back to Sidel.

"And what was a captain from Naval Intelligence doing at a state dinner in Czechoslovakia?"

"I wasn't privy to POTUS's private talks with President Ludvik," Sarah said.

Ramona couldn't stop scratching. "Didn't it have something to do with Franz Kafka? Wasn't POTUS on a pilgrimage at the taxpayers' expense?"

Sarah pursed her lips. "That was the subterfuge, I suppose. The Czechs are in deep shit. Their currency is worthless. And President Ludvik needed POTUS's presence to bail him out."

"How? With a magic wand? " Ramona asked with a slight tremor in her voice.

"As I said, ma'am, I wasn't privy to their private talks."

"And were these talks worth the death of Colin Fremont and the maiming of two Secret Service men?"

"Stop that," Bull Latham said. "We all agreed to the talks, Ramona. Don't crucify the captain."

"I'll do my best, Mr. Vice President. Captain, aren't you currently residing in the White House attic?"

"Yes, ma'am, on orders of the president. I'm part of his staff." Ramona licked her tongue.

"That's curious. I never assigned you a berth in the attic."

"You'd have to discuss that with POTUS, ma'am."

"And who else resides in the attic at the moment?"

"Captain Oliver. His son Maximilian has a learning disability. And POTUS thought—"

"I'm aware of the boy's condition," Ramona said. "And who are the other occupants?"

"President Karel Ludvik. He's sort of in limbo, ma'am. I'm not sure the Czechs want him, and he doesn't seem to want the Czechs."

Ramona went right on scratching. "And who else?"

"A pair of Izzies, ma'am."

Ramona whipped her head around. "And what about you, General Ben-Zion? Ain't we pals anymore? I thought you guys shared information that was vital to our security. Why's Ariel Moss still here with the fucking founder of Shin Bet? How long has that lunatic been dancing under your radar?"

Ben-Zion would have loved to slap her face. He was answerable only to his prime minister, but he didn't want to rile the relationship between Israel and Uncle Sam. His own purse strings suddenly depended on Ramona Dazzle, who seemed to have all the covert agencies under her spell. Sidel had been adrift from the moment he entered the White House.

"Ari was always under surveillance," he said.

"Even when he robbed banks in Tel Aviv?"

"Ah," Ben-Zion said. "The banks were a myth. He took a few shekels, mostly counterfeit coin."

"And was Mordecai Katz also a myth?"

"Enough," Bull Latham said. "We're among friends here."

Ben-Zion was much more comfortable talking to this Dallas Cowboy, though he didn't have much faith in the FBI and their starched white shirts. They were more like preachers than gatherers of intelligence.

"We read all of Ari's mail. There were vague threats. We checked them out. It was a lot of gibberish."

"But that gibberish brought him here," Ramona said. "Right before an attack on the mountain—and suddenly he resurfaces after the bombing of Ludvik's dacha." She whipped her head around again and turned to Sarah. "Isn't that a strange coincidence, Captain?"

"Damn you, Ramona," Bull Latham said. "You're not at that killer law firm of yours. Captain Rogers isn't a hostile witness. We're lucky to have her."

"And what if the football was stolen by some foreign agents?" Ramona asked with an inquisitor's crooked smile.

"Who cares? They couldn't do anything without the biscuit."

While the president was incapacitated, it was only Bull who could authenticate the codes. But Ramona didn't give a damn about Bull's biscuit.

"Get real! Does someone have a fucking clue about the mental state of Isaac Sidel?" Ramona kept scratching at the same raw wound. "I think you ought to go on the tube, Mr. Vice President—talk to the country, tell the people what's happening."

Ben-Zion didn't have to be a rocket scientist to catch the battle lines. Ramona had reached too far. She turned her own office in the West Wing into a travesty of a command center, sat with a "ghost" from Tel Aviv and a lovely intelligence officer with limited powers, and tried to *invent* a new crisis—the unraveling of Isaac Sidel—with Bull Latham as her partner, but the Bull wasn't buying it.

"I'm not gonna create a worldwide panic, Ramona, just to satisfy your own whims."

Bull watched the Witch of the West Wing blow her cool. Her hands were shaking. "My whims? We have to walk around on tiptoe and protect a president who's an utter incompetent, who doesn't have the least conception of his own responsibility, who's put all of us in harm's way?"

"Not here," Bull whispered, "not now."

The Bull winked at Sol Ben-Zion and walked out of Ramona's office with him. He hijacked Ramona's chief deputy and locked her out of her own office.

"Sol, Ramona doesn't have the weight to pull you into her orbit. And yet here you are. What's going down? You're not a meddler, Sol. Or a tinkerer. And yet you're tinkering."

"I am not," said the chief of Shin Bet. "I didn't make up Ramona. She's as powerful—and mischievous—as Haldeman ever was."

"Solly," Bull said, "you don't know shit about American politics. Nixon was a wounded man after Watergate. He ceased to exist as president, and Haldeman crept into the vacuum."

"What's different now?" Ben-Zion asked, taunting the Bull. "Sidel is a clumsy magician in the midst of his own disappearing act."

"He's visible enough," the Bull said. "You aren't fond of him, are you?"

"We worry," Ben-Zion said. "A Jew in the White House, the first of his kind, and we don't know a thing about the Big Guy. He could dance with Arafat, and leave us out in the cold. Has he ever shown an interest in Tel Aviv?"

"But you can't measure him that way," the Bull said.

"Why? Is he unmeasurable? He talks of visiting Beirut."

"Yes. He says it's like the South Bronx."

"Wonderful! The Jewish St. Francis. The South Bronx is paradise compared to Beirut. Sidel would be flayed alive by all the different factions. Yes, Ari may have stumbled onto something, but it's no simple plot. Sidel is a very soft target, racing around like a knight in armor. He should be undone."

"That's treasonable stuff," said the Bull.

Sol Ben-Zion laughed. "Half of what we do is treasonable. I came here because I'm curious. Two of the men I most admire, Ari Moss and Motke Katz, have been swindled, caught up in some deceit about Sidel—tell me, that young captain in Ramona's office, how can I find her again?"

"You can't, Sol. Go home."

"I'd like to recruit her."

"Go home."

And the Bull returned to Ramona, who must have banished the young captain to Isaac's attic. Ramona hissed at him, her mouth full of venom.

"Don't you ever humiliate me like that again, mister. Not in front of Shin Bet and Miss Steel Toes. I could have relegated you to the back kitchen, like other vice presidents, and I still can. We agreed to get rid of Sidel."

"Sure, we'll rip him right out of his hospital bed. The nation would love that. And you should never have invited Ben-Zion here. You wanted to deliver a coup d'etat in front of that fox catcher. Now he knows all our weaknesses."

"Come on," Ramona said. "He was so busy eyeballing Miss Steel Toes, he didn't have time for anything else. And I wanted to know if Ariel was acting on his orders—if he was on some covert mission."

Bull Latham stared at the wintry garden outside Ramona's window, then his eyes turned inward, and he grabbed her by the throat. There wasn't a fleck of pity in his pale blue eyes. He could have strangled her right in the West Wing. Her throat was rattling.

"Be quiet," the Bull said. "You told the Izzies more about us than they could have dreamt up on their own. Ben-Zion spotted all the cracks in our command—that the president has a team of piranhas ready to devour him at any moment. You should never have invited Shin Bet into our playground."

The Bull released a little pressure on her throat. She was sobbing now.

"But Sol's our friend," she muttered between sobs.

"Little Sister, we have no friends."

"You son of a bitch," she said in a scratchy voice, "I could have you arrested for assault."

"But you won't."

And he walked out of the West Wing, whistling to himself.

17

The White House butler brought Sidel his slippers and one of the winter robes that the Big Guy had plucked from the barrels of Orchard Street. Isaac had the beginnings of a beard; he wouldn't allow the butler to shave him, although he might have looked a bit less like a tramp with a brand-new pink face. The president seemed incongruous among all the sick soldiers, walking around in some ancient subaltern's robe, yet it was the kind of robe that Lincoln had once worn in the White House. And with his sad eyes and the scruff on his chin, Isaac was *almost* Lincolnesque.

He went from ward to ward; the soldiers and their families were startled to see him. This wasn't the president's hospital—it was Walter Reed, where mice scuttled about, where soldiers lay for months on some extended leave that felt like half an eternity. And here he was in his bathrobe, clutching a soldier's hand, and Isaac tried to imagine what it must have been like when Lincoln visited hospital tents with Mary and Tad during the Civil War, surrounded by amputated limbs and drunken, delirious officers who were battle crazed.

He sat with a blind soldier from Oregon in a room of blind soldiers. They were all curious about Isaac's Glock, which had been lost in the debris at Karel's dacha and suddenly reappeared in a plastic envelope sent to Walter Reed. They didn't ask about Air Force One and all the other presidential perks. They liked the idea of Isaac as the sheriff of Manhattan, a Golem with a Glock. And so he amused them with stories of his mishaps as mayor, and his adventures, too, of gunfights outside Madison Square Garden and wrestling matches at City Hall, of how he'd gone into Rikers and rescued young men and women who had been incarcerated by some lame judge's orders and utterly forgotten, of how he'd rushed into an abandoned fire station in the South Bronx that had been taken over by sex traffickers and managed to walk out with all the traffickers and their string of slaves—girls who hadn't seen sunlight in six months.

"Mr. President, didn't you feel like executing those sons of bitches on the spot?" one of the blind soldiers asked. "Didn't you have the urge?"

"Yes, I did. I wanted to glock them inside the fire station. But I had to resist the urge."

"Why?" another soldier asked. "Did it have anything to do with the law?"

"No," Isaac said. "I've broken every law in the books. But there's something much worse than execution—the court system. It's like navigating through hell."

Isaac could feel a hand on his shoulder. He had a guest, his helicopter pilot, with blue marks under both eyes.

"Boss, I just got back from Germany. Captain Sarah sent me. She has all those damn admirals at Quantico squatting on her ass. But she says you have no business being here. She calls you the Prisoner of Zenda."

"The docs haven't released me," Isaac said.

"You're commander in chief. You can write your own release."

The Prisoner of Zenda. Perhaps his chief of staff had done him a favor. He might have been better off at Walter Reed. He had to deal with all the sudden fury around him—the recriminations, the death threats, the talk of impeachment, congressional reprimands, editorials against his imperial presidency, cartoons of Isaac in a bowler hat, with Kafka's long nose and burning, rabbinical eyes. He couldn't escape the constant barrage.

His one solace was the attic. He now had a family—Karel Ludvik, pursued by every sort of secret police; Ariel Moss and Mordecai Katz, without legal status in America; Captain Sarah, his own spy who also spied on him; Colonel Oliver, his son Max, and Karina, Max's live-in maid; and the Golem himself, who sprang to life whenever he stood on the attic stairs.

Karel Ludvik cried in Isaac's arms. He'd lost fifteen pounds since the bombing ten days ago. He wore a rumpled shirt and a mothballed sweater that must have come from one of Tim Vail's supply closets. His shoes weren't shined. The president of Czechoslovakia didn't have much of a portfolio outside his native land.

"Isaac, your vice president was going to send me back to Prague, trade me in for a handful of captured American spies."

"The Bull can't move you, Karel. Moscow and Prague can cry bloody murder. You're safe—with me."

But there was intrigue, always intrigue. Isaac found a note in the pocket of his windbreaker.

> *Mr. President, we have important matters to discuss. If you could schedule an exam at Walter Reed tomorrow at noon, I would be most grateful. You needn't look for me. I will find you.*
> *Sincerely, General Solomon Ben-Zion*
> *Shin Bet*

He showed the letter to his mavens in the attic.

"It's a fake," Ariel insisted.

"That's not Sol," Mordecai said. "He was once my second in command. He would never write such a letter. It didn't come from Shin Bet."

"I'm afraid it did," Sarah said. "He handed it to me."

"Ben-Zion is in America . . . on a state visit? That's not his style. I know him. That man never strays from Tel Aviv."

"He's still in Tel Aviv," Sarah said. "Boss, your chief of staff invited him—as a ghost."

"But he could have had you whisper in my ear," Isaac said. "Why use my windbreaker as a dead letter box?"

"He's old-school," Sarah said. "He's read too much le Carré."

Isaac looked into her hazel eyes. "I love le Carré."

"So do I, boss. But I get a little sick of all the tradecraft—that esoteric language of spies."

"Still," Ariel said, "you'll have to meet with him, Isaac. But don't trust a word he says."

Karel stood in the corner, stroking his chin. "It sounds fishy. Why a soldiers' hospital?"

"Because all the American generals are in love with Israeli intelligence," Ariel said. "And Sol must have found a friend."

So the Prisoner of Zenda returned to his roost at Walter Reed. He scheduled an appointment with the cardiologist who had looked after him and the calcium in his heart, advised Matt Malloy, and the next morning he boarded Dragon; the entire caravan crossed the District, snarling traffic wherever it went, and arrived at the old army hospital, which looked like a red brick outpost in the middle of a reservation at the edge of Rock Creek Park.

The Big Guy had to admit that his calcified heart was beating like a little boy's. Isaac admired Sherlock Holmes and Sam Spade, but he worshipped George Smiley, who was always coming out of retirement to fix something broken at the Circus—MI6—and practice his tradecraft. Isaac had almost none. He would have made a feeble spymaster. He met with his cardiologist, his blood pressure rising like a wayward pump, and as he left the office, an intern took Isaac aside, touched his arm, and led him to another office.

"Wait here," Isaac said to Matt Malloy and went through the door. A huge man with a monstrous face that could have been stamped out of metal stood near the window in a doctor's white coat.

"Sidel, how many minutes do we have before that kindergartener comes crashing through the door?"

"Three, I'd guess."

"Good," said this Frankenstein with a metal face. "I never liked you. You're no friend of ours. You've probably done us harm with all your nonsense about Beirut. But you were once a good policeman."

"And what am I now?"

"A fool. A clever one, but a fool nonetheless. It's not entirely your fault. Your intelligence teams gather little intelligence, or no intelligence at all, and you're left to fiddle in the dark." There seemed to be a crack in the metallic mask. "You must not visit Beirut."

"Ah," Isaac said, "I would have felt at home. I thought it might remind me of the Bronx."

"You would not last five minutes. Prague should have taught you a lesson."

Sidel couldn't decipher much beyond the crack in Ben-Zion's mask. "I wasn't allowed to enter Prague. I couldn't have protective cover, I was told."

"And still you went—to Terezín, where Hitler had his show camp, his favorite Follies. And you barely survived. You must not travel. There's only one city in the world where you would be safe—Tel Aviv. We have our share of rogue agents, but none of them would ever harm you, or allow you to be harmed. We have our pride. Our people are obsessed with the image of a Jewish police chief, mayor, and president. You even have a nickname at my headquarters. King Saul, the unlucky one, who was deaf to God's voice."

"I'm not a king, lucky or unlucky."

"You most certainly are," Ben-Zion said. "Otherwise you would not be in such danger. I cannot hope to count your enemies. But I'm like a weasel when it comes to gathering information. Shall we start with an industrial tycoon and publisher who works out of Hamburg and West Berlin? Herr Rainer Wolff. You've become a threat to all his enterprises. Rainer's a worrier. He trades in currencies. And you're too unpredictable as—"

"Prince of the Western World."

"Yes, the man with the sleek blue-and-white thunderbird, Air Force One, the perfect symbol of American might. Rainer would rather have the thunderbird remain on the ground. And he will have you killed—unless you kill him first."

There was a knock on the door. "Sir, are you okay?" Matt Malloy called through the frosted glass.

"Matt, I'm fine."

"May I come in?"

Ben-Zion talked in pantomime, nodding no with that Frankenstein face.

"I'll be out in a few minutes," Isaac said. He felt manipulated by General Ben-Zion.

"Why don't *you* have the publisher killed?"

Isaac heard a metallic roar. "Rainer? He's one of Israel's biggest friends."

"Then why are you sharing his secret?"

"I told you. You're our King Saul."

It didn't feel right, this sudden revelation, a gift from the chief of Shin Bet, a wandering ghost who never left Tel Aviv. It felt more and more like a setup, a fancy deal. Ben-Zion could have met Isaac in the Oval Office, no matter how secret his presence was. There was a little too much tradecraft in Ben-Zion's insistence on Walter Reed.

"General, I should warn you, I'm wearing a wire."

The mask fell away, and Isaac saw an actual smile, no matter how metallic it was. There was a marked amusement in Ben-Zion's silver-gray eyes. The general was having a hell of a time. "I would expect nothing less from the Pink Commish."

"Were you going to tell your comrades at Shin Bet how you recruited the president of the United States in an obscure office at Walter Reed? Not a chance. I'll never be one of your assets. And if I holler once to Matt Malloy, he'll handcuff you in front of every nurse and doc, and send you back to Tell Aviv on an El Al express. Why are we here? What is it you want?"

"An oath," Ben-Zion said, "that you will not visit Beirut. Hezbollah will see it as a triumph, and suck us back into the war. You're a hero who's risen right out of the ruins."

Isaac was perplexed. "Hezbollah will celebrate a Yid from the Lower East Side? That's a laugh."

"But children have your picture on their walls with your Glock—a gun like your own is outside any definition of an infidel."

Ah, Isaac remembered now. There'd been a siege at the first mosque in Manhattan, on Riverside Drive. It was during Isaac's time as police commissioner, at a low point in his career. He was battling with the mayor, who had her own blind addiction against drug dealers. It was at the height of the Rockefeller Drug Laws, when a college sophomore hard up for cash could spend her most fertile years in prison for trying to traffic a few ounces of grass.

The mosque had been seized by several religious fanatics. Her Honor wanted Isaac to storm the mosque. But he knew the fanatics would slaughter the worshipers and the clerics inside and then set fire to themselves, in their last lunatic act of faith. So Isaac defied Her Honor, wore a white handkerchief, and went inside the mosque, with his Glock tucked inside his shirt. He didn't bargain, didn't cajole. He listened to the leader of the fanatics, a boy with angelic blond curls and a rabbit's flaming red eyes, who saw the mosque as the Islamic devil's first outpost in Manhattan.

"There's more to come," this curious angel said. He and his crew were armed with automatics, but it wasn't their firepower that disturbed Isaac, who grasped the charismatic force of the boy with blond curls. He held his entire little menagerie together with the glue of his rhetoric. The boy was a born preacher.

"Satan is under every stair, in the prayer rugs, in the women's veils."

Isaac did make one final try. "Son, you'll be murdering children and old men. Grant them some kind of innocence."

"No," the boy said—he must have been nineteen or twenty. "They are Satan's assistants."

Isaac had no choice. He glocked this boy preacher through the heart. The boy's entire crew collapsed and dropped their automatics. And Isaac marched out of the mosque with clerics and worshipers and defeated fanatics.

This is what Hezbollah must have seized upon. The strange Jewish prince who was *almost* a child of Islam. And General Ben-Zion couldn't afford to have Isaac near Beirut's Green Line, among Hezbollah, Christian militias, civilians, refugee camps, Israeli commandos, and American spies—he would reignite the civil war in Lebanon.

"General," Isaac said, "I swear to you, Beirut isn't on my list. I have no list. Consider me a man without a travelogue—once I did walk Dublin's streets, visited Leopold Bloom's address, lit a candle for James Joyce, but that was before I went into politics. Presidents shouldn't have literary predilections. It could ruin them, as my love of Kafka ruined me."

"You'll recover," Ben-Zion said. "America worships a true original. But a favor for a favor. You have an assassin in the White House."

Isaac wanted to glock the Israeli Frankenstein, who'd nearly been burnt alive in Beirut.

"Now you volunteer this information?"

"I needed to extract that promise from you," Ben-Zion said.

"And if I'd refused you that promise?"

Suddenly Isaac could read the pain that knit all the scars and ridges together on the spymaster's riven face.

"Then, dear King Saul, I would not be in your debt."

"And who is this hypothetical assassin?"

"I assure you. It's far from hypothetical. If you aren't careful, you won't survive the month."

"Then should I close down the mansion, General Ben-Zion, and arrest everyone, including myself? I'm also an assassin."

"It wouldn't help. The assassin will follow in your footsteps. You're the cop. Think like a cop. You can turn off your tapes. It's time to go."

"I'm not wearing a wire," Isaac said. "It was a bluff."

"I know," said Ben-Zion.

And Isaac walked out of the office, abandoning the chief of Shin Bet in his doctor's spotless white coat.

Assassin.

The Big Guy's sudden exhilaration—he was back in Sidel country—terrified him. He worried about the collateral damage. What if Max was caught in the crossfire?

"I'll have to warn Stef," he muttered, before he disappeared into the cushions of Dragon, and the caravan left Walter Reed, with Isaac's double in one sedan, and his doctor in another. That was the madness of a president's logistical maneuvers.

18

Isaac didn't have time to reconnoiter and rub his gold shield. How could he search for a hired gun when the DNC kept stabbing him in the back? His own party wanted to run him out of the District on a rail. It was politics, always politics. Genevieve Robinson, alias Brenda Brown, his former chief of staff, advised the Big Guy to sit down with the Senate Republican Caucus.

"Don't say a word, Isaac. Just nod your head and listen."

The Republicans wanted to rob from Social Security and get rid of every fucking entitlement program. Isaac had a bad case of vertigo. He still kept nodding his head.

Ramona came marching in once the Republicans left the Oval Office. "You can't invite them here again. It's an insult to our own Caucus."

"I'm meeting with the House Republicans tomorrow."

"Cancel," she said.

"If you don't put an end to your palace coup, I'll caucus with the Republicans and cut my ties with the DNC."

"That's political suicide," Ramona said.

"No, it's Russian roulette."

An officer arrived from Fort Meade, a rabbi who was also a second lieutenant, a big burly fellow who declared himself the unofficial White House chaplain. His name was Elijah Silvers.

"Who sent you, Silvers?"

"Genevieve Robinson, sir. She said I could be your equalizer. Since you're not a member of any congregation—"

"And have never been."

"I could serve as your spiritual guide." And this army chaplain from Fort Meade whispered in Isaac's ear. "The voters will love it, Mr. President, particularly the religious right."

Isaac was suspicious. "Why didn't Brenda clue me in herself?"

"She said you wouldn't go for it. So I took the initiative."

The chaplain had to be vetted, of course, and he was. He followed Isaac around like a hunting dog.

"Are you sorry that you killed people, Mr. President?"

"Silvers, you're not a priest. You can't absolve me of my sins."

"I'm curious," the chaplain said. "And I could lighten your load a little."

"I don't have one," Isaac said. "I glocked whenever I had to glock."

Isaac got used to the chaplain's lumbering gait. But there were other issues, outside regret and remorse. The clock was ticking, and

Isaac had an assassin in the house, unless it was all a big lie, and Shin Bet was trying to frighten him for his sins. Still, he couldn't stop worrying about Max. The Pink Commish had to plead with his helicopter pilot. "It's only temporary. Until we find the fuck."

But Colonel Oliver kept postponing his move back to Arlington with Max and Karina. "Boss, we'll do it tomorrow, I swear. You know how Max loves the attic. And Karina has her washing machine and ironing board. She's in heaven."

Isaac put pressure on the Bull, and forced the FBI to stop harassing Stef's Serbian maid. Karina had arrived in America with the help of a rich uncle in Arlington. She was a tall, *zaftig* blonde who reminded Isaac of a forgotten TV actress, Dagmar, who'd had a moment of fame in the fifties. Karina was gentle with Max, and her malapropisms made the boy feel a little less anguished about his own duel with the English language.

Karina had a pungent perfume. Her body moved with its own kind of lazy lightning under her housedress. Isaac couldn't deny that he was attracted to this Serbian Dagmar. Karina seemed to grow fleshier under Isaac's gaze, with all the frightful tremors of a sudden metamorphosis. She wore nail polish and a hint of mascara—a blond femme fatale in a housedress. But she never flirted with the Big Guy, never played the seductress. She was always proper near the boy, protected him without trying to replace his lost mother. Karina had aspirations. She hoped to work with the blind at Gallaudet University. She was teaching herself to "sign" at night, and she would practice with the boy. She had the very best sponsor. She lived in the White House.

Isaac would have to send her and the boy away until he found the hired gun. He wondered how much of an oracle Sol Ben-Zion really was. Yet that Frankenstein from Shin Bet had been adamant, and Isaac began to meditate. Ben-Zion must have lived through unbearable carnage in Beirut—massacre after massacre along the Green Line. It was the Israeli incursion into Lebanon and the Camp David Accords that had driven Ariel out of office. He resigned in '83 and became the Hermit of Haifa. And all the carnage had bound up Ariel, Mordecai, and Sol Ben-Zion in one great broth of blood.

Isaac began thinking of that blond boy inside the Manhattan mosque. His name was also Elijah, like the army chaplain. The boy preacher had an infernal poetry. He could sermonize like Satan. Isaac had to look into his raw red eyes.

He would often sit in the Cosmetology Room with Rabbi Silvers. Isaac loved the reclining chairs. It was a beautician's paradise. The Big Guy had a wife somewhere in Miami, the Countess Kathleen, but the salon lacked a genuine First Lady.

"Do you suffer remorse?" the chaplain asked.

"About the boy preacher? I dream of him sometimes. His rabbit's red eyes."

"You might have convinced him to leave with the others."

"There was no time for talk therapy," Isaac said. Young Elijah had begun to twitch. He wanted to destroy everyone in the mosque. All he could see was Satan.

"I had to glock him," Isaac told *this* Elijah.

"I like that word—*glock*," the chaplain said. "It has a wonderful flavor, but you executed that boy."

"I did. And I would do it again. But righteousness doesn't rub away the bad dreams."

"Do you glock the boy in your dreams?" the chaplain asked.

Isaac rose up in his reclining chair like a sea lion. "Silvers, since when are you a shrink?"

"I'm your rabbi," the chaplain said. "I have a right to ask."

"I never glock him in the dream. We dance."

"*Dance*," the chaplain said, rolling that word around on his tongue. "Isn't it peculiar?"

"He's wearing lipstick. I mean, he's not a girl. He's Elijah, the cracked prophet. But he's wearing lipstick. And we dance. He has tears of blood in his eyes."

"Like a suffering Christ," the chaplain said.

"Yeah, a Christ with murder on his mind."

Perhaps Isaac did want absolution. He wasn't sure. He noticed a tall, busty blonde come toward him with a sway of her hips—he could have sworn it was Dagmar, broken loose from the fifties. Then the vision vanished. He saw the Serbian maid with Max. She crept down onto the carpets like a four-legged beast, while Maximilian rode on her back. But there was something remiss in her pose, something *malaprop* and perverse, as if it was designed for Isaac's benefit, not the boy's. Yet Max was delighted.

"Karina, are we g-g-going to China—or Bethlehem?"

"Is China on next floor?"

Isaac was startled by her prowess, and the rich purpose of each move as she crept along the carpets. It excited him. He'd been as solitary as a monk at the White House.

"Karina, I command you—f-f-fly to Bethlehem."

"Maxy," she said with a hoarse laugh. "I have not dragon's wings, or motor in my heart. I will never train to fly. We must borrow your papa's wagon."

Isaac could see the amazing curve of Karina's spine. She drove past Isaac with the boy, into some unknown interior of the attic, while Isaac sat with the military chaplain and imagined himself gripping Dagmar's broad back. He had such unholy thoughts, he had to look away from Rabbi Silvers.

19

H
e must have dozed off in the Cosmetology Room. Had the chaplain gone back to Fort Meade? Isaac was wearing his subaltern's robe, like Abe Lincoln. He must have gone down to the residential floor and come back upstairs, a sleepwalker in disguise. The salon was dark, but Isaac could see a crack of light in the attic. He glanced at the green glow of the numerals on his watch. It was well before midnight. He could hear a hissing sound. He stood up and marched into the narrow mezzanine.

Dagmar. . .

Karina hovered over the attic ironing board in her panties and bra. She didn't seem brazen. She was humming some Serbian tune. Isaac crept up behind her, could sniff that powerful perfume.

"Karina," he said, "didn't you leave for Arlington with the colonel and Max?"

She twisted her head around with all the aplomb of a television queen. Karina didn't hide her succulent flesh. Isaac was a bit ashamed. He had a king-sized tent sticking out the front of his subaltern's robe.

"Mr. President," she said without a waver in her voice, "I had to finish ironing. Maxy left me behind."

He wasn't even certain what happened next. He found himself licking the armpits of Max's live-in maid. He loved the salty aroma. He was ridden with guilt, even as he hovered over her, like some Dracula. Had he used the power of his office to brand this Serbian Dagmar with the mark of his own spittle? She had the Big Guy's number. She was still at the ironing board all the while he caressed her. She was pounding away at a pair of Max's pants. Isaac heard the iron's white-hot whistle.

"Mr. President, we play country girl and big bad wolf?"

Yes, he wanted to say, *yes, yes, yes.*

But he wasn't a big bad wolf. He was bemoaning his fate as a prisoner of the White House when he noticed a nasty curl on Karina's lip. There was little seduction in her eyes. He managed to swerve under her elbow as she brandished the iron in her fist. She batted at him with her free hand. She must have had military training somewhere. She shoved him right across the mezzanine. The ironing board collapsed. Isaac could have shouted for help, but she must have known he wasn't a shouter. She was toying with Sidel. She meant to push his face in with the iron.

And he thought to himself. *This fucking madness has to stop.*

All the malapropisms were gone. She was suddenly as fluent as that boy prophet, Elijah.

"The attic is empty," she said. "It's Karel's birthday. I made a reservation at the Old Ebbitt Grill. They'll get drunk on chicken wings. Sidel, you should have known better than to come at me with your prick like a battle lance. You'll pay for that."

"You aren't from Serbia, are you?"

"I couldn't tell Serbia from a cat's ass," she said with a murderous chuckle, though her laughter shaved off a bit of her heat. And now Isaac took a leap of faith. Fuck the presidency! He'd been a mayor with his fists, and had never been more or less than a street cop with the crippling shrewdness of the streets.

"You trained with General Tollhouse."

He'd startled her. But her toughness returned.

"Does it show, Mr. President?"

"You must have been with Wildwater at Warm Springs. But Tollhouse didn't send you. That's not his style. Tollhouse wouldn't have been so oblique."

She was still stalking him with the iron. But Isaac had derailed her a bit with his own gift of gab.

"What's your real name, Karina?"

"Karina," she said.

"And who sent you here to give me a goodbye kiss?"

"Rembrandt," she said.

"I should have seen it," Isaac said. "All the talk about Gallaudet. You got that from the master himself. Gallaudet is one of his escape routes in the District."

Karina nodded her head. "And I'm gonna give you one of my own tats," she said, rattling the iron. "I'll burn it right into your fat brain. A wolf's eyes and ears."

"And you're the gal who left those greeting cards in the beauty salon, under a hair drier."

"Yeah," she said, "that was my personal touch. Viktor relied on my ingenuity a lot."

"He helped you create that Serbian myth, with the uncle in Arlington."

"I was bulletproof," she said. "I picked out a pathetic maid who lived in a closet. I strangled her. We dumped her body in the Chesapeake, and I became Karina."

"You vampirized her."

"Yeah," Karina said. "That's a fancy way to look at it. You're a poet, Mr. President. Would you like one last tumble? Close your eyes, and I'll do you with my panties on."

Keep her talking.

The Big Guy was recovering his ground, even while she lunged at him with the iron. She could afford the luxury of keeping him alive a little longer. She was as agile as an acrobat, but now it was Isaac who tugged at her invisible tail.

"Tell me, sweetheart, did you ever really like Max?"

"That stupid little stutter boy. I wanted to stuff a rag in his mouth. I was going nuts. But Rembrandt wouldn't make his move. You would have been a corpse months ago if he hadn't attached himself to your heartbeat. And I can't have the FBI combing through all my shit. Those idiots could stumble onto something, even if I am bulletproof."

She shouldn't have been so dismissive of Max. Dagmar didn't deserve that little boy. And while she pondered, his wind had come back. He was as wily as Odysseus.

"So you found another sponsor."

"Yeah," she said, with an insane glimmer in her eye. "And he wasn't so finicky—not about you."

"Rainer Wolff," Isaac whispered.

"Rembrandt's on the run. Half his partners have dumped him. That guy has a lot of balls. But he went too far. He clipped his own banker, and he can't move money around. Can you imagine? A billionaire who's short of cash."

Her eyes were fluttering now. She'd forgotten Sidel for a moment, caught in the monsoon of her tale. He'd talked her to a turning point. The iron had stopped whistling. He leapt at Dagmar, slapped the iron out of her fist. She laughed at him, mocked his maneuver. That crazy curl appeared on her lip.

"Papa wants to play," she said. He wondered where she grew up, if she was a street urchin like him, and if he was staring at his own distorted face in a funhouse mirror. She shouldn't have come to this attic—it was Isaac's lair. Her flesh shivered as she laughed, and Isaac felt no pity. He didn't need one of Rembrandt's tats. He'd always been a werewolf—alone, alone.

Dagmar couldn't have reckoned on the ferocity of his attack. He ripped at her, seized her ears, knocked her head against the wall, struck her with her own iron, as her lip uncurled and the first sign of fear registered on her face, with blood welling in her eyes, blinding Dagmar.

"Here's something for Max!"

All the humiliation he'd endured—being babied half the time, with a panoply of protectors who couldn't protect him—roused Isaac, and his rage fell upon Dagmar with blow after blow. He was willing to suffer the consequences.

He looked at himself in a real mirror on the mezzanine wall. He was speckled with blood, like someone maddened by the moon. Dagmar lay on the carpet, one arm stretched out, as if she'd just performed in a ballet. Sidel was the choreographer here. He didn't bother to feel the pulse in her neck. He had the White House operator call Bull Latham and ask him to bring his cuffs. He'd rather not be arrested by a stranger.

He wouldn't clean the blood off his subaltern's robe, wouldn't cover Dagmar in a sheet.

The Bull arrived, saw the carnage, squinted at Isaac's robe. "Jesus, I was worried for a minute."

"Aren't you gonna arrest me?" Isaac had to ask.

"Come on, boss. She was bent. But you wouldn't give us a chance to prove it. Forgive me, I have to bring in my border patrol."

The Bull began whispering into his mobile. Isaac had never heard of border patrols in the District. Half a dozen men appeared in the attic, wearing identical blue suits, crisp white shirts, and striped ties. They could have been their own fraternal order. They carried two of the biggest satchels Isaac had ever seen. They didn't put on work clothes, like house painters. They padded about in rubber soles. One of these sextuplets reached into a satchel, pulled out a portable vacuum cleaner, and sucked up some of the debris Dagmar had left behind—a broken bracelet, a brassiere strap, bits of hair.

Another sextuplet wiped the blood off Isaac with a cotton ball bathed in alcohol. "Mr. President, you'll have to give these lads your robe," the Bull said. "They'll have it cleaned for you. They'll return it with the same wrinkles—come, sit with me." The Bull led Isaac back into the Cosmetology Room, and they sat in reclining chairs, the vice president and the president in his winter underpants.

"Where will your lads put the young lady?"

"What young lady?" the Bull said with a smile. "You've been by yourself all evening."

"But the ironing board . . . she must have been logged in."

"And we'll log her out," the Bull said. "Leave it to my border patrol. But that bitch shouldn't have been allowed to share your quarters, sir."

"Bull, I've been bombed, shot at, and nearly brained with Karina's iron. And I can't counterattack with a whole caravan of cars."

"That comes with the terrain. The president's like a diva . . ."

"Yeah, I know all about it—the Prince of the Western World.

"Isaac, what do you want?"

"Lightning. And I can't have it without a much slimmer machine."

"Done," the Bull said. "You'll still need a babysitter. And you'll have to call the White House switchboard on the hour. We can't afford to have you vanish into the twilight zone. The country would go wild."

Isaac's eyes lit with pure delight. "Bull, that's the only way I can win—from the twilight zone."

"You'll still need a babysitter."

The sextuplets stood near the doorway with their satchels. They shook Isaac's hand and left with the Bull. Isaac was bewildered. There wasn't a trace of Dagmar in the mezzanine, not a splotch of blood. Not a single ridge in the carpet. That was the beauty of Bull Latham's border patrol. The sextuplets had erased the very fact of Dagmar's existence. It wasn't a matter of dried blood and powdered bones. Dagmar was a figment of Isaac's imagination, a maid and a murderess who had never been.

20

Viktor should have fled to the white hills of Lisbon, where he knew every winding path that dove down to the river, and where he could have survived on pink wine and Crackerjacks while he waited out his enemies. Or he could have gone to Bilbao, a medieval city where his father had made a fortune opening a passel of ice cream parlors with exotic flavors, and where foreigners rarely went. But he couldn't seem to get Paris out of his blood. It had nothing to do with high fashion, monuments, and museums.

He sat in the Zeyer, a brasserie in the fourteenth that Henry Miller had frequented fifty years ago and held court with other artists and writers who had to scrounge for every meal. The Zeyer's habitués had tales to tell about the bald American with his Brooklyn accent, who limped along in French, and wanted to fuck every female in the brasserie from sixteen to sixty. It amused Viktor, made him laugh. Miller fucked the wives of friends and lived off Anaïs Nin and her husband while he wrote *Tropic of Cancer.*

Viktor could have gone to the Coupole, in Montparnasse, where his father, *Pakhan Karl,* would often meet his lieutenants at the bar. Sometimes, Viktor came along. His father had adopted a drunken poet with a long, grizzled face, who would wander into the Coupole, swaying from side to side. His father called him Sam. This Sam never had a sou in his pockets. He dressed like a *clodo.* Spittle flew from his mouth. The *pakhan* had to wipe Sam's face with a silk handkerchief. Years after his father's death, Viktor finally realized that Sam without a sou was the Nobel laureate who had written *Waiting for Godot.* But even that bit of news couldn't bring him back to the Coupole. Besides, he might have been spotted by Rainer's henchmen in the middle of Montparnasse.

Viktor clung to the Zeyer, a poorer cousin in the heart of a modest neighborhood at the Carrefour Alésia, near the Porte d'Orléans—it was an artisan's paradise. He closeted himself at a corner table, drinking a blond Belgian beer, and could see across the terrace and into the street, as plumbers in hip boots went past, glaziers with shivering sheets of glass on their backs. He was still at war with Rainer Wolff, but his own allies were dwindling. His orphans—the *besprizornye*—had begun to abandon him. He was more involved in tattoos than in counterfeit currency.

He kept his needles and dyes in a wooden box at his feet, like some religious monk. He had a new fiancée, a young widow who wasn't at all like Viktor. She had a fixed abode in Georgetown. She loved ballet and Washington's winter galas and balls. She belonged to the Republican National Committee. Viktor had stuffed the committee with cash like a golden goose when he was trying to sabotage Sidel. But he was drawn to the widow and her muscular American blondness that seemed so bland on the surface, yet was scratched by its own peculiar passion. The *pakhan* had fallen in love for the first time perhaps . . .

He was reckless. He shouldn't have been daydreaming at the Zeyer. Still, he smiled when Rainer sat down at the next table, superior as ever in a coat with a mink collar.

"Rembrandt, we could have had the best sea bass in Paris at the Dôme, picked it right out of the tank, and I have to find you here. How are you adjusting to our reduced circumstances?"

"Don't cry, Rainer. You have a million commodities."

"But I had to sell short," Rainer said. "Should I tell you how much I lost in a single day? Did you have to garrote our own banker?"

"I didn't garrote Pierre," Viktor said. "I slit his throat."

"*Mensch*, it comes to the same thing. Either we have a truce, or you don't walk out of here alive."

Viktor smiled into the teeth of Viktor's remark.

"And how will you orchestrate my disappearance in a brasserie full of clients drinking orange *pressé* and Belgian beer—ah, I forgot. You were once with the Abwehr. Choreographing disappearances was your specialty."

"It still is. I'll create a diversion, a fire in the toilets. Why the devil did you come back to Paris? It's teeming with Michael Davit's men. Davit has a grudge against you. You strangled two of his very best employees, sworn to protect Pierrot. You made a fool of Davit. He couldn't deliver. And he wants to deliver now. Your partners are very cross. Rosa Malamud has put a bounty on your head."

"How is dear Rosa? Are her fashion shops flourishing? Has she stabbed anyone in the heart with her knitting needle?"

"Rembrandt," Rainer said, "she's sharpening it especially for you."

Viktor should have been more alert. Rainer had manufactured a little homecoming party for Viktor, who recognized Michael Davit's men in their plaid jackets with leather elbow patches, like country squires. They were thugs with split eyebrows, despite their aristocratic attire. And then he saw Rosa herself at the bar, too involved with Rembrandt's destruction to count her millions.

"It's hopeless," Rainer said, "can't you see? Give us your plates— your precious plates—and you'll walk out of here in one piece."

Viktor laughed. "But they're my intellectual property. You're a publisher, Rainer. Would you ask any of your authors to surrender their rights?"

"Rembrandt, you're wasting my time. Either we deal or we don't."

Viktor knew the Zeyer's exits and entrances by heart. He couldn't duck out on Davit's men. He had to move right into the squall. "Rainer, your spotters didn't find me. You couldn't have taken some magic wheelbarrow from West Berlin. You figured I'd come here."

Rainer pretended to yawn. He should have been a *Schauspieler.* He had to act out different parts when he was with the Abwehr—he was once a butler in the house of a British spy for two weeks, and had to play a transvestite to trap a clerk in the Foreign Office who was selling secrets to Stalin. "Rembrandt, you're so predictable. You can't resist a proletariat café. Paris is where your father made his mark. Only an idiot or a clever man would hide right under our noses. And I learned how to be patient. I told myself, *He'll come to the Zeyer, sooner or later.* And here you are."

Viktor leapt up, tossed his blond beer into Rainer's eyes, skipped between two of Davit's thugs with their fancy elbow patches, clopped another one on the head with his wooden box, but he couldn't maneuver fast enough. Rosa Luxemburg ripped into his coat with the savage point of her knitting needle. He still knocked the needle out of her hand, and clutching his side for a moment, he danced into the stairwell that went down to the toilets. He nearly tripped, but he clung to the banister rail. The Zeyer was his terrain, even if he'd brought his enemies here. He went through an unmarked door that led to a tunnel where most of the Zeyer's deliveries must have been made. He climbed a flight of stairs and found himself at the side of a little church on the Avenue du Maine. He opened the gate and hopped across the avenue, with a trickle of blood on his hand.

He arrived at the Mistral, a dump of a hotel next to the rue Daguerre. Sartre and Simone de Beauvoir had both stayed here when they were penniless philosophers. But that's not why Viktor had chosen the Mistral. He liked its random sense of decay. He climbed up to a room on the second floor, where the young widow was waiting. Renata would have preferred the Ritz. But the Ritz was outside Viktor's realm of reliability, though he had stayed there once, had sat with his *besprizornye* at Hemingway's bar. He would have been noticed at the Ritz with his odd flamboyance, that cavalier disregard of decorum by a billionaire who walked around with a child's paint box . . .

"I was worried," Renata said.

Viktor couldn't even calm her. He would have smeared blood on Renata with his own hands. She'd walked out of one disaster on an errand for him, and he didn't want her to walk into another. She was a casualty of sorts. She still had a twitch under one eye, from that explosion in the castle. She whimpered in her sleep. He'd rock her in his arms half the night.

Viktor made a call from the phone in his room, whispered a few words. Within five minutes there was a knock on the door. He welcomed the ancient *toubib*, Muhammad, who had once been part of his father's clan. The *toubib* dug a needle into Viktor's arm that was almost as large as Rosa's knitting needle. Muhammad spoke Russian, English, and a little Arabic with Viktor. He cut away Viktor's clothes with a surgeon's scissors, cleaned and cauterized the wound, then wrapped him in a bandage of tape and gauze.

"I'll have to travel," Viktor said. "I can't stay here. It's too risky."

"Sir," Muhammad said, "the kind lady, she should hold your hand. It will be like a transfusion."

This *toubib* without a doctor's diploma wouldn't accept cash from Viktor.

"You have rewarded me many, many times. Allow me this one bit of service."

And he was gone. Renata didn't ask any questions. She followed the *toubib*'s advice, clutched Viktor's hand. The *toubib* had been right; a kind of electric current passed through Viktor, energized him. He shouldn't have brought her into this mess, made her his private ambassador to Karel Ludvik. But she hadn't been better off on her own; her dead husband's bankers and lawyers had preyed upon Renata, had robbed her blind. Viktor had to threaten this band of thieves with dire consequences; he'd kidnapped the nanny and daughter of one banker, but he didn't have the heart to hurt a child. Luckily the warning worked. Yet the bankers weren't done with Renata; they hovered over whatever bits of property she had left, preparing to pounce when the time was ripe.

So she'd become a vagabond like him, by default. But he couldn't travel with her. He'd have to slip across borders, worrying about betrayal after betrayal. One of the *besprizornye* whom he could still trust would pick her up in an hour, drive her to Brussels, where she would board a commercial flight under an identity he had picked out for her: *Desdemona Roth*, an heiress without an heir. But he hadn't told her all this—he didn't want to spoil this last little hour at the Mistral.

"Whatever happens, you'll have enough cash," he said. It was a rotten habit he'd inherited from his *pakhan* father. Money was always on his mind.

"Stop it," she said. "I'm staying with you."

The blueblood and the besprizornye.

He didn't argue. She held his hand. He'd profited from that transfusion the *toubib* had talked about—the beat of her heart, the warmth of her blood.

She must have deciphered her own fate in his dark eyes, realized that the werewolf was sending her away. "Darling," she said, "let me go with you. I'll become a washerwoman, I swear. We can hide in Ibiza."

A rumble of laughter rose up from Viktor's belly. He wouldn't have lasted five minutes on that island of castaways, counterfeiters, informants, and retired British agents.

He kissed her as hard as any man could with a cauterized wound. He was crazy about Renata, more than crazy—it was a genuine affliction.

"Ibiza," he said. "We'll see."

"Or Prague," she said, with a sudden fire in her eyes. "Yes, Prague. We'll have our own palace. Didn't they promise us a palace, dear?"

A palace, he muttered to himself, like a dreamer with a stitch in his side from Rosa's knitting needle.

21

saac's little family began to fall away. Ariel and Mordecai returned to Haifa with the blessings of Sol Ben-Zion and Shin Bet. "Itzik," Ariel said before he got on an El Al flight, "how can we save you if you won't save yourself? This is not your home. It's a haven for diplomats." Isaac would miss his pair of crusaders in trench coats. They, too, had lived outside the law.

And then Karel Ludvik, the self-deposed president, decided to disappear from the attic. This former colonel of state security must have arrived at some agreement with the Soviets and the Czechs. "Mr.

President, I have what they want—Rembrandt's paper. I hid as much as I could before I left."

"And once you turn it over?" Isaac asked. "They're torturers, for Christ's sake."

But that didn't seem to trouble Karel Ludvik. Perhaps he would create his own pact among torturers, since he'd been one himself. He'd never tattled on Renata Swallow, never talked about what she'd been doing at his dinner table the night of the bombing, but suddenly he volunteered. It was his parting gift to Sidel. She hadn't come to barter with Karel in Rembrandt's behalf, or to sell him a bundle of Ulysses S. Grants. Besides, Rembrandt had already sold him half a ton of paper. It was a much more vital matter than counterfeit currency. Rembrandt wanted to relocate to Prague, with Renata Swallow. He was buying his way into Czechoslovakia, with the doyenne of Washington's Cave Dwellers at his side.

"She's in love with that crime czar," Karel said. "And love always distorts the picture."

"So you're a philosopher now," Isaac said.

"No, a pragmatist. Rembrandt is banking on Prague's future in a free Czech state. But it doesn't really matter. He's an outlaw where other outlaws will prosper. It will be frontier capitalism in another few years. And I told you once. He already owns half of Prague. He'll be a little king."

Isaac peered at him. "And what will you be, Karel?"

"The king's accomplice."

And he was whisked away on Aeroflot. Isaac's own intelligence teams hadn't gotten their money's worth from Karel. The folks at Langley must have sweated him for a while, but the CIA was in disrepair. Its agents had been running drugs in Nicaragua to help finance more and more rogue ops. Langley was under Bull Latham's thumb.

"Don't bother fixing the unfixable," the Bull loved to say. And Isaac had to wonder how many rogue agents were out there, floating around in the fourth dimension—1989 wasn't a good year for spies. A randomness had settled in. Members of MI6 had turned on their own masters. There was an international crisis. Agents could be bought and sold by the bushel. And private contractors like General Tollhouse prospered among all the confusion; he could raid Isaac's mountain retreat at will, and put one of his assets—a female soldier of fortune—in Isaac's attic. Wildwater was its own CIA.

Isaac would have been all alone if Captain Sarah hadn't returned to the attic with the president's pilot and the pilot's son. Max was very blue. He'd grown fond of Dagmar's musk; it had become ambrosia to a stuttering boy. And Sidel had a difficult time skirting around the maid's magical disappearing act.

"She had to leave, Max. Her Auntie was sick."

"Uncle Isaac, will she ever be back?"

"Soon," he said without missing a beat. Isaac was like any rogue agent. Worse, even. But he couldn't fool Captain Sarah and Stef.

"You got rid of her," Sarah rasped, the moment Max had fled to another part of the attic. "She wouldn't have disappeared on the spin of a dime. She was much too loyal to Max."

"She was loyal to no one but Mr. Wildwater."

Stef was furious after Isaac told him the entire tale. "She might have hurt my little boy. Tollhouse shouldn't have taken advantage of me like that—planting one of his own operatives as my live-in maid."

But they couldn't wreak vengeance on Wildwater right away. Isaac had a much more urgent matter. There'd been a riot and open rebellion at Rikers, the nation's largest penal colony, which held fifteen thousand souls on its island fortress. It was a turnstile jail, with inmates moving in and out. More than half of them didn't even wear prison garb; they sat for months and months if they couldn't make bail. There was a unit for pregnant women, another for psychopaths and suicide cases, and yet another for adolescents. Guards openly had sex with inmates, and beat others half to death. Rikers was considered an extension of the Bronx, on the East River. The jail was run by two gangs, the Bloods and the Latin Kings. Rikers had become their honey pot and their private crib. They had their very own day room, where they initiated new members into their ranks, and hired themselves out as contract killers. They could disappear for an afternoon and return to their cell blocks without ever being noticed. They'd learned the art of tattooing from some forgotten master and loved to display their tats. But the Kings and the Bloods hadn't caused the riot. They had little to rebel about.

The riot had been started by a lay preacher, Martin Teasdale, who called himself a rabbi and minister of the dispossessed. None of the correctional officers seemed to know why he was at Rikers. The COs couldn't find a record of Martin Teasdale. He wasn't an inmate. Somehow he had slipped into the penal colony and remained, moving from dorm to dorm, from block to block. Perhaps the COs had adopted him, perhaps not. He taught impromptu classes in religion and philosophy, organized inmates who weren't involved in the war between the Bloods and the Kings, and managed to outmaneuver them. And one winter night, he took over every single facility at Rikers, with his captains beside him—pale boys, pregnant women, and mean hombres. They'd reversed the order of things—locked the COs inside their bunkers, contained the Bloods and the Kings, trapped the warden and his deputies inside their offices, and communicated with the press via the warden's mobile. They had firearms and smoke grenades, but they hadn't harmed a living soul in the penal colony.

Teasdale had made one request: he would surrender to Sidel, and Sidel alone. Ramona Dazzle went ballistic when she heard that on the six P.M. report. "Mr. President, there's already too much Manhattan in your blood."

"But Rikers is a piece of the Bronx."

"It's still like going back to grade school," she said. "You graduated from the mayor's chair. This might play if that demented preacher were calling out to you from some jail in Iowa. Then Colonel Oliver could ride you right onto the roof. It would be gangbusters! But not a lousy dump on the East River. You've already been called the Ghetto President. You shouldn't return to your roost."

It was a political landmine for the mayor and the governor. Neither one wanted another Attica, with the blood of inmates and COs on their hands. And why did this lone white man who called himself a preacher appeal to a population of Latinos and blacks? Martin Teasdale didn't seem to have a prison record. He was reared in Vermont, attended a rural school and later a teachers' college, returned to the same rural schoolhouse, where he taught second grade until he was hospitalized. Teasdale suffered from a crippling chronic depression. What whiff of steam or air had brought him to Rikers Island? And when had he begun to preach? He wasn't registered as a Republican or a Democrat. The man seemed apolitical. And here he was creating a firestorm in a penal colony and seeking out Sidel.

S tef had to prepare the lift package. He had little lead time. An entire penal colony sat in some sandbox, waiting for the president. Stef rode in advance with his crew to JFK, where the lift package—two White

Tops—had been assembled. They could have dropped the package off at LaGuardia, which was less than a hundred yards away from Rikers. But the arrival of Air Force One would have disrupted the entire airport. The runways weren't really long enough, and Air Force One might have landed in the East River, or crumpled onto Rikers. Also, LaGuardia didn't have the space to house White Tops in its hangars.

The colonel was already in the cockpit when his radio started to crackle.

"Red Rider to Rio, Red Rider to Rio, the Citizen is on the way. Thirty minutes to touch down."

"Roger that, Red Rider. Over and out."

Stef was grateful that they could skirt Manhattan on this part of the lift, and wouldn't have to bring that same old nightmare of gridlock every time the president was on the ground.

The Citizen had arrived with Captain Sarah and half his White House detail. He was wearing his windbreaker, as usual. His cuffs were slightly frayed. He wouldn't permit the White House butler to arrange his wardrobe. The Big Guy dressed and shaved himself. He climbed the air stair without a nod to the cockpit.

And Stef rode the currents, rocked and cradled Marine One above the plains of Queens with its high-rise villages that looked like battlements in some bittersweet dystopia. He had to skirt LaGuardia's airspace. The White House liaison officer had mapped Marine One's route with air traffic control.

He snaked along the edge of the East River and peered down at the penal colony that inhabited its own windswept island like a rubber pancake with white and red bunkers. Stef could see the rolls of razor wire that surrounded the penal colony like a lethal bracelet. He landed his bird on a patch of lawn without grass. It was cluttered with reporters come to see the mishaps of a president whose numbers dropped precipitously in poll after poll. Stef felt like he was part of a circus sideshow. The mayor and the governor had to be there—it was a prime-time crisis—but they weren't looking for a photo op with the commander in chief. Isaac had become his own isolation ward, a president who never had his proper honeymoon.

Teasdale's command center was "the Bing," the nastiest jail on the island. It housed the incorrigibles. The Central Punitive Segregation Unit—CPSU—was a supermax facility, in permanent disciplinary lockdown. Yet Teasdale had penetrated the bitter heart of this bunker, the most ancient and run-down unit in the penal colony. The warden had declared a red alert—a total lockdown of the island—once Teasdale went on the warpath, but this lowly teacher from Vermont was able to override the warden's red alert and seize control of every facility, trapping the master and many of his screws in their own bullpens. Of course, the dreaded Ninja Turtles of ERU—Rikers' Emergency Response Unit—had rushed the Bing with their batons. The Turtles were unmistakable in their fatigues, padded coats, helmets, and steel-tipped boots. The Turtles had solved every crisis on the island. ERU had never failed. But Teasdale disgorged the Turtles, sent the warden's paramilitary unit howling from the Bing, their faces covered in feces and blood.

Isaac walked into a swirl of elite units from the NYPD; the police commissioner had arrived with his sharpshooters and SWAT teams clad in black. But the new Commish, who was little more than the mayor's attack dog, had been given no instructions at all. The mayor couldn't afford a massacre. And the governor stood on the sidelines, yapping with reporters, while the Bronx borough president, who was swept into office with Isaac Sidel, seemed to care about the island's population of undesirables. He was shrewd enough to talk to Sidel in front of the cameras.

"There are kids in the Bing, Mr. President, and old men with diabetes and heart conditions. What can you do?"

"Go inside and talk to Mr. Teasdale."

"And if he won't reason with you?"

"Well, we'll have to reason with the unreasonable."

Isaac was no stranger to this island. He'd taught classes at one of Rikers' high schools, had met with boys in their "junior" jail—sixteen-year-olds were treated as adults and sent to the penal colony. He'd tried to secure scholarships for the brightest ones, and gave reading lessons to boys who had never learned to spell. He'd wanted to get rid of Rikers, but he had neither the power nor the will—it was a gulag on the East River, with a tundra all its own; more than half of the young men who did time at Rikers returned within a year. Even as president, he'd petitioned the Federal Bureau of Prisons, but nothing came of that petition; it was mired in politics. Jails and penitentiaries brought in big bucks. And there were always stats about the little "dips" in violence, while the prison population boomed. Democrats and Republicans alike clamored for additional wardens and screws.

Teasdale still remained a mystery. COs weren't allowed to wear guns inside the cellblocks. They could arm themselves outside the jails, since they might encounter former inmates with a grudge against them. Teasdale's band must have broken into the COs' lockers and swiped their pieces. That's what Isaac had heard on the news. But perhaps there was another explanation. Some of the inmates went out on furlough; they would leave Rikers aboard the Department of Correction's orange and blue buses, volunteer at homeless shelters and hospices for men and women with full-blown AIDS, and then return on the same orange and blue buses in the middle of the night. And Isaac wondered if Teasdale had smuggled warriors and weapons into Rikers on these buses. If so, this wasn't a spontaneous eruption and riot. It sounded more and more like a Wildwater op. And Martin Teasdale wasn't some preacher out of the wilderness. He was a mercenary, a soldier of fortune. But how could Isaac be sure?

Neither the Ninja Turtles nor a single screw would welcome the most popular mayor the city had ever known. The governor conferred with his aides, and finally approached Sidel. *That prick*, Isaac muttered to himself.

The Gov had abandoned Isaac a month after the elections and sided with the Democratic Caucus. "You'll have to solve this thing, Sidel," he said on camera.

"You numbskull," Isaac said, "you nitwit, why don't you wave your handkerchief and come inside with me?"

The Gov fled from the TV crews without a word, as Isaac shoved around the cameras. No one volunteered to accompany him.

A janitor had to steer Isaac toward the hellhole where Martin Teasdale had barricaded himself, a corral for the most violent inmates—CPSU. The janitor wouldn't follow Isaac on his journey.

"The crazies are in there, Mr. President. Good luck."

But Isaac wasn't alone. A tribe of stray cats had swarmed around him, caressing his heels with their scarred heads. They didn't bother with mice or insects. They hunted rats on this little razor-wired plantation. And the leader of the tribe, known as Desirée, an enormous white she-cat with many scabs, had fallen for the Big Guy at first sight. She had a strange, high-pitched voice in Isaac's presence, though she snarled at other cats who inched too close. Desirée had adopted Isaac, and led him into the Bing, her curled tail like a crusader's flag.

Isaac stepped on crumbs of shattered glass. Cockroaches climbed the walls as Isaac went through a gate that opened for him and Desirée, and shut behind them with an electrical scrape. The aroma here was much worse than the stench of shit and sweat and unwashed linen at the city's homeless shelters—it was the perfume of perpetual rot, and it made Isaac giddy for a moment.

The metal detectors were unmanned, but one of Teasdale's rebels sat in the control booth with his own button mike and ushered Isaac into the facility. The Big Guy passed a cell block cluttered with screws in their winter underwear. They looked frightened and forlorn.

Who the fuck is Martin Teasdale?

A voice shot out at him with its own grit.

"Are you bearing arms, sir?"

"Yes," Isaac shot back into the stinking wind that blew across the Bing. "I've come with my Glock."

"Dangle it from your left thumb."

So Isaac dangled his Glock and stepped deeper into a stench that debilitated him.

"Is this your bodyguard?"

"No," Isaac said, pointing to the mountainous white cat. "My welcoming committee."

He went through another rumbling gate and arrived in a tiny room that must have been a holding pen, where he spotted Martin Teasdale and his motley band of rebels. Some must have been high on coke or meth; others looked deranged. They had a variety of weapons: stun guns, grenades, hand cannons, firemen's hatchets, and swords from another century. The men—Latino, white, and black—wore head scarves, stocking caps, and doo-rags made of silk. None of them were in jailhouse green. Several sported CO uniforms, with the shirts unbuttoned and cuffs rolled up. They couldn't have been professional soldiers. They had the swollen cheeks and split lips of inmates who'd been manhandled. Isaac sensed a piercing beauty and defiance in the sad, bitter faces of these men—outlaws sentenced to solitary confinement. The women looked as fierce as the men. Some were pregnant;

others wore the uniforms of female COs. The preacher stood out among them. He was very tall, like a skeleton in a sheath of yellowish skin.

"Reverend Teasdale," Isaac said, "I feel silly with my gun resting on a finger."

"You can put it back in your pants, Big Balls."

Who is this guy?

Isaac was touched by Teasdale's army. Pregnant women, psychopaths, desperados, and pale boys with filth on their faces. How had they managed to overcome a penal colony with the population of a small town? Perhaps Isaac miscounted their numbers and misconstrued their mission. Was the reverend a genius of disorder?

"Are you hungry?" Isaac asked. "I can give a shout and have some food brought in."

"We have command of the kitchen," Teasdale said. "We're not hurting for grub."

"Then why did you summon me? Why am I here?"

"I'll ask the questions," the talking cadaver said. "Sit."

They sat down at a table that was infested with rat droppings. Teasdale offered Isaac a Mars bar that had come from one of the facility's vending machines. Isaac unwrapped the bar, took a bite, and soon the caramel clung to his teeth.

"Big Balls, why haven't you shut down Rikers? It's the worst penal colony in creation. It reeks with shit."

"Reverend, I sent in reformers while I was mayor. I got the children out of there. I did what I could."

"Don't talk mayor to me," Teasdale said. "You're president. You could have the Justice Department shut down Rikers."

"It's not a federal facility," Isaac said, with a sudden lameness in his voice.

Teasdale cackled at him. Tribe members in doo-rags glared at Isaac.

"Big Balls, that's no excuse. Federal marshals could swoop down on this island and create their own red alert. The warden would shit his pants. I voted for you, voted for the first time in my life. And you play your war games with the Pentagon."

"What war games?" Isaac asked. "You won't find generals crowding the Situation Room."

"*Situation Room*," Teasdale said with spittle on his tongue. "That's a laugh. The real war is right here. Rikers is crowded with crazies—men and boys who have no business being inside a jail. And this isn't even a jail. It's a holding pen for undesirables."

Teasdale was right on the mark. But Isaac couldn't admit that in front of this band, or he would have had to surrender himself to Teasdale.

A boy with a teardrop painted on his cheek—the mark of a murderer—pointed a Colt .45 at Isaac's heart. He couldn't have been much older than eighteen. Isaac recognized him instantly: Oswaldo Corona, who'd been one of Isaac's best students on the island. He'd been elected to *arista*, the honor society. Isaac had talked to Columbia and Yale about him. And here he was in the Bing, with that ominous teardrop.

"Mr. T.," Oswaldo said, in that sweet, childish voice of his—he even wore his arista pin. "Should I whack him in the right eye or the left?"

"Homey," Isaac said, "did you forget me so fast?"

"I'm not your homeboy," Oswaldo said. "You're the master, and I'm the slave."

"'Waldo," Teasdale asked, "what will we accomplish by shooting out his eye? Go easy on Big Balls. He's better than most."

Isaac couldn't stop squinting at that teardrop. How had a boy who had written about vegetable gardens in the barrio, who adored his *moms,* and wanted to be a novelist or an astronaut, have ended up killing someone and having a teardrop painted on his cheek as a sign of respect?

Oswaldo wouldn't talk about his past or his present. It was this rabbi of the dispossessed who had to explain what had happened to the boy scholar. A CO at the jail for "juniors" had tried to punk Oswaldo out to another CO, and Oswaldo had punctured his throat with a ballpoint pen. The boy had gone back into the maze of the court system, and would soon be transferred to a facility upstate, where he'd probably spend the rest of his life. Meanwhile, he wore a teardrop and carried a cannon, like Isaac's own Secret Service.

Isaac swore to himself that he would look into the case. No, he would have to do better than that, or he himself would be trapped in the maze.

"Mr. T.," Isaac said, "Rikers should be shut down, but it will only rise out of the mist on another island, the ghost of a ghost. I can't reform the courts. No president can. I can shuffle around my federal prosecutors, but the numbers will still come up short. How the hell did you trap the warden and all his disciples in their own cages? You got around their red alert, locked them inside their lockdown. And you took the Ninja Turtles and tossed them out of the Bing. You're no rabbi. You trained will all the other mercs at Warm Springs."

"Didn't I tell you?" Teasdale said. "No questions. If I surrender, Big Balls, there has to be a press conference."

"I can't protect you," Isaac said, "once we're outside the Bing. I can't call the shots."

"Yes, you can," Teasdale said.

"Rabbi, don't be so damn naïve. The might of the whole system will rain on your head like a shitstorm."

"But not while you're standing beside me. Shut the Bing for thirty days. Talk to the press. The warden will have to dance on a bed of nails—for a little while."

Isaac agreed to the rabbi's terms. He left the COs in the cellblock and marched out of the Bing with the Reverend Teasdale and his rebels. Isaac had secured their weapons, including the cutlass, and carried them in a metal container, with Desirée at his heels. He held off the Ninja Turtles and the SWAT teams. He was still commander in chief.

"Rabbi," Isaac said, "I think you'd better free the warden, or this will never go down."

Teasdale whispered into his button mike: a siren blasted, and soon every gate on this island gulag opened with a maddening screech. Teasdale had handed back Rikers to the little despots of the Department of Corrections.

Suddenly Isaac was some kind of a hero. Reporters from all over the planet wrapped a necklace of microphones around the Big Guy.

"Mr. President, how did you get the fiend to surrender?"

And for a moment Isaac's glamour had returned. He wasn't the recluse of Pennsylvania Avenue, marauded wherever he went. He had freed an entire facility from its captors, had walked unscathed out of the lions' den.

"Mr. Teasdale is not a fiend. I can't concur with his methods. He broke the law, and he's willing to pay for his transgressions. But you'll have to consider this an extreme form of protest. I'm going to ask Justice to shut down the Bing for thirty days. We'll have another look at this island."

The Big Guy didn't blink or squint into the lights. Half the world was watching the metamorphosis of Isaac Sidel—resurrection, really.

This was the man who had helped elect the unelectable Michael Storm, and now stood in his place. The cameras seemed to settle on his windbreaker. He was a president who was willing to enter the maelstrom.

"And what about that feral cat?" asked a journalist from *El País*.

"Desirée? I'm taking her with me to the White House."

22

Dragon hadn't been part of the lift package. Isaac didn't want to ride through his own town in an armored cradle. Marine One delivered him to the Wall Street helipad, where he climbed into an anonymous sedan with Desirée, Captain Sarah, Stef, Matt Malloy, and another member of the White House detail. The sedan delivered him to an Italian grocery on Ninth Avenue that also had three dinner tables with waxen cloths; it was a Mafiosi joint, and he'd been coming here ever since he was a deputy chief inspector with the NYPD. His daughter Marilyn and Joe Barbarossa, his son-in-law, were sitting at one of the tables.

The Big Guy had a special dispensation. He could bring his feral cat inside the store. The grocer's other cats scattered behind the counter at Desirée's first hiss. Sidel was pleased. *His* cat was territorial. She curled up at Isaac's feet, her meow like an asthmatic trumpet. Marilyn barely had room under the table for her legs.

"Isaac, did you have to adopt such a monster?"

"The cat adopted me," Isaac muttered.

"That's even worse," Marilyn said. "All the strays collect around you. Isaac, you're a bag of bones. Joe, tell my father that he looks terrible."

But Barbarossa couldn't do that. He'd gone out on kills with Isaac Sidel. Isaac was the only boss he'd ever had who understood his erratic nature, his mood swings, his gift for violence. Every other cop on the force had feared him, not because his father-in-law had once been the Pink Commish and was now president, but because Barbarossa was volatile and dangerous to have around. He wore a glove on one hand; it covered the burns he'd received in Nam fighting other drug dealers. And Barbarossa's glove could rip at you out of nowhere.

He decided to play the diplomat and not contradict his wife, who could be as warlike as her father.

"Ah, Dad," he said, "I'll bet you haven't had a decent meal since you left the Apple."

They drank Chianti together from a bottle wrapped in straw, had roasted red peppers soaked in olive oil, a chopped salad, grilled sardines, spaghetti pomodoro with the thinnest noodles Isaac had ever seen, and a hazelnut cake that the grocer's wife had prepared for the president. Isaac had to sign his autograph for the grocer's tribe of nephews. He'd sent one of them to Sing Sing. But the grocer and his wife didn't bear a grudge.

Marilyn scrutinized her father across the table without the semblance of a smile. "I still say he's thin."

Isaac would never recover from Marilyn the Wild. She ruled him and rifled his dreams. She was like a burglar inside the Big Guy's gut.

"When are you coming to DC?" Isaac asked.

"Never," she said. "I told you not to run. You can't breathe outside the boroughs."

Matt suddenly appeared at the table with his mobile. "Didn't mean to interrupt, Mr. President. But I think it's urgent. Renata Swallow just called the White House, and the switchboard patched the call through."

"Renata's on the line? But she wouldn't take any of my calls . . ."

He grabbed the mobile from Matt with its two rabbit ears. He always felt like a Martian with that machine. He had to juggle with the rabbit ears before he heard Renata's voice; it sounded as if she were stranded in an echo chamber.

"Renata, I hope this has nothing to do with Balanchine. I'm not in the mood to talk about the master."

She was crying, and Isaac regretted that he was so nonchalant with her; like a ping-pong player fending off a vicious serve with one eye shut. "What's wrong?"

"Viktor wants to see you."

"Fine," Isaac asked. "We can meet in one of the tunnels at Gallaudet—tomorrow."

"He's not at Gallaudet," Renata said. "He's in Manhattan—on the Lower East Side."

Ah, Isaac reasoned with himself. Viktor Danzig must have inherited his mother's flat—the seamstress Pauline wouldn't take a nickel from her billionaire son. Rembrandt had buried her in Woodlawn.

Isaac got the *pakhan*'s address from Renata. "But why is he in Manhattan?"

"Because, darling, he has no other place to hide."

"Is he hurt? Is he in trouble?"

Renata told him about Michael Davit, the Manchester entrepreneur who had his own school for assassins. Viktor had remained one hop ahead of Davit's hitters. But where were Rembrandt's Ninja Turtles, the *besprizornye?* They'd abandoned him and vanished with their own hard cash, their holdings, and counterfeit plates. Rembrandt had become too unpredictable, falling in love with a Washington blueblood, neglecting his Ulysses S. Grants while he maneuvered *against* the Swiss bankers' lottery in order to spare Sidel's life. The *besprizornye* had come to terms with that publishing baron, Rainer Wolff, and may even have been hunting Viktor on their own. The Sons of Rossiya were disbanding without their *pakhan.*

"But is he hurt?" Isaac had to ask again.

"Yes," Ramona said, "and the cops are after him."

"What cops?"

"Your own boys in blue," Ramona said; her voice turned to static, and a long silence rippled right through Sidel, as he began to saddle up.

He whispered in Barbarossa's ear, and Barbarossa whispered right back.

"Dad, I'll have to call from a pay phone, just to be safe."

Barbarossa left the little restaurant in his black leather coat and returned in five minutes.

"Joey, were there any problems?"

"Dad, don't ask."

But Isaac understood the score. Rainer Wolff, or one of his agents, must have hired several homicide detectives to track Rembrandt to the Lower East Side. There had always been freelancers like that, and Vietnam Joe was part of the same club.

"Dad, I stopped the hemorrhaging, but there's still one lone wolf out there, and we'll have to take our chances."

Marilyn could never seem to decode all this cop talk.

"Isaac," she said, "fatten yourself. Finish the cake before you disappear altogether. And Joey, don't you let him walk into an ambush."

Barbarossa stroked his glove as a warning sign to Isaac's enemies, wherever they were, while the Big Guy began to brood. He wasn't even sure if he was allowed to kiss his own daughter. "Marilyn, the Secret Service will drive you home."

But she hugged Isaac and Joe. "My two idiots," she said, with the taste of hazelnut in her mouth.

Isaac groaned when he saw Dragon outside the grocery.

"Boss," Matt said, "I took the initiative and had that baby brought here on my own."

They all climbed into the president's cradle. Desirée had already captured a mouse. She delivered her trophy to Isaac and leapt onto his lap, while Marilyn stood inside the curtained window and waved to her husband and Isaac, as Dragon disappeared into the night.

It was an old-line tenement on Attorney Street, a firetrap that should have been torn down. Perhaps it was Isaac himself who had spared the building when he was the grand seigneur of Manhattan real estate. He wouldn't allow a single tenant to fall into oblivion inside New York's labyrinthine bureaucracy. Promises were always made, and often produced nothing but a subway token and a berth at a public shelter.

Dragon was much too conspicuous. The Big Guy didn't want to advertise his own *razzia*. So he left Dragon a block away, and while Barbarossa and Captain Sarah approached Rembrandt's building from the roofs, breaking into an abandoned building a few doors away, Isaac, Stef, and Matt Malloy marched into the firetrap on Attorney Street, with Desirée weaving around them and bumping into their heels with her bullet head.

Isaac knew it was some kind of a trap. The lampposts were all unlit. Some motherfucker must have knocked out the lights with a long stick. The firetrap itself was dark as Moses. Matt had to use his pocket flashlight, or they would have stumbled about on the stairs like straw dolls.

Up they went, one stair at a time, mired in dust and filth. The banisters creaked; it was Isaac's old bailiwick. He loved every moment. He was back on his native ground, removed from a world of monuments and antiques, and the must of history. He didn't have to be reminded of Lincoln's footsteps, as much as he admired the Great Emancipator. He had a rawness here, not Marines in harness, butlers on parade. He was on a president's holiday. And then he heard the cat hiss—it was like a deafening whistle. Desirée hunched her back and leapt into the air, her enormous body twirling, as she attacked with her claws.

Someone groaned on the second floor landing. "Stop, stop, I beg you. Get this creature off me."

Isaac called once. "Desirée."

And the cat returned to his heels. A man stepped out of the shadows, with deep runnels of blood on his face.

Isaac recognized one of the lazy lieutenants from his own time at headquarters, a worthless bagman who fetched coffee and delivered the Department's pocket money from a local bank.

"Hirschhorn, is that you?"

The bagman blinked at the president.

"Jesus, Isaac, nobody said you were part of this package."

"You're a lucky guy. Barbarossa will be here in a minute. If he catches you, he'll knock your brains out."

And the bagman rumbled down the stairs.

"Is that wise, Mr. President?" Matt asked. "Letting a crooked cop back out on the streets?"

"Matt, if we grab him now, we'll overplay our hand. Don't worry, he'll turn in his badge by tomorrow and run from Joey as fast as he can."

They didn't have to grope very long in the dark; Desirée led Isaac's search party to a crack of light under a door. Isaac didn't bother about a bell. He wrapped once with his knuckles on the rotting wood.

"Who's there?" a disembodied voice broke through the other side of the door.

"A friend."

There was a long silence. And Isaac began to feel bewitched, trying to explain himself to some guy he couldn't see.

"I'm looking for Tollhouse's tin man—a tattoo artist. This is your late mother's apartment. I'm Sidel."

The door opened. And Viktor did seem disembodied in the dim light. His face was bloodless. He stood in his undershirt, with a bandage around his middle.

Isaac entered with his search party. The apartment was nearly barren. It had a bureau and a bare-bones bed. There was a battered sofa in the sitting room and several chairs. It saddened Sidel, this ruthless stamp of love. Had Viktor's mother waited year after year in this railroad flat for a *pakhan* who would never come, Siberian Karl, a mystic, a murderer, a forger and a thief?

"Is this how your mother lived?" Isaac asked. "In a monk's cell? What happened to you?"

"I got careless," Rembrandt said.

"Why aren't you in Czechoslovakia? Karel told me that you were about to become the little king of Prague."

Rembrandt laughed with a certain bitterness, and it must have pained him to laugh. His face screwed up into a tantalizing half-mad look.

"A sovereign without his scepter. Karel promised that Prague was for sale."

"But you've been eating up all the real estate," Isaac said.

"That doesn't amount to much in Prague—it's Kafka country, or did you forget? I have all the documents from the banks, but Karel still holds the key to the kingdom. He's gone into business with Rainer Wolff, and both of them want me dead."

Now Isaac realized why Karel had been so eager to bolt. It had nothing to do with the Kremlin or his own conniving minions at Prague Castle. He'd used Isaac to climb out of the Bull's black hole and position himself as his own little king. Isaac wasn't the real fall guy. Rembrandt had ruined himself with his lottery.

Isaac turned to Matt. "Have the White House find the Bull, will ya?"

"Boss," Matt said, "I have him on the line."

Isaac swiped the mobile away from Matt with one of his paws.

"Bull, we have a problem. I need your pals at the Bureau to babysit for Rembrandt until we can relocate him."

"Isaac," Bull Latham said, "I wouldn't use the Bureau. You'll leave some residue, like a snail. We're better off with Wildwater."

"Wildwater," Isaac said, "always Wildwater." And he pressed down hard on the rabbit ears.

Within twenty minutes, three men and a woman arrived in Ray-Bans. Isaac felt uncomfortable around such civilian soldiers until Barbarossa came down from the roof with Captain Sarah.

"Joey, I'll feel much better if you put together a little unit to watch over these mothers. I'll pay your boys out of my own pocket."

"It won't be necessary, Dad. I'll call in a couple of favors."

"And if you catch hell from the Commish, you tell him I'll cut off all his federal funding . . ."

"Dad," Barbarossa said, "I'm untouchable."

"And take care of Marilyn, will ya? Ah, I almost forgot. Bring a doc along, some guy we can trust. We have to patch up this package. He's as pale as my cat's belly."

Isaac glanced at Rembrandt for the last time. "Hey, you owe me a tat."

And he left with his search party. Desirée had already discovered a mouse in this dump. She left it on the cracked sill of Rembrandt's door and scampered down the stairs like the absolute queen of the Lower East Side.

PART SIX

23

It was serendipity, something like that. Rainer Wolff, the Berlin publishing baron, had been invited by the Library of Congress to a symposium on the future of the printed word, and Isaac seized upon the symposium for his own concerns. Yes, he still had his collection of Modern Library classics from Columbia College. Yes, he would have killed to maintain the hegemony of the printed word. But he hated all the clatter of symposiums. Books would live or die without the constant screed of librarians, authors, and publishing barons. And, of course, POTUS was one of the invited guests.

He was asked to speak at the gala in the Great Hall of the Thomas Jefferson Building. Isaac was a commodity again, a precious piece of merchandise. The honeymoon he'd never had suddenly began. He'd given Rikers back to the warden and his Ninja Turtles, had gone into the bowels of a supermax facility—the Bing—and disarmed a band of desperados. He was pictured on the cover of the *Daily News*, below a banner headline:

POTUS TOP COP

The Democratic Caucus reversed itself and chased after Sidel. Republicans couldn't stop courting him. Even Ramona Dazzle was nice. All Isaac wanted to do was look into Rainer Wolff's eyes, so he could measure the man.

He always had a bad case of vertigo whenever he entered the Great Hall; he couldn't adjust himself to the dizzying heights, as if he was floating around in an Arabian bazaar, with a ceiling of blue glass and gold tidbits that seemed to swim in front of his eyes. There was a mosaic of blinding colors, a white marble floor inlaid with bands of brown, and twin statues of some goddess who represented both war and peace. Isaac was lost in this palace of infinite space. He didn't belong here, a college dropout like him. But he had a rabbinical streak.

"For one semester I lived inside a cradle of words. I read until my eyesight weakened. Sentences had their own perfume, sometimes the stink of death. I was like a hunter on an endless battlefield, strewn with marvelous debris. I had no existence beyond my reading self. Then I had to quit college, and I went into freefall. I became a cop, and I had to endure the metallic grip of handcuffs, but I can't imagine a world without books."

The guests at the gala stood around in their tinseled clothes and clapped for this curious president, who would have come to the Library of Congress in his windbreaker had his butler not shamed him into wearing a velvet bowtie, a crisp shirt, polished shoes, and an ancient Tuxedo from his tenure as the Pink Commish. Ramona Dazzle couldn't keep her hands off the Big Guy; she kept stroking the worn patches of his tux. She introduced him to a man in his eighties with exquisite white hair and the startling profile of a handsome hawk. The man wore a plum-colored velvet jacket.

"Saul, I'd like you to meet President Sidel."

Saul's Bellow.

The Big Guy was shaken. He knew Bellow might be at the gala. But the encounter itself was beyond his ability to dream.

"Augie," Isaac muttered. "I've been living all these years with Augie March. I can't forget Caligula, the cowardly eagle."

"There's a little bit of Caligula in all of us," the master said. "But I admire what you did at Rikers, Mr. President. You went into the heart of darkness and came out a winner."

"I'm not so sure," Isaac said.

"But it was almost *novelistic*. Perhaps you are what Augie might have become."

"I doubt it," Isaac said. "I'm more like the eagle."

Both of them laughed. Isaac had much less vertigo in this palace. Perhaps he had conquered his fear of heights. Guests grabbed at him, and he was pulled away from Saul Bellow. His chief of staff couldn't stop showing him off. He hadn't been a hero inside the Bing. He'd averted a slaughter, had saved the lives of inmates who'd been beaten and mauled by certain screws, and perhaps he'd also saved the screws. But now he was as cunning as Caligula. He kept shaking hands, whispering, shouting, kissing women's cheeks among all the tumult until he happened upon a man with an executioner's crystal-blue eyes.

Rainer Wolff.

And like Caligula again, he removed himself from all the tumult.

"I liked your little speech," the publishing baron said. "I, too, believe in the primacy of the written word, Mr. President."

And much, much more, Isaac mused. Bull Latham had told him about Rainer Wolff, an *Übermensch* of a different sort. Rainer had come from a distinguished merchant family with a hint of Jewish blood and might have fallen into the hands of the Gestapo and the SS. But Rainer was rescued from oblivion by Admiral Wilhelm Canaris, master of German military intelligence, who declared that he couldn't get along without his *"Jüdische"* protégé. Uncle Willie was a real enigma. He had little taste for Hitler's atrocities and delusions, yet his commandos at the Abwehr could cross borders like invisible men and sabotage whatever resistance there was to the Reich. Canaris had a monk's purity and a spy's contradictions. He was one of the earliest plotters against the Führer, but he couldn't participate in the failed July '44 plot. Hitler had removed his puzzling spymaster. Uncle Willie was held under house arrest, and was later delivered to one of the Abwehr's own dungeons at Flossenbürg castle, where he was hanged to death from a meat hook.

Rainer had also joined the plotters, but his role was never uncovered, and somehow he managed to remain loyal to military intelligence and its deposed master, Uncle Willie. The admiral had a mad daughter, Eva, who was locked away in a public *Krankenhaus* after his fall and might have died of neglect if Rainer hadn't moved her to a private clinic. He visited Eva as often as he could, wooing and threatening her keepers.

Rainer had another mission. He was in charge of the Abwehr's counterfeit currency. When his own forgers failed to produce, he was sent to the Eastern Front and suffered from a severe case of frostbite. Herr Kapitän Wolff came out of the war with two permanently crippled toes. He was both a hero and a villain, depending upon the angle and the mirage of history's own mirror. He took over his father's moribund publishing empire and made millions.

Rainer still had the look of a spymaster, Admiral Canaris' greatest disciple. Nearing seventy, he had a panther-like gait, even with his crippled toes. Isaac could tell from a glance that he'd never frighten Rainer into any kind of retreat. But he had to test the publishing baron, claw at him a little, reveal that he was aware of Rainer's murderous tricks.

"Herr Wolff," he said, "I have greetings from an old friend."

The blue eyes were no less alert. "But you must call me Rainer. We are almost comrades, Mr. President. Both of us were born in a brew of words. We are book lovers. What could possibly keep us apart?"

"Rembrandt," Isaac said.

The Berliner smiled. "You mean that gangster who walks around with a wooden box and paints pictures on people?"

"I believe Rembrandt was a partner of yours."

"Yes," Rainer said. "I had dealings with him and his little army of aging orphans. But I'm a businessman, Mr. President, and we cannot foresee the directions that our business affairs will take." He patted his mouth with a silk handkerchief that he kept in his sleeve. "Do you have a literary agent, Mr. President? You are also a painter, I suspect, but you paint with words, and not silly little bottles of ink. I would be very interested in publishing your memoirs."

Isaac wasn't going to let Rainer off the hook. "My memoirs might not be very flattering—to you."

Rainer smiled, his tobacco teeth glistening under the lamps of the Great Hall.

"Ah, but it would tantalize your readers, Mr. President. We would both make a killing. And if you gave me world rights, I could put together quite a package. Imagine, your memoirs could come out in Germany, England, America, France, and ten other markets within the same week. But I can't think of a title, and titles are important. What shall we call your book?"

"*The Death Lottery Rider.*"

Rainer sucked at Isaac's words. "That sounds like a crime novel, Mr. President, not a memoir."

"True," Isaac said. "But your own memoir, Herr Wolff, would amount to the same thing—a crime novel."

"I'm not ashamed of my past," Rainer said. "I served under Admiral Canaris. I led a team of saboteurs. We undermined Czech patriots, we slit their throats. But we did not butcher women and children."

"And you were kind to the admiral's crazy daughter."

Isaac must have found a secret niche. The crystalline eyes withdrew inside his skull, and his face rippled with anger.

"That was a private matter, Mr. President."

Isaac meant to claw a little deeper, rile the publishing baron, even if he had to rattle the dead. But he imagined Eva Canaris at the sanitarium, and it stuck in his craw. He didn't want to feel sympathy for a spymaster who had shielded a delicate girl from Gestapo bloodhounds.

"Herr Wolff, your past doesn't concern me. I'm worried about your future."

The Berliner's face stopped rippling. That arrogant, superior smirk had come back, and his eyes were crystal-pure again. "But the future is sealed," he said. "I will publish your memoirs."

Rainer bowed like a Prussian aristocrat—he was a gutter gangster, an assassin who had sipped from a silver spoon—and he quickly mingled with other guests at the gala with his panther-like gait.

I'll never nail that prick.

Sidel was filled with fury. He was ready for a massacre. He'd learned the art of war from Joe Barbarossa. *When in doubt, go to your guns.* But he couldn't shoot his way to Berlin, even with Joey at his side. So he finagled. He moved his financial wizard, Felix Mandel, from Treasury to the West Wing. He appointed Felix director of the Office of Management and Budget. It was a fancy title for the president's bagman. Felix had to oversee federal spending and sculpt the president's budget out of some invisible clay.

The Big Guy had invited Bull Latham to his first skull session with Felix in the Oval Office. Isaac didn't give a crap about his archives. Not a word was recorded, not a whisper was saved for posterity. It wasn't a matter of learning from Nixon's mistakes, of muffling another Watergate. Isaac had all the slyness of the Pink Commish.

There would be no Sidel presidential papers.

Felix sat on a plush white sofa next to Sidel, while the Bull sat on that sofa's twin on the far side of a teak coffee table. Felix could hear a rustling behind the president's purple drapes. It confused him; he couldn't believe that a large rat inhabited the Oval Office; then a creature with whiskers whirled through the air and plopped on Isaac's lap. Felix felt like a fool. He was face to face with the president's feral cat, Desirée, rescued from Rikers Island. She'd become almost as famous and coveted as Fala, FDR's black Scottish terrier. But Fala never tore the president's drapes, Fala never snarled, never frightened the White House staff. This mountainous white cat was meowing as she stared at Felix with some kind of fascination in her olive eyes.

"She's crazy about you," Sidel said. "Would ya like to hold my little girl?"

"No thanks, Mr. President."

The butler knocked, entered the Oval Office, and served them coffee and almond macaroons on the teak table. They drank their coffee out of porcelain demitasse cups embossed with the White House seal. Isaac fed Desirée a macaroon; she devoured it like a lioness and licked at the coffee in Isaac's cup.

"Felix," Isaac said in front of Bull Latham, "do we have a reptile fund?"

Felix's brows knit with consternation. He was jittery around the Bull and this monstrous cat on the president's lap.

Isaac had to repeat himself. "You know. Reptile fund. Le Carré."

The Bull winked and tried to educate Felix Mandel. "Actually, it wasn't British at all. It existed long before MI6. Bismarck had his own *Reptilienfonds* to bribe journalists and do other damage. I'm not including our intelligence services, and their black operational budgets. That's strictly academic. The question is, Felix, can we shove cash into someone's pocket without the scrutiny of Congress?"

Felix nodded once, while the cat devoured a second macaroon.

"Well," the Bull said, "that cash would be considered a reptile fund."

Felix didn't nod again. "Mr. President, I can thread the needle as well as any man, but I won't lie and steal."

"Not even to save the presidency?" the Bull asked.

Suddenly, without a warning sign, or even a meow, Desirée leapt onto Felix's lap. He let out a little scream, then calmed himself. But Felix was more confounded than ever. "I'm a numbers cruncher. I can create as many reptile funds as you want, but I have to have a good reason."

Now Isaac intervened. "Suppose some guy in Berlin—"

"You mean Rainer Wolff," Felix said, as if the White House had made him omniscient with a magical cat on his lap. "I saw you with Herr Wolff at the gala. I met him last year in Davos. He has quite a reputation. He was Hitler's chief counterfeiter, who nearly froze his ass off on the Eastern Front. I believe he was one of the first publishers to encourage Günter Grass. That's no small accomplishment."

"He's still a counterfeiter," Isaac insisted. "He manipulates currencies all the time. And Herr Wolff would increase his profit margin by having me dead. Didn't you once tell me I had zero chance of survival, that the biggest hedge fund managers were betting I wouldn't complete my *maiden year*? Your very words."

Felix found himself stroking Desirée's wild white mane, soft as velvet, despite the scabs. He had a triumphant grin. "I know, I know. *Statistically* you're a dead man. But I was a mite too clever for my own good. You can't kill a president just like that. It's not cost effective. It would rattle the markets and create a worldwide recession—the dollar would slide and slide. He'd never be invited to Davos again."

Isaac hunched his shoulders. "Felix, what if Herr Wolff did the markets a favor? I've gone after Big Tobacco. I'll take on pharmaceuticals next. I'm on the *Wall Street Journal*'s most wanted list."

"There's no such list," Felix said. "Yes, some of the papers have called you a pinko, but FDR was called a lot worse, and he survived in a wheelchair."

"But FDR was a patrician," Isaac said. "And I rose out of a pickle barrel on Essex Street. Bull, tell him the bitter truth."

The Bull rolled his eyes, as if he were talking to a child and not the savviest economist at the table, a demon who could destroy a nation's wealth with his phantom currencies and now had conquered the Boss's feral cat. Desirée was purring with both eyes shut.

"Felix, did you forget that there's a lottery with Isaac's number on it, started by the bankers themselves? The payoff increases exponentially the longer Isaac lives. It's become an assassin's bullet, and Herr Wolff is behind the bounty."

"I don't believe it. The honchos at Davos would have known about this dark side of Rainer. Industrialists certainly have their own secrets. I'm not part of that privileged club. But you can't hide something like this."

"It's not such a secret," Isaac said. "I have a ghoul on my back wherever I go. There are sockers waiting for me, even at the White House. My helicopter pilot is living here in the attic. He has a little boy, and the socker was posing as the boy's maid. She whacked me with a white-hot iron. Ask the Bull."

Felix turned pale. He should have realized that the presidency itself was a statistical nightmare. He'd created ghost currencies, knew what a flood of fake fifty-dollar bills could do in a volatile market, but figured POTUS could ride out the worst storm, at least at the White House. He scratched his lip for a moment. It was a nervous habit he'd picked up at Davos. Desirée licked his hand, and he almost licked her back. Soon he'd be as mountainous as the cat. *Concentrate*, he told himself.

"And I suppose Herr Wolff selected this socker, as you call her?"

"No," the Bull said. "But he paid for her upkeep."

And now Felix was in his element. "We don't really need a reptile fund, Mr. President. I can ruin Herr Wolff, bring him down on my own. It's not strictly legal. But I can juggle behind his back. I'll tap into his holdings. A publishing empire isn't that different from a nation. Instead of a phantom currency we'll introduce phantom paper. He'll become a pauper after six months."

"Felix," Isaac said, "that won't do the trick. He'll build another empire, and he'll continue coming after me."

"Then he's a barracuda," Felix said. "And we'll need a reptile fund. But what is it for?"

"To hire sockers of our own," Isaac said.

And Felix started to tremble. He was caught in POTUS's whirlwind, and he couldn't get out. He'd lose face if he returned to Treasury. He was Isaac's secret chancellor of the exchequer, not a hatchet man exactly, but the financier of hatchet men. And he'd have to get used to that label.

"There no point dancing around," Isaac said. "We have to get rid of Herr Wolff."

Felix was as cautious as a chancellor of the exchequer could be. "Mr. President, I'll get you your reptile fund, but I'd rather not know who these reptiles are."

"Then you'd be a straw man, a clerk among clerks. You wouldn't like it very much, being on my B-list, a wizard kept on a string. Is that what you want?"

"No," he muttered, with Desirée still on his lap, creasing his trousers with her claws.

Isaac tossed his head back, like FDR. "That's grand. We'll have to hire the hitter behind the hitters, General Tollhouse."

Now it was the Bull who groaned. "Isaac, I thought you hated Wildwater."

"I do. But we have limited options. I can't run to Berlin wearing a mask. I'm only a guy with a Glock. I have to travel with a whole fucking fleet. It has to be a Wildwater op."

"But Rainer Wolff is probably Wildwater's biggest client."

"That's why we need the reptile fund," Isaac said. "And a little pressure from you."

"And what if he picks up his tent and moves to Switzerland?"

"Then we'll come down hard on the Swiss."

"So," said the Bull, "we remove Herr Wolff's options and shove him toward the kill zone."

"Please," Felix said. "I'd prefer not to hear that word—kill."

Isaac tugged at Felix's necktie. "My budget director can't be a big baby. Bull, how can we scare the shit out of those Swiss bankers and put an end to their lottery?"

"Isaac," the Bull said, "Herr Wolff has his own Secret Service."

"So do I. And that didn't stop Wildwater or one of its affiliates from planting a bomb right under my ass at Karel Ludvik's dacha."

"But you walked out of that explosion in one piece," the Bull had to insist.

Felix's head was swimming. In one day he'd gone from a master of phantom currencies to a phantom himself, employed by Isaac Sidel.

"Felix," Isaac said, "you can go now. The Vice President and I have certain details to discuss."

Felix panicked. He felt evicted, left out. But he couldn't contradict POTUS, and he couldn't get up.

"Mr. President, I have Desirée on my lap."

"So tell the little girl to jump in the lake. Ah, I'm joking Felix."

Isaac cooed at Desirée, and the cat leapt onto his shoulder.

Felix climbed off the sofa with cat hair on his wobbly, leaden knees. He was about to return to his own office in the West Wing when he banged into Ramona Dazzle, who seemed in the dumps.

"What's going on?" she growled at him.

"Nothing much," Felix said. "POTUS and the Bull are plotting the end of the world. And they can't do it without me and my numbers."

Felix hopped away from Ramona Dazzle without another word.

24

ch, the Americans and their Marshall Plan, Rainer muttered to himself.

Only such creatures could have built their Great Hall in homage to Thomas Jefferson, a slave master with slave mistresses. Rainer loved books and the miracle of warfare, the constant rustle of spies. War was like Mozart, not a science, not an art, but pure music, the melody of melodies, with blood and bones as the excrement, the waste matter that couldn't corrupt the music. He was happiest at that nondescript gray building on the north bank of the Landwehr

Canal, the Abwehr's hidden headquarters, so secret that the Führer himself didn't have a clue where Uncle Willie spent his days and most nights. Rainer was a bachelor then. He preferred to visit brothels. He was second in command of the Brandenburg Brigade, the admiral's specialized unit of soldier-saboteurs. Their barracks was right in Berlin. Uncle Willie could have arrested Herr Hitler and his whole hierarchy—cleaned the slate in one swoop. Rainer had planned the op half a million times—the streets, the routes, the hours, the calling in of firemen to stop traffic, while the Abwehr's black buses sped across Berlin with the culprits in hand. He would have hung them all in the rear yard of the barracks. But Uncle Willie had that touch of reticence, along with the tremor in his right arm.

Herr Admiral, you are not one of them, and when they find that out, they will rip you apart. We have our boys. We must use them before it is too late.

But it was always too late for Uncle Willie. The SS stripped him of the Brandenburgers, and without his boys he was a sly old fox who'd lost his teeth. The admiral's boys became ciphers rather than saboteurs until the SS integrated them into their own units. Rainer was left behind, even after Uncle Willie was arrested, and the Abwehr itself was a symphony of ghosts.

He'd been in love with Eva, the admiral's older daughter, and his love was a little like the melody of war. He'd kissed her once, only once, when Uncle Willie wasn't looking, and had to clutch Eva's fist behind the admiral's back; this strange, furtive romance of pecking and patter was also the language of a spy. She was a gentle creature who had nightmares of the world's end, and Uncle Willie didn't want her involved with one of his own saboteurs. "My brutal boys," he would say, "my brutal boys." But the admiral was plucked from his gray building by the SS, beaten and abused, and his best saboteur had to shield Eva from the Gestapo, who would have shipped her off to one of their euthanasia hotels, filled with mental defectives and dwarfs. He kept her at a clinic, had to bribe the nurses with Reichsmarks he printed at his own press. And then Rainer himself was sent to the Eastern Front, not as a Brandenburger, but as a lowly officer with a bundle of raw recruits. He survived with his own tricks of the trade, a captain who lost every single one of his boys.

And then he vanished into a normal, anonymous life. He married an heiress, took over his father's firm. Yet what could business affairs mean to him, a saboteur at heart? He had his own secret headquarters, like Uncle Willie. He found a replica of that old gray building on the north bank of the Canal. It remained empty for years, a warehouse of memories, until the memories began to congeal. Rainer hired his own clerks, involved them in shady deals. He siphoned off assets from his publishing empire.

He'd stumbled upon Viktor Danzig—*Rembrandt*—at a high-class brothel in Hamburg a dozen years ago. They were both wild, warring creatures, both without a pinch of fear; they could read their own ambitions in one another's eyes, their secret delight in uncovering avenues of disorder and smashing other men's idols. They signed a pact on the spot, created a partnership in crime, while Rainer revived his old counterfeit currency section from the Abwehr. But none of his counterfeiters had Rembrandt's masterful touch, none could provide paper without a flaw. Soon he and Viktor had their own Swiss bank, their own properties in Basel and Berne. Meanwhile, his family prospered. He had two lovely little girls, Gretel and Wilhelmina. They grew up, married, had children of their own, while *Großvater* Rainer bribed politicians, sat on economic councils, dealt with the Stasi on both sides of the Berlin Wall. But Viktor proved unpredictable. He went around with a wooden box and didn't take care of essential details. That's why Rainer had to strike—like a commando from the Landwehr Canal.

He had Rembrandt on the run. But things went sour a day after that gala in the Great Hall. Rosa Malamud's boutiques on Paris' Left Bank were all firebombed. And Rosa was ruined overnight. Her accounts disappeared, her credit cards were frozen, as if she had been visited by a whirlwind.

Michael Davit fared even worse. He lost his holdings in Manchester, and the school for assassins he had nurtured for years—his flagship enterprise—suddenly fell apart. The premises had been vandalized; all the assassins were gone. And Michael Davit was found with a broken neck in an abandoned barn near his country manor.

Rainer had inherited Uncle Willie's cool head and cool heart. He wouldn't check out of his hotel near the White House. He was still at the Washington, a floor above Pesh Olinov's suite. He marched down one flight and rang the Russian's bell. It was Olinov himself who came to the door—his bald thug of a bodyguard must have fled. There were bruises under Olinov's eye. His mouth was bloody. His velvet bathrobe had been turned inside out.

"Was it the soldier?" Rainer asked.

"Yes," the Russian whispered.

They entered Olinov's suite like two conspirators. The Russian couldn't stop shivering. There was a great rent in the carpet that ran like a lopsided river across the sitting room. A plush chair had been overturned.

Olinov was crying now. "We cannot continue," he said.

"When have I ever failed you?"

"We cannot continue," Olinov whispered again.

And Rainer realized that the soldier was also in the room.

"Come out, General," he said with the same imperturbable smile. And Tollhouse appeared from behind the lavender drapes in his Baltimore Orioles cap and one of Isaac Sidel's signature windbreakers.

Rainer marveled at Tollhouse's fire-marked face; the *soldier* looked almost like an albino. The cap must have covered the wig that Tollhouse had to wear.

"Rainer, tell me, why does Gorbachev tolerate this little pest who lies and steals and has a monopoly on toilet paper?"

"It's simple," Rainer said. "Without Pesh, he could never navigate the many mousetraps of the KGB. It's Pesh who keeps him in power."

"Then Gorbachev must be a very lonely man."

Tollhouse dismissed Olinov without bothering to wave his hand. "You can go now. Get the fuck out of here. I've already paid your bill. You've given up your residence at the Washington. Gorbachev will need his court jester in Moscow if he intends to survive."

"General, I haven't packed," Olinov said with a whimper.

"*Out.*"

And Olinov vanished into the hall in his velvet robe turned inside out.

"You shouldn't be so harsh," Rainer said. "Pesh has his good points. He was once very loyal."

"But this isn't the Boy Scouts. I never admired merit badges."

Rainer sat on one of Pesh's sofas. "And what manner of fate have you prepared for me?"

Tollhouse stroked the torn bill of his cap; he could have been a baseball manager who'd seen better times. His mind had begun to drift.

"General, I paid you a fortune—to rid the world of Sidel. You never lost a penny on my account. You had every chance, and still you failed."

"I didn't fail," Tollhouse said. "I always worked for Sidel. He just didn't realize it."

Rainer considered strangling the general with the velvet sash that clung to the drapes. "Yet you took my millions without a qualm."

"You got your money's worth," Tollhouse said. "Sidel was stranded on Pennsylvania Avenue for months. You maneuvered around him, sold off whatever paper you had, manipulated the markets around the *possibility* of POTUS becoming a corpse. You didn't need much more than the myth of his destruction. I made a rich man even richer. So stop crying those crocodile tears. He couldn't even travel to Prague, his dream town. But he should have gone to your island metropolis. West Berlin was the place for him, with its Turks, its whores, its spies, its squatters, hunched inside a wall. He'd love Berlin. It would remind him of another ghetto—the Lower East Side. But it's too late. You won't be there to greet him."

Rainer could see the madness in Tollhouse's eyes, plots spiraling out of control. But if Tollhouse really wanted Rainer dead, he would have gone for the jugular and not toyed with Michael Davit. Rainer had some kind of protective cloak that wasn't clear. Ah, it had something to do with that little gray house on the Canal. Tollhouse worshiped Uncle Willie and the Abwehr—that band of aristocratic saboteurs, who would suddenly appear behind the enemy's lines, speaking Polish better than the Poles. They were consummate actors in the theatre of *Kriegspiel*. So Rainer used the general's own skills against him.

"*Mensch*, if I don't leave the capital alive, the Library of Congress will never forgive you. I was an honored guest at the gala. Thomas Jefferson will rise out of his grave."

"Let him rise. I told you. I work for Sidel."

Rainer squeezed as hard as he could. It was *Kriegspiel*. But the targets were much less distinct. "Big Balls has turned the tables. You've been hired to get rid of me."

Tollhouse laughed for the first time, but his burnt skin had little elasticity. And he wore a grimace like a death mask.

"Yes, your body count is in the package. But it's difficult to ice a Brandenberger. It's against my principles. You know, I'm sentimental about certain things. Rainer, you were my Roman Legion. Will you promise to stay clear of the president?"

"No," Rainer said.

Tollhouse must have been hit with fatigue. Even the grimace was gone.

"I'll kill your wife, your children, and your children's children. I'll decimate entire blood lines. The whole population of West Berlin will suffer on account of you."

And now Rainer went on the attack. He'd trapped the general. He had much better terrain.

"Dear general, my answer won't be any different no matter how many you kill."

"Good," Tollhouse said. "The Library of Congress can go fly a kite. You're now officially Wildwater's guest. You can have safe passage to West Berlin. But if you go near your corporate headquarters in Hamburg, I promise, you'll never get back."

He'd run to Hamburg, visit the Red Castle, his favorite bordello—it had had several facelifts over the past forty years, had started in a grungy cellar, then climbed several flights of stairs to the attic, with its glorious harbor view. He no longer went to the bordellos in Berlin. They were filled with black marketeers, spies and gangsters from Istanbul, MI6 outcasts, and American generals and millionaires; and the girls wouldn't shave their legs or sponge themselves between clients. He wouldn't mind dying in a tub, like Marat—at the Red Castle. Tollhouse could hire one of the little darlings to slit his throat, as long as she shaved her legs.

He'd have his last glimpse of the harbor, a lyrical wasteland with its endless rotting warehouses and wharves, its derricks, its cranes that seemed to scratch the sky, and the ships themselves, like hulking pharaohs that could barely keep afloat—that was Rainer's little paradise. But Tollhouse was much too curious about the wonder of Rainer Wolff to have him killed. His hooded eyes suddenly brightened like those of a little child.

"Tell me about the admiral?"

Rainer had him hooked, this Moby Dick with scarred white flesh. "*Mensch*, what is there to tell? He was a little man in lumpy clothes."

"But he had the precision of a celestial clock. Your brigade was always there first, at every fucking battle."

And now Rainer scolded this mad general. "We were saboteurs— we had to be first. It was *Kriegspiel*. We had a whole warehouse of uniforms next to the Canal. We liked to parade around Berlin as British troops—it scared the pants off people. The admiral loved practical jokes. We could have fooled Churchill himself. My cockney accent was impeccable."

Tollhouse grew wistful. "Get the hell out of here. Go back to Berlin."

Rainer wasn't sure if it was a death sentence, a battle cry, or both. Tollhouse had his own sense of *Kriegspiel*. Wildwater was now part of the West Wing.

Tollhouse left him there without a word of goodbye. Rainer hiked upstairs to his own suite. And he went down to the lobby with his luggage and an old leather briefcase that had been repaired a dozen times by an old Jewish tailor near the checkpoint at Chausseestraße. The tailor was ninety years old. He'd worked exclusively for the Abwehr until the admiral smuggled him out of Berlin, and into one of his safe houses in the hinterland. The tailor lived in England for a while after the war. But Rainer begged him to return, and he bought the tailor his own shop. Rainer never had to buy a single article of clothes after that; everything he wore had been sewn by hand. He often had lunch with the tailor, who never discussed the war and the death camps with his benefactor, but still looked at Rainer like a live bullet burning into his head . . .

Tollhouse had paid the publishing baron's hotel bill, and had a black limousine waiting for him outside the Washington. Rainer entered the limo like a willful, walking target. Would the chauffeur drive him to Dulles International or a Wildwater warehouse on the banks of the Anacostia? Rainer didn't seem to care. It was *Kriegspiel* all over again. He didn't think of his wife, or his children, or the mistress he had in Milan above a Louis Vuitton shop. He thought of Eva Canaris, of her squirrelly hand, like some secret weapon of desire. All his life he had to find sustenance in the memory of a single kiss. Rainer shut his eyes and fell into a profound sleep.

25

W e'll do it at David."

Sidel hadn't forgotten the art of the Lower East Side. He loved to play *shadkhen*—marriage broker and wizard—with his helicopter pilot.

It gave him a measure of delight that Colonel Oliver had given up his widower's weeds, moved out of the White House attic, and rented a flat in Georgetown with Captain Sarah.

"We'll do it at David."

"Boss," the colonel muttered. "I can't follow you."

"Your engagement party," Isaac said. "We'll do it at David."

Stef shivered in silent protest. "Wait a minute. I never said we were engaged. It's an experiment between Sarah and me—a trial run."

"Terrific," Isaac said. "And when the trial run is over, we'll do it at Camp David."

It was wiser not to argue with POTUS when he was in one of his moods. "Yeah, I get ya, boss. We'll do it at David."

The White House rocked with madcap energy. Sidel's ratings hit the roof. Seventy-nine percent of the voting population agreed that POTUS was the best damn cop and commander in chief to have around in a period of uncertainty, when the Eastern Bloc was unraveling and Gorbachev made overture after overture to the West. *Glasnost*, what the hell could it mean? Did Moscow want to move into the wild lands of Alaska and become our fifty-first state?

There were Kremlinologists at every little corner, including the White House, where Isaac met with all his mavens in the Situation Room. East Berlin had become the capital of the hardliners, according to the Kremlinologists. Erich Honecker, first secretary of the East German Central Committee, didn't want *glasnost*. He hewed to a strict socialist line. And when there were riots in the streets, Gorbachev wouldn't come to the rescue. He was more interested in the humming capitalist music of West Berlin.

"It's a ploy," Tim Vail said, "a trick. Honecker's his man. Gorby will have to prop him up."

"No," said Felix Mandel, Isaac's budget director. "He'd rather let East Berlin sink."

The Kremlinologists in the room trained their daggers on him. But that couldn't stop Felix. "East Berlin is a phantom city, an apparition, a poisoned fairy tale, a porous myth."

"And West Berlin?" rasped Ramona Dazzle, who sided with the Kremlinologists. "Gorby will strangle it out of existence."

"No," said Felix. "No, no, no. It's sucked all the energy out of the East."

And now Ramona gave him one of her demonic smiles. "What about the Wall?"

"Another apparition," said Felix.

"The Wall Jumpers wouldn't think so," said Tim Vail, who pressed a button on his new silver wand; four screens hummed with competing images of a raffish man in a ripple of bullets—an unemployed clown perhaps—as he fell from the Wall like a wayward pin of flesh caught in a flicker of light; some graffiti artist had decorated this particular piece of the Wall with sunflowers and dragonflies in garish, defiant colors.

Suddenly Isaac began to mourn the ghost of Stalin inside him.

"But I ruled New York as a socialist town."

"Sure, boss," Felix said. "The tycoons let you have your little toy palace. But where did the *gelt* come from for your pet projects? You could bob and weave around all the contradictions."

"And you're saying East Berlin will perish?" Isaac asked with a waver in his voice.

"That Wall will be around for another fifty years," said Ramona, who leapt into the fray.

The Kremlinologists nodded their heads. "Another fifty, at least."

"And what should we do in the meantime?" Isaac had to ask his mavens. He felt bewildered, like little Alice surrounded by the Queen of Hearts and her royal retinue.

"Nothing," said Tim Vail. "Gorby will fall flat on his ass. The KGB will put in one of their cronies, and Honecker will prevail."

"Then it's business as usual," Isaac said.

The Bull had been sitting there in silence, his eyes beetling across the Situation Room. He was usually rhapsodic with all the mavens around. Isaac had to drag him into the conversation.

"It's a different ballgame," the Bull said in that cryptic manner of his, as if he had some overwhelming truth he was about to reveal.

"How so?" asked one of the Kremlinologists.

"We have POTUS. And he's the best weapon in our stockpile."

"But I thought it was too dangerous for him to travel," Ramona said.

"The danger days are over."

And the meeting was adjourned. But the Bull signaled to Isaac, and they sat alone in the Situation Room. The Bull chuckled to himself like an intelligence chief after some great coup.

"Rainer Wolff is toast."

"Bull, I haven't read about his demise in any obit."

"It doesn't matter," the Bull said. "It was a classic Wildwater op. Tollhouse met with the Nazi, and set him straight. That old boy can't hurt us—dead or alive. But we have one small wrinkle, sir."

Isaac could feel a shower of shit swirling over his head. "And what's that?"

"Tollhouse thinks he deserves the Medal of Freedom. And he would like the ceremony performed in the Blue Room in front of all the cameras."

"He's a murderer," Isaac muttered. "I won't do it."

"But you commissioned that murderer to save your life. We paid him a handsome fee. Felix had to juggle all our books to find the cash."

"I won't do it," Isaac said. "Mr. Wildwater stays in the shadows, where he belongs—and that's final."

But everything was more complicated than it appeared to be. Isaac couldn't have a rogue general wandering about with a grudge against the commander in chief. So he pinned the medal on Tollhouse at a secret ceremony. And Mr. Wildwater promised never to wear it in public. Such were the compromises a president had to make.

He had no guests at the White House other than Desirée, and needed none. The monstrous white cat invaded all of Isaac's meetings with his cabinet. She frightened the wits out of Ramona Dazzle, hissing and arching her back every time Isaac's chief of staff left her corner suite. And Desirée was still in love with Felix. She would serenade the budget director, sitting near his office, and meowing like a moonstruck frog. Still, she revealed her matted, warlike belly to no one but Isaac, leaping onto his desk in the Oval Office, scattering papers and penholders until the boss stroked her religiously. Desirée demanded the Big Guy's complete attention, and didn't always get it.

There was a logistical problem: what part would she play in a presidential lift package? She could fly with him to David, sit on his lap in Dragon, when he had to ride around the capital to meet up with some diplomat, but what about all the other packages? Queen Elizabeth had invited him to Windsor Castle, and would Desirée fit in with the queen's corgis? Would she rip these royal dogs to shreds? Should a mongrel like her—a cat as chaotic as Rikers itself—be permitted on Windsor's grounds?

A European junket was being planned for POTUS, a kind of jubilee. He would sit with Elizabeth at Windsor, chat up the British prime at Chequers, meet with the French president at the Élysée, visit the house where Beethoven was born in Bonn, with the German chancellor at his side, take a White Top to West Berlin, ride down the "Ku damm" in Dragon, and deliver a speech in front of the Wall.

The itinerary still had to be polished to perfection. The Secret Service didn't want him near the Berlin Wall.

"Boss, there will be a whole bunch of squatters, Lefties, and anarchists," said Matt Malloy. "We won't be able to protect you."

"Stop it," Isaac said. "I had the same squatters, Lefties, and anarchists in Manhattan, and I managed."

They solved the riddle of Desirée. The delinquent cat wouldn't be allowed near Windsor, out of respect to Elizabeth and her dogs, but she would have a special basket and litter box on board Air Force One. Still, Isaac's interns had to anticipate the difficulty of having a cat with the appeal of a movie star.

"Sir, the foreign press will want photo ops with you and Desirée."

"They can have all the photo ops they want, at their own risk. Desirée might not take kindly to their cameras."

The Big Guy was on a roll. He was more coveted in the Deep South than Republican Party bosses, and was called the Pistolero President in the heartland of Illinois. He wouldn't stay on script—there was no script that could handcuff Sidel. He would walk into a fundraiser, attack Wall Street donors, and speak about financing schools in the nation's worst barrios. "We have to lure our best teachers into the poorest districts, so that billionaires will beg to have their children enrolled in these schools. Make them better and better—that's how you solve de facto segregation."

But reporters had to remind him that New York City had been one of the worst offenders, that it had its own invisible wall.

"Not so invisible," Isaac said. "I failed. I had Merlin, but Merlin didn't make much of a dent."

"Then how will you find a solution, sir?"

"With blood, sweat, and volunteers. I'll teach in one of the problem schools myself."

The reporters smiled and winked at one another. "And it will cost the taxpayer millions just to solve the logistics of getting you in and out of there."

That realization also cost Sidel. He was still trapped within the confines of the presidency, no matter how much freedom he had to travel. Windsor Castle would have the same hot wind as the West Wing. He could have bullied his way into Prague, followed Kafka's steps, stone by stone, and he'd have been just as blue. He was as much a prisoner of circumstance as the Queen of Hearts. And while he wandered about the residence with his own crazy cat, who was ruining the White House carpets with her claws, he looked up and found Colonel Oliver in his flight jacket.

"Stef, why the hell are you here? Am I part of some secret lift package?"

"We'll do it at David."

Isaac was still caught up in a woeful dream of self-entrapment.

"Kid, have I missed something? Am I out of commission?"

"We'll do it at David," his pilot repeated. "Sarah and I have agreed—to an engagement party."

Isaac was the last to learn about the lift package. That's how low he'd been, how far down in the dumps. The Bull himself had arranged the lift. The engagement party was meant as a surprise to Sidel. He put on his cap and his windbreaker, had to coax Desirée into her travel cage, while the White House butler bundled up her litter box and portions of wet and dry food, and within ten minutes they were on the South Lawn, with Marine One revving up. Isaac was the sole passenger—with his cat and a pair of Secret Service agents, who clung to the shadows.

The White Top danced and swerved above the lawn, and Sidel felt a strange lightness about him, a lifting of the soul. It lasted deep into Maryland as they rode the mountain range. And when he glimpsed the rudiments of his presidential retreat—Cactus, as his own protectors called it—that lightness of soul was still there. The cabins, lodges, barracks, and roads were laid out like some abandoned village caught under a spell. And perhaps Isaac was the enchanter—with his cat.

They were all waiting at Aspen Lodge. Captain Sarah, young Max, the Bull, Felix Mandel, Ramona Dazzle, who rarely accompanied the Big Guy to David, Matt Malloy, a few interns and aides, and Isaac's own private Seabee, Charles, who had once lived near Willie Mays in Harlem Heights.

Isaac's mind was playing tricks. For a moment he could has sworn that General Tollhouse was at Aspen, wearing the Medal of Freedom Isaac had forbidden him to wear. But it was one more apparition that flew away. Captain Sarah kissed him on the cheek.

Ramona was subdued around such company. She couldn't seem to find a proper role.

Bull Latham edged her aside, since he was both maestro and master of ceremonies, and part-time president when the boss's head was in the clouds.

"Ladies and gents, we've assembled here at Aspen Lodge to honor the engagement of Colonel Stefan Oliver and Captain Sarah Rogers, in the presence of their *rabbi*, Isaac Sidel, who brought them together in his own inimitable way. A toast to the president—and to the colonel and his fiancée."

"*Their* fiancée," said Felix Mandel, who was a bit tipsy in the miasma off the mountain.

"To the president!" shouted Isaac's guests, clutching glasses of ginger ale. "And to the honorees—Stef and Sarah."

The Secret Service joined in the merriment. Isaac swayed about the room with Max on his shoulders. He even danced with Ramona, whose body stiffened. He had little sense of modern music. His temperament remained in the '40s and hovered around Franklin Roosevelt's war. Bandstand stuff—Glenn Miller, the Andrews Sisters, Benny Goodman, Dinah Shore, and the Golden Toothpick, Frank Sinatra. He'd followed the Toothpick's career, had seen him perform at the Paramount, amid a battalion of bobby-soxers, screaming, clutching their scalps, as the Toothpick swayed on the bandstand, hitting notes that Caruso might have envied—there'd never been another balladeer like the Toothpick. Isaac's own history was wrapped around FDR, Eleanor, too, William Bendix in *Back to Bataan*, or was it *Guadalcanal Diary*? Isaac was a little thief during the war years. He and his baby brother Leo had their own black market. Leo Sidel was the dirty little secret of the Sidel administration. Leo lived in a trailer park. He was an alcoholic and a writer of bad checks. Bull Latham's pals in the FBI looked after Leo, who'd been bribed and pampered, and forbidden to go near the White House.

"Leo Sidel's a poison pill," Brenda, Isaac's first chief of staff, had warned. "He'll drag you down into the abyss." And Isaac had to take all of it into his final reckoning. But he missed Little Leo at the party in Aspen Lodge. The Big Guy had abandoned his own baby brother.

He whispered in the vice president's ear. "Bull, are you sure Little Leo's alright?"

"He's thriving, boss."

"In a trailer park?"

"That's the style he likes," the Bull said. "We clear all his bad checks. We'd diaper him if we had to."

"But suppose a reporter finds out who the fuck he is?"

"Such a person would never get close enough to Leo. And if some wise guy ever did, we'd haul his ass off to Quantico and put him in a reeducation program."

"But couldn't I visit Leo once?" Isaac whined.

"Boss, I beg you, don't go near that fire. We'll all get burned. That brother of yours is a publicity hound. Once he gets a whiff, we'll never put the genie back in the bottle."

The Bull shoved away from him, but Isaac wasn't finished yet.

"What sort of alias does my brother use?" Isaac shouted within earshot of all his guests.

"Leo Little," the Bull said.

Leo Little.

How poetic, and appropriately cruel. Leo had stayed little all his life, while Isaac burgeoned around him like some man-eating plant. Desirée wasn't the monster in these parts—it was Isaac Sidel. He'd let his cat out of the cage the moment he arrived at Aspen. She sniffed all the food. She didn't want her cat fare. Isaac had to feed her hummus and hot dogs from his own plate. She licked ginger ale out of the Big Guy's glass and leapt onto Felix's lap, sat there like a princess with wounds in her white coat, while Isaac watched Stef and Sarah dance to the elegiac sounds of the Golden Toothpick.

The lovebirds danced and danced, and then Sarah herself coaxed Isaac out onto the floor.

"You were the matchmaker, boss. I first made love to Stef in your flannel robe. And don't you play the innocent party."

"So I'm the culprit now."

"Yes," she said.

"And you be nice to Max, hear?"

"He'll never adore me as much as he adores you. You're his Uncle Isaac."

And Sidel returned her to Stef. He didn't climb into bed until well past midnight. It was his Seabee who cleaned up all the mess.

Isaac had a wet dream. He was making love to a woman with beautiful flanks. It was full of heartbreak, as the woman vanished from his bed. He woke like a silver bullet at the crack of dawn. The light burst through his picture window. The Seabees must have attended to the salt lick. Isaac watched a lone male fawn dance tentatively toward the lick on its long legs. The little whitetail tumbled once, and got up, like a soft bridge repairing itself. Where was the rest of its herd? Isaac prayed that there wasn't a gray wolf or any other predator lurking around.

But the real predator was inside Aspen. Desirée stood on her hind legs and followed the movement of that fawn with hungry eyes.

"You harm that little fellah and it's curtains for you, understand?"

The cat bumped Isaac with her bullet head and disappeared from the picture window. That's when Isaac saw a man in a worn winter coat limp toward the lick with a wooden box in his hand. Another apparition, damn it. But this apparition wouldn't go away. How did Rembrandt get inside the compound's electric walls?

Isaac had a more urgent problem. Desirée must have broken through a porch screen; she leapt toward the wobbly little whitetail like the Rikers cat that she was. And then the fawn's mama appeared from behind the shrubs. And while Desirée sailed in midair, the doe batted at her with one hoof—the cat shot across the yard like a blurry football.

Isaac was prepared to mourn until he heard Desirée howl. She rose on her paws, her back curled in defeat, and withdrew to her own hidden lair, while Rembrandt climbed the steps to Isaac's patio. The Big Guy didn't have to ask any questions—it was Bull Latham who had let Rembrandt through the gate. Either Rembrandt was in the Bull's pocket, or they had reached some kind of an accord. Isaac wasn't an absolute imbecile. While he reigned as president, the Bull ruled. Isaac had the ceremonial robes, but he was like a blind horse who raged—the Bull called him "boss" and kept control. It wasn't anything like a bloodless coup. The Bull was loyal to Sidel in his own fashion. Isaac was as much of an infant as Little Leo. He'd burst through City Hall with his Glock, but what mark had he really left? Rikers was still there . . .

"Viktor, did you give the Bull a long lease on your paper?"

"Not at all," Rembrandt said. "I promised to give up Ulysses Grant."

"And what if you come up short one day?"

Rembrandt shuddered in his worn coat. "Big Balls, I didn't come to Camp David to discuss my affairs."

"Then why did you come?" Isaac had to ask.

"I think you earned your tat, Mr. President. Soon you'll be one of my registered werewolves."

A registered werewolf.

"I like it. Where's Renata?"

"Best not to ask," Rembrandt whispered, pointing to the microphones he imagined in Aspen's walls.

"Would you prefer to live in Prague? I can put the squeeze on Karel Ludvik."

Rembrandt perused Isaac with his own piercing eyes. "Mr. President, I had to sell off my assets to survive."

Desirée appeared, with a bruise on her bullet head. She climbed on Isaac's lap the moment he sat down. She was purring like a ghost in a graveyard.

"That's quite a beast."

Rembrandt set his box down on Isaac's coffee table, opened it, fiddled with his needle, his brushes, and pots of indelible ink.

"Take off your shirt, please."

Isaac removed his pajama top, and Rembrandt frowned at the hair on Isaac's chest.

"I can't work in that forest. It will soak up all the ink."

He shaved Isaac's chest with a pearl-handled razor that had once belonged to a barber in the gulag; his father had won it in a bidding war with another *pakhan*. Rembrandt's wooden box was a portable tattoo shop. He didn't have mirrors with retractable necks and an electromagnetic "gun." He had to use a primitive electric pen with his pots of ink. He hunched in the light that glanced off the picture window. He wore a surgeon's gloves and kept wiping the wounds in Isaac's skin with swabs of alcohol. Isaac winced as the pen's knifelike needle cut into him with Rembrandt's design. There were no lunch breaks. Even Isaac's Seabee wasn't allowed to interrupt. And Isaac had to imprison that wild cat in the crate Charles had prepared for her, stuffed with old towels, or she might have jarred the path of Rembrandt's pen with a sudden leap.

Rembrandt toiled for sixteen hours, letting the ink dry before he went back to his electric pen. It was a maddening process. Isaac had to gulp half a gallon of water, while Rembrandt didn't wet his lips once. He couldn't even look at the tat after all the artistry was done. He wore a bandage over his heart like a soldier plucked from battle.

Rembrandt had to leave before the "unveiling" of his tattoo.

"What if I don't like it?"

"It's not an ornament, Big Balls. You're a *chelovek*. You have to like it."

"When can I take a peek?"

"Not for two days. The cuts have to heal."

Rembrandt packed up his wooden box, squinted at the cat, and went out the door.

Isaac panicked. "What if I want to get in touch?"

"You can't. Didn't the Bull tell you? I don't exist."

He climbed down the patio stairs and got into a bulletproof car with black windows. Isaac realized he wouldn't hear from Rembrandt again. The tattoo artist had fallen into one of Bull Latham's black holes. Big Balls was feverish with that engraving on his chest, wrapped in gauze. What did he really know about Latham? He'd never visited the Bull's own Little White House at the Naval Observatory. Suppose there was a *second* Situation Room? And Isaac was the country's court jester, the seasonal clown? He summoned his vice president to Aspen Lodge.

The Bull arrived with his nuclear football and his military aide, like an uncommon commander in chief. Isaac had the Bull's aide sit outside on the patio with the football. "What the fuck is going on, Bull? Am I under house arrest?"

The Bull stared at the little blots of blood in the bandage. "Boss, are you delirious? I can resign if you prefer another vice president . . ."

"You're running Rembrandt, aren't you?"

"I've slowed him down, that's all. He tried to have you killed, for Christ's sake."

"He also saved my life."

The Bull hunched his linebacker's shoulders. He seemed exasperated. "Rembrandt would have made a nifty profit from your death. He set that murder machine into motion."

"What changed his mind?" Isaac asked.

"He's an artist. How should I know? But I won't lie. Rembrandt's licensed to me. He's *my* counterfeiter."

"That's grand," Isaac said. "And I'm kept in the dark."

"Boss, it's best if he doesn't exist."

"That's what Rembrandt said. 'I don't exist.' What the fuck does it mean?"

"It means I put him in deep cover, where he can't harm us and no one can harm him."

The Bull marched out of Aspen, and Isaac was left with Rembrandt's hieroglyphics under the gauze. His fever mounted and waned. He followed Rembrandt's instructions, undid the bandage after two days. He didn't know what to make of the riddle on his chest. It wasn't at all like Pesh Olinov's griffin with its magnificent sweep of talons and claws. Rembrandt had painted a very peculiar cat on Isaac Sidel. This cat had Desirée's features, but with donkey ears; its whiskers were in gold; its tail was knotted like a torture instrument; its eyes sat like silver pecans in its skull; one of its paws had been mutilated, and the other was soaked in blood. Rembrandt had etched some kind of sibyl with a cat's face on Sidel.

He was now a registered werewolf, whatever that meant—a *chelovek*, with a sibyl near his heart. His skin burned like the devil where Rembrandt had cut into him, and blood kept leaking from the wound. It was like some crazy circumcision. What would the doctors at Walter Reed and Bethesda make of Isaac's tattoo?

He didn't give a damn. His Seabee had prepared some soup. Isaac walked the trails near Aspen with Desirée. She was used to the roaches and rats and sickening sweat at Rikers. Isaac's cat wasn't countrified. Her instinct as a lioness had been to run down a frightened fawn, but she was puzzled by the tangled growth of the forest; the tiniest squirrel eluded her. The dark, clotted earth made her sneeze. She clung to Isaac's heels.

"You sissy," he said. His chest seemed to rip with every word.

He climbed back up the stairs of his citadel, with Desirée still at his heels. He stared out his picture window. The telephone rang. A call had been patched through from the White House. Ariel Moss was on the line.

"Itzik, it's good to hear your voice. *Mazel*—you're lucky to be alive."

Isaac wondered how many machines were recording his conversation with the Hermit of Haifa? Was Bull Latham listening in at his own lodge?

"Bull," Isaac said, feeling frisky, "say hello to Ariel Moss."

There was dead silence, and then Bull Latham hopped aboard.

"How are you, Ariel?"

And the three of them kibitzed like old comrades for half an hour. The Bull had no shame. He took part with gusto in the very call he was monitoring. Isaac laughed his ass off, and every peal of laughter pinched like hell.

"Yeah," he said, "I'm lucky to be alive."